ABOUT THE AUTHOR

Sam Youd was born in Lancashire in April 1922, during an unseasonable snowstorm.

As a boy, he was devoted to the newly emergent genre of science-fiction: 'In the early thirties,' he later wrote, 'we knew just enough about the solar system for its possibilities to be a magnet to the imagination.'

Over the following decades, his imagination flowed from science-fiction into general novels, cricket novels, medical novels, gothic romances, detective thrillers, light comedies… In all he published fifty-six novels and a myriad of short stories, under his own name as well as eight different pen-names.

He is perhaps best known as John Christopher, author not only of *Pendulum* and *The Death of Grass* but also of a stream of novels (beginning with *The Tripods Trilogy*) in the genre he pioneered, young adult dystopian fiction.

'I read somewhere,' Sam once said, 'that I have been cited as the greatest serial killer in fictional history, having destroyed civilisation in so many different ways – through famine, freezing, earthquakes, feral youth combined with religious fanaticism, and progeria.'

In an interview towards the end of his life, conversation turned to a recent spate of novels set on Mars and a possible setting for a John Christopher story: strand a group of people in a remote Martian enclave and see what happens. The Mars aspect, he felt, was irrelevant. 'What happens between the people,' he said, 'that's the thing I'm interested in.'

John Christopher

The Death of Grass

The Caves of Night

The White Voyage

The World in Winter

Cloud on Silver

The Possessors

A Wrinkle in the Skin

Sam Youd

The Winter Swan

Babel Itself

A Palace of Strangers

Holly Ash

Hilary Ford

Sarnia

A Bride for Bedivere

PENDULUM

'England swings like a pendulum do'

SAM YOUD *as*

JOHN CHRISTOPHER

PENDULUM

THE SYLE PRESS

Published by The SYLE Press 2017

First published in 1968

Copyright © John Christopher 1968

Cover design by David Drummond

ISBN: 978-1-911410-04-1

www.thesylepress.com

PART ONE

I

THEY DROVE BACK FROM PALLISTER through the dusk of a fine June day. At first the sky was obscured by the brilliance of the city's lights, but as the Rover cruised north along the Broadway, buildings gave way to parkland, dark beyond the immediate orange sodium glare, and it was possible to see above the trees a calm deepening blue with one or two bright stars. The radio was on, playing a Victorian music-hall revival. 'Goodbye, little yellow bird ...'

Rod was pleased with the evening. He always took Hilda's parents out for a meal on their wedding anniversary, along with Hilda herself and her brother and sister. Last year he had tried a new place, out in the country, but it had not been successful. Hilda's mother had praised everything, but scarcely touched her food. Her father had eaten his, but with a disapproval that started from seeing that the menu was entirely in French and grew throughout the dinner, becoming audible when there was not a single English cheese on the cheeseboard. Tonight they had gone back to the Steak House, and everyone had been happy.

His elation stemmed partly from this, partly from being well fed and wined, but grew also out of a more general satisfaction. He totted up credits and debits, and found the balance good. His health, first. A touch of rheumatism in one knee, sharpening when the glass fell, half a stone excess weight – well, perhaps three-quarters – spectacles for reading ... but fit enough for a man in the middle forties. And his private life: a good home, wonderful wife, three children who were not always easy to understand but basically all right. In business ... successful by any standards, immensely so in relation to what he had started with.

The Rover turned off the main road, and into the quiet curving streets of the Gostyn Estate. His major achievement: Gawfrey-Town, it might have been called. These had been open fields when he was a boy. He could remember cycling out here, on the second-hand bicycle he had bought with money earned by delivering groceries, looking for mushrooms. A cold bright morning in September, the hedges jewelled with dew, mist clinging to the grass. And now, 'Santa Clara', 'Chez Nous', 'Cherry Trees' … solid well-painted houses, set back from close-mown verges, a car in every garage and in some cases a second parked outside. An atmosphere of peace and security; a community of bank clerks, minor civil servants, junior executives.

At the end, in fifty acres of parkland, approached through wrought iron gates (renewed, though now permanently open), Bridge House. The gates had been closed on that morning more than thirty years ago. He had looked through, between rusting bars, half-curious, half-timid, and seen the distant house, with the early morning sun on its peeling shutters. Closed, locked up, deserted. It must have been the time when old Colonel Leslie had gone to live in Italy. His son, after the war, had opened it up again, but circumstances were against him. In the end he had sold out – the house and the surrounding land – to the Gostyn Development Company.

It still belonged to the company. Matthews, his accountant, had worked that out. It was also the head office of Gawfrey (Constructions) Ltd, which meant that most of the upkeep was tax deductible. He had had to overcome Hilda's reluctance. She was glad of his success, but opposed to any form of show. She had accepted in the end when he had persuaded her that the decision was a business one: that was a sphere in which she accepted his views unquestioningly. (She did not in other respects. The question of schools for the children had provided another long and amiable battle, which she had won. They went to local grammar schools.) Now, he thought, she was used to the place, and liked it. The size of the house certainly made it easier for them to have her parents and Jane living with them.

The car turned in at the gates and along the drive, tyres whispering on the new surface, dull red in colour, which had been put down last year. He noticed a deterioration at one point, and made a mental note to have it checked. Then, as they came out of the cover of the rhododendrons, his eye was caught by something else: a blaze of lights from the windows of the house ahead.

From the back, Jane said:

'Looks quite a party.'

Hilda, with steel in her voice, said:

'A bit too good.'

The party was being given by their elder son, Stephen, who was sixteen. Hilda had been opposed to him having it on an evening when the adults were going to be out, but Rod had persuaded her. There seemed to be lights everywhere except in the office wing. He was struck also by the number of scooters and motor-bikes parked outside; there looked to be fifty or more. He said:

'How many were supposed to be coming?'

Hilda said:

'About fifteen or sixteen, he said. Less than twenty, anyway. You know how difficult it is to pin them down. I managed to get that much out of him because of the food supplies.'

He felt the beginning of anger.

'Something seems to have got out of hand.'

Instead of putting the car away, he left it at the front door. The door was open, and a blare of pop music came from that and the windows, also open. In the hall, a couple were standing in a corner, kissing, their bodies pressed together and motionless; the girl's hair was dyed in the fashionable shocking red. Beside the Pembroke table there was a mess of vomit; on it, a couple of half-empty glasses and a third which had been broken.

The racket, at this range, was tremendous. He went through to the green sitting room, and found it full of teen-agers. They paid no attention to him – most of them were doing the new step which involved hands on each other's shoulders, a fixed mutual but blank stare, and a sideways oscillation of the torso. One girl was leaning perilously backwards from a window, with a boy seemingly pushing her out. She had a blue sweater rucked up under her neck, and a black brassiere underneath that had been undone. She was no-one Rod had seen before. Cigarettes had been ground into the pale lime nylon carpet, the cocktail cabinet was open and littered with bottles. Someone had drawn a phallus on the wall with a fibre marking pen.

He went through to the room beyond, where the Grundig radiogram was on at full blast. Four couples were dancing there, avoiding a corner where someone else had been sick. Rod switched the set off. One couple continued to jerk to and fro; the others stared at him.

He said:

'Where's Stephen?'

There was a pause. A girl giggled. A boy said:

'Who's he?'

Three youths came in from next door. They were older than Stephen, eighteen perhaps, all wearing embroidered silk waistcoats, all with their hair elaborately combed up and back. The one slightly in advance said:

'Who are you, Charlie?'

He had the local accent, a whine but an aggressive whine. Rod said:

'Get out of my house.'

'You stopped our music. You're killing the scene, Charlie. You ought to switch the music back on. You're acting like you want someone to say please or something. That's not very polite when you got guests.'

He was the tallest of the three, his hair glossy black, face thin but heavy, cheeks hollow under prominent bones, nose long with flaring nostrils. There was the beginning of a boil on his chin, an ugly red patch against the bluish white of his skin.

Rod said:

'Get out. I won't tell you again.'

The youth took a deliberate step forward, and the two behind followed suit. He said:

'We don't like being told that, Charlie. We don't like being told to get out of anywhere. Put the music back on, so we can think better. That's something I'm not telling *you* again, Charlie.'

More had come through and were watching. Rod wondered if they had weapons; the under-sized one on the left, with gingery hair and greenish-looking teeth, was feeling for something in his pocket. He did not think of himself as a brave man, and was aware of the dangers: teen-agers had beaten up a man in Pallister a couple of weeks earlier and left him in the gutter with a broken jaw and badly bruised kidneys. But anger outweighed caution. He went forward and swung at the face in front of him. Taken by surprise, the youth pulled back, lost his footing, and fell against one of his companions. They tottered a moment, and both went down.

Rod saw Jane enter the room as the black-haired one got to his feet, rubbing an elbow and grimacing with pain. Rod felt cooler. He also felt that he had lost the initiative. He thought they were going to rush him. He called past them:

'Jane! Did you get through to the police?'

She hesitated only for a moment before picking it up.

'Yes. They're sending a car.'

The short gingery one said:

'She's bloody lying.'

'Stay and find out,' Rod suggested.

The leader took another step forward, but this time the others did not follow. He said:

'Even if it's true, I don't care about the sodding police. You've got nothing on me. I could have you for hitting me.'

Those behind them were melting away. A girl said loudly: 'I'm buggering off. Come on, Dave.' The three were left, with a couple who clearly wanted to get past them but could not. The black-haired one said:

'I'll remember you, Charlie. I got a memory for faces. I'll remember yours.'

He swung an arm as he went, catching a standard lamp and pulling it over and shouldering Jane roughly out of the way. Something else fell in the next room, and glass splintered. Outside, a motor-bike started up and was followed by others. Jane picked up the lamp. One of the arms holding the shade was bent, but that seemed to be the only damage. The bulb was still alight.

The sound of two-stroke engines rose to a crescendo and moved away. Rod saw them streaming off along the drive, in most cases with a girl riding pillion. There were footsteps and Stephen appeared, accompanied by other boys, his friends. The adult pose he usually put on had been shaken. He said:

'They've gone, Dad.'

'Right,' Rod said. 'Now I want to know who they were.'

'I don't know.'

'What do you mean – you don't know? You asked them, didn't you?'

'No. I didn't.'

'Then how did they get here?'

'They just rolled up.'

'And just knew we were out, and you were having a party?'

'One of them was Perry's brother.'

This was said by a boy wearing a black silk sweater with a golden dragon on the front. Rod turned to him.

'Who's Perry?'

'He's in our form. I mean … he may have heard us talking about it – the party.'

It could account for it. Talking about having the house to themselves, and the hint picked up. Rod said:

'You can clear the mess up, anyway. Including the vomit, and that drawing on the wall.'

He was addressing Stephen. Someone else snickered, suppressing it when Rod looked that way. He said:

'Does anyone find this funny?'

They stared in silence. The scared look was passing. It was finished now, had been assimilated.

'All right,' he said. 'You can go. The party's over. Unless you want to help Stephen clear up.'

They filed out. There was desultory muttering, and the sound of furniture being put to rights. Jane said:

'He was probably jealous – the boy in their form – at being left out. So he talked to his brother, and his brother brought this gang along.'

'Yes.' There was a cigarette scar on the glossy top of the radiogram, which he rubbed ineffectually with his fingers. 'Where's Hilda?'

'Checking upstairs.'

'They went upstairs?'

Jane shrugged. 'Into a couple of the bedrooms, I think.'

'The little bastards!' A thought struck him. 'Linda …'

'She's at the pictures with a girl friend, isn't she?'

'Yes. I forgot.'

'And I gather Pete had the sense to shut himself in his room. No damage except to property. Won't your insurance cover that?'

He felt himself getting angry again, but in a colder, less confused way. He said:

'Pity your Professor can't view the scene. It might teach him something about the rightful demands of youth.'

She smiled. 'I doubt it. He's a teacher. He's given up learning things.'

There was a bottle of whisky standing on the floor. She picked it up and examined it.

'They didn't finish this one. I'll pour us a drink, if I can find a couple of clean glasses.'

II

WALTER HAD LECTURES the whole of the morning, and Jane did not see him. She did not go to lunch until half past one and, with some shopping that needed doing, it was a quarter to three when she got back. He was at his desk, leaning back in his executive chair and listening to his own voice on the tape recorder. He switched off, came round the desk, and kissed her. The embrace lasted, and developed. She released herself to lock the door, and returned to him. They made love on the carpet she had chosen the previous year, a Hafiz of subtle colours and design.

He was disposed to a lingering aftermath, but she would not permit that. He lay sprawled while she tidied herself.

'What's the hurry? Not much work on hand.'

Jane unlocked the door. 'I was thinking of possible visitors.'

'Unlikely.'

'Not impossible, though.'

He said complacently: 'Well, my reputation's not very high, anyway. Or were you thinking of yours?'

His selfishness amused her. 'It crosses my mind from time to time.'

He looked at her with affection. 'You are a pretty remarkable girl, you know.'

'Am I?'

'So cool. I like that. No scenes. No hysterical demands for divorce and re-marriage – all the rest of the blackmail.'

'You're not suggesting you would stand for it, if I did?'

'It still makes you remarkable.' His gaze was appreciative. 'I like you better in a frock than in hip-shorts.'

She smiled. 'I know.'

'For one thing, you're slightly bandy.'

'Thank you, darling.'

'Only slightly, but I hate to see you falling below your best.'

She dug a toe into his side, below the ribs. He was putting on weight; there was a roll of fat there.

'Get up.'

'Now you're being vicious.'

'Just practical. There are your letters to do. We'd better make a start if you want them off today.'

He caught her leg, and pretended to bite the bare calf.

'Plenty of time.'

'Not really. You've got drinks with the TV boys at six thirty. And you've got to get home and change first, so you'll need to leave by half past four.'

'But I'm not going home.' He got to his feet, and struck an attitude of mock intensity. 'Home is where you are.'

'Do stop clowning, darling.'

He returned to his desk. 'I'm not going home this afternoon, though. I'm staying at the flat tonight. I can change there. Look, why don't you …?'

'Come back with you, for another frenzied ten minutes? I probably won't have a better offer today, but no, thank you.'

He looked aggrieved. 'You're too quick with your conclusions, and bloody unfair as well. What I was going to suggest was that you came with me to Andrew's, and that we had supper together afterwards.'

'And go back to the flat for coffee and a nightcap?'

'Well, yes. But that's entirely different. Isn't it?'

She gave it rapid thought, and agreed that it was different. She had no particular plans for the evening. The thought of being with him away from the office for a few hours was attractive. It was several weeks since they had had a meal together.

'I'll think about it.'

'For God's sake! What is there to think about?'

'After we've cleared the mail. Is this all that came this morning? Distinct signs of slipping.'

'There's more in the right-hand drawer. From yesterday.'

She went round to get it, and he caught her hand.

'Don't keep me in suspense. Say yes. I don't ask much from life.'

'You don't ask anything.' He grinned at her. 'It's one big bellowing demand.'

Someone said: 'What's a tit, after all?'

'Not just a tit. A tit on the telly.'

'There have been before. African dancers.'

'Nig-nogs are all right. No sexual stimulation.'

'*Isn't* there?'

'Not officially. It's like nursing mothers.'

'I don't see how anyone could.' This was from a very thin girl, lankly blonde, in a red dress with an open midriff. 'Feed a baby in public, I mean. I mean – feed it.'

'Old Jonas …' One of them adopted the characteristic manner of the television announcer referred to. ' "The BBC deeply regret … a most unfortunate accident …" '

The imitation broke up among general laughter. A squat young man who looked like a bank clerk – what was he doing here? – said:

'I suppose it could have been an accident.'

The laughter was louder, almost a howl. They thought of themselves as insiders, but had to accept that they were in the provinces, not at the centre of things. Their knowingness was the more determined for that. One called Canaway said:

'I happen to have heard the real dope. From people concerned.'

'The bird?'

'Alas, no. Not yet, anyway. I'm working on it.' He was in sound broadcasting, Jane remembered, but had ambitions to get into television. She also remembered that he had once made a pass at her, at a party much like this. 'It's a chap who knows Benny Hillman. That's her agent.'

'Go on.'

'It took some doing, I gather. A specially designed bra, and a frock built round it. Quite ordinary, not to say demure, when she went on camera to sing her little song. Then a clonk of scenery falling behind her – he paid twenty quid just for that – round she whips, all startled like, and out it pops. The left breast, because it's bigger than the right, with the bra constructed for maximum upthrust once it was loose. And twenty million eyeballs snapped to attention. A stroke of genius.'

The bank clerk said: 'I thought she really did look surprised. And embarrassed.'

'You mean you saw it?'

It was a point of honour that none of them watched television, apart from the programmes with which they were connected or which were professionally 'in' at the moment.

He said defensively: 'It seemed genuine.'

'So it was.' More hoots of mirth. 'No foam rubber about that one.'

'I mean …'

Tolerantly explaining, Canaway said: 'After all, she's done her stint with RADA. And three years in rep. And she once had an audition for Sadlers Wells. Adding up to absolutely nothing before last night. But now … Moira Miller's the name to watch. I'm told she's been booked for the Palladium already.'

A news cameraman said: 'She won't get on the BBC again.'

'Want to bet? Next year's Royal Command Show, I'd reckon. And Benny's made, of course. Three of the biggest names have switched to him so far, and the line is forming fast. There's a heavy premium on a good idea, as long as it really is good.'

Jane looked for Walter, and saw him in a corner, talking to a small dark girl who was staring up at him, engrossed. The subject was very likely abstruse, but the intense mellow voice, the podgy boyish face and coarse dishevelled hair, black with two wings of white, above all the concentration on the person addressed, were having their usual effect. Sexy Staunton. He knew of his nickname, and professed to find it hilariously amusing, but he was proud of it, too.

Boxes within boxes, she thought. The family man with the distinguished looking wife and two handsome children. And Sexy Staunton, the flutterer of female undergraduates' hearts. And inside that, to the few who really knew him, a shy man, flirting with women but afraid of them, keeping them at a distance. Inside that again, her lover. She wondered if his wife, Angela, knew anything of it. She had broached the subject once, and he had passed it off with a joke. There was a lot she did not know about him and, somewhat to her surprise, she was not particularly curious.

He caught sight of her watching him and, without stopping talking to the girl, gave a small jerk of the head. That meant: come and rescue me, I'm bored. Obediently, Jane went to get him. The girl made a poor show of concealing her annoyance. There was no doubt about the way it seemed to her. Walter Staunton and she had been having such an interesting, you might say *intimate,* conversation, when that secretary of his dragged him away. Obviously jealous.

'Let's get out of here,' Walter said. He gave a big smile to a passing account executive. 'I've had this lot. Besides, I'm bloody hungry.'

His physical appetites were strong and, in the case of food and drink at least, quite uninhibited. It was a heartiness which in other people would have repelled her, but which in him she found attractive.

They went to an Italian restaurant, where he sucked and chewed spaghetti with gusto, washing it down with draughts of Valpolicella. Jane watched him with fascination. There was a blob of tomato sauce on his chin, which she wiped off with her own napkin. Like a mother with a child … probably that was part of the attraction. A child, but with that sharp powerful brain, that expressive intelligence. He was talking about the threatened students' strike, in which, as usual, he was renegade from established academic opinion.

'It's a direct and naked attack on students as such. And if those bloody fools in the Senate House could only see it, it's an attack on them as well. The old English hatred of the intellectual again.'

She had no particular view on the issue, but she rather enjoyed opposing him, and he himself relished argument: perhaps because he was never defeated in it, or at least never admitted defeat.

'Aren't you making it sound a bit too sinister? The increased allowances were only a half-promise, and the country is in economic trouble.'

'The country's always in economic trouble, or heading for economic trouble, or having to tread carefully on its way out of economic trouble. And that was no half-promise. They're quoting the small print now, but verbally it was an unqualified assurance.'

'It's not just the students. There's a general wage stop.'

'It's the students who were put off year after year with ridiculous excuses, and who only last winter were persuaded to accept a quite inadequate increase, on the absolute guarantee of it applying to the next academic year.'

'There's a difference, surely. Between wages and – well, grants.'

'Yes, and the difference is simple. The wage-earner has economic power, through his ability to withdraw his labour. The student hasn't, though his importance to the future of the country is greater than any other element in it.'

'They don't have families, and they do get help from their parents in some cases.'

He topped her wine up a quarter of an inch, and refilled his own empty glass. A quick annoyed glance searched for the waiter with their pudding.

'Point one. The position of the worker and his family has been well looked after – that big increase in family allowances last year, and tying them to the cost of living, which they rejected out of hand in the case of students' allowances. Point two. Not all parents, by a long chalk, are Rodney Gawfreys, subsidizing their relations out of capital gains.'

Jane smiled. He and Rod had met a couple of times, and registered a mutual dislike.

He went on: 'The overwhelming majority have already been stripped to the bone by the cost of school life, before the child comes to University. Take the Marshall boy. We accepted him last December, and a week ago he wrote to say he had decided to go into some business job instead. He had a fine potential, but he's lost, and I know why. Two younger brothers at school, and his father a country solicitor with a modest practice.'

'Cardew said …'

'I know what Cardew said.' Cardew was the Minister of Education. 'That disgusting anecdote about his little pal at school, who went to University and, although a teetotaller himself, worked in a bar in the evenings and at weekends, with a book beside him to pore over when business was slack; and who even managed to send money back home to his unemployed father. And now he's a Civil Servant and a pillar of the realm …'

He broke off while the waiter set down Jane's sorbet and his own zabaglione; he was unashamedly sweet-toothed. Between spoonfuls, he continued:

'Even if one counts that as a praiseworthy case-history, it's impossible to apply as a generality. For one thing, there aren't enough part-time jobs to which a student can take books to read when things are quiet. But personally I don't regard it as praiseworthy except as a response to an undesirable and really monstrous challenge. I can just see Cardew's buddy, with his house at Wimbledon, his carefully folded copy of *The Times*, his room in the Ministry, with the carpet and the hat-rack and the

Canaletto print on the wall. I can see him taking his measured walk to the local with his Boxer dog of an evening, to drink his two halves of keg bitter. I can just hear the bastard patronizing the arts – though not financially, of course. A barren disaster of a life, and we're supposed to accept it as a success.'

His zabaglione was finished, while she had only started on the sorbet. He caught the waiter in passing, and demanded cheese. Jane objected:

'That's a flight of fancy, and altogether unfair. You haven't the faintest idea what the man's like.'

'Oh yes, I have. I've had dozens of them pass through my hands, God help me. Hard grinding workers, good examinees, and not an original thought in their heads. The object of a University is not to get people through certain examinations which will qualify them for certain executive jobs. That was the system that took the guts out of China for a thousand years. The object is to encourage the creative ferment which springs from adolescence, not to batten it down.'

He was in full and enthusiastic flight now. He took a wedge of Camembert and, after a fractional hesitance, a larger wedge of Double Gloucester, with a handful of biscuits. Slapping butter on them, he said:

'This is exactly what people like Cardew and the PM can't stand. It's not just that they regard the cultural and liberal activities the University offers as unnecessary – they see them as dangerous. And from their point of view, of course, they're right. A properly educated generation would never stand for shysters like that in positions of political power. There's no difference between government and opposition as far as that goes. They both look at things from the same standpoint. Union debates were all right: little microcosms of the Mother of Parliaments, where the right people were broken in to follow the right rules. A high premium on presence, rhetoric, formal logic – everything that stultifies the mind. Teach-ins are something else again. Spontaneity, irreverence … the rules flouted and the gods mocked. They can't understand it, and they fear it, and they are hell bent on crushing it. But they won't find it as easy as they think.'

Jane put down her spoon. 'The student has no power, though. You pointed that out.'

'No economic power was what I said.'

'What other kind is there?'

'Economic power is effective within defined and agreed frameworks. When you bring passion and conviction into the scheme, all the values change.'

'If they had power, could they be trusted to use it? At their ages?'

'I don't see why not.'

She told him about the take-over of Stephen's party, of what they had found when they got back. He listened, frowning.

'That's exactly it. Don't you see? The challenge already exists. With stupid louts, it takes the form of loutishness. You can't blame them for it – they are what a mercenary and ruthless society has made them. The urgent need is to apply that energy to creative rather than destructive ends.'

The waiter came and asked about coffee. Walter looked at her interrogatively.

She said: 'You did say something about having coffee at the flat.'

His face relaxed in a grin of simple impish pleasure. In his forties, he was a boy himself still. He said fondly:

'One of the things I like in you is that you never get carried away by argument to the extent of forgetting the important things.' He looked at her with frank and greedy admiration. 'A real bed, and a whole night. And my first lecture not till eleven.'

'I'll have to be in at nine as usual.'

'The energy drain is less for a woman. And you're younger. But you could leave it till nine thirty, I think.'

'Thank you.'

'That would give you time to make me breakfast.'

III

MARTIN STAYED THE NIGHT at Bridge House, but was up early the following morning for his return to Pallister. He made himself Nescafé and buttered toast. The Austrian girl, Elke, was in the kitchen before he left and they exchanged good mornings, his propitiatory, hers, he thought, contemptuous. Embarrassed, he crammed the last of the toast in his mouth, swallowed the coffee, and went out.

It was a grey morning, chill for the time of year. He got his old motor-bike started with some difficulty, hoping the noise would not disturb those still asleep, and chugged off down the drive. He had the usual mixture of feelings as he drove through the gates into the suburban calm beyond. Relief and regret, and guilt for his own inadequacy. Towards Rod, in particular. Rod had done so much for him, for them all, and his response had been so inadequate. Rod had seen him through University, which had meant three years of drifting followed by a Pass degree. And Rod had wanted him to come into the business. He knew he had been right to refuse that. The disappointment would have been greater, more drawn out, if he had said yes. He would have made a terrible mess of anything so practical and complicated.

But awareness of this did little to lessen his sense of failure. It must be galling for Rod that his brother-in-law, for all the opportunities he had provided, was an ordinary school teacher, and in a Primary school at that. He made jokes about the family's bent towards education, linking him and Jane, but Martin felt that the jokes, as far as he was concerned, sometimes had a sour note. He himself enjoyed his job, and was content with it, but he knew how it must seem to men of wider ambition.

Moisture dripped from the steel sky, a fine drizzle which thickened, wetting the surface of the road. He reduced his already moderate speed, but was aware of the small knock of fear, lifting to a peak when a Jaguar passed him, seemingly close, on a bend. He prayed, but did not expect it to do much good. More of a coward than a Christian. Last night he had seen the motor-bikes, sensed the possibility of trouble, and kept out of the way while Rod went into the house, making the excuse of looking after his parents. Jesus, he thought, dear Lord, I don't ask for great courage – just to be able to cope with fear the way ordinary people do all the time. But one should want that out of love, not out of self-disgust.

He was drenched by the time he reached his digs, and Mrs Johnson fussed over him, insisting on warming the clothes he was to change into, making him tea and trying to get him to eat another breakfast. He was glad when he could get away again.

His first class was Form Three for Geography. They were doing Australia, and he talked to them of the flora and fauna of that continent. There were animals there which were called marsupials. Did they know what marsupials were? It was an unlikely shot for seven- and eight-year-olds from homes dominated by pop music and commercial television, pub and club, Bingo hall and supermarket, and most of them looked blank. Joey got it, though.

'Like kangaroos, sir?'

Martin nodded. 'Not only kangaroos. There are a great number of different marsupials. What is it that's special about them?'

Joey again: 'They carry their young in their pouches.'

'That's right. The little ones are very tiny when they are born. They travel to their mother's pouch and stay there till they are much bigger. That's different from mammals. What happens with mammals, anyone?'

Henry Livingstone this time, Joey sitting tight. He rarely intervened when he thought someone else could answer.

'Suckle their young at the breast, sir.'

There was a titter at the back, and someone said: 'Dead sexy!' Gregory Tofield. Not to be outdone, the pale fat boy who was known as Porky called, in a louder voice:

'Like the girl on the telly last night!'

More tittering, particularly from the girls' desks. Martin kept his patient smile. Behind it there was love and pity for the children, disgust for those who surrounded them, smeared them, with dirt. It meant nothing here and now, but it was the beginning of the process of perversion. The meaningless word, the misunderstood innuendo, would become provocation, temptation, an acceptance of nastiness and eventually a wallowing in it.

There was such beauty there. Not physical beauty, though often that, too, but the beauty of innocence, minds opening, flower-like, to the sun, Even Porky, and Gregory Tofield. Their end was not in their beginning, but their end was certain in a world where men profited from the vices and weaknesses of other men. Cigarettes for manliness. Beer for strength. Puff and guzzle and fornicate. Hate and lie and cheat, like the other good fellows. Go for the easy shilling, the dishonest quid. It lay in wait for all of them, even Joey. Perhaps especially Joey. A cramming at the Comprehensive for an Oxford scholarship, and then the gates opening on the broad road to luxury and power. Balkan Sobranie instead of Players, whisky instead of brown ale, expensive motor-cars and expensive mistresses. A waste and a horror.

Turning from the thought, he said: 'Marsupials are a very important group of animals and, of course, the kangaroo is the largest of the marsupials. Does any of you know how the kangaroo got its name? Well, I'll tell you.'

They were talking in the common room about an incident on a

television show the previous evening in which a woman's breast had been accidentally revealed: Martin realized this must have been what his class had been sniggering over. Price was doing most of the talking, with interjections from Sheila Kennedy, who fancied herself as a wit. Moncrieff, the Headmaster, sat in his armchair, pulling judiciously at his pipe. Miss Garside went off into peals of laughter which showed that, although thirty-five now, she was a girl at heart.

Martin took his tea to the table on the far side of the room, picking up a newspaper on the way. The headlines said: POUND IN DANGER. Underneath, MINISTER FORECASTS STERN MEASURES. There was nothing very new in the story – just one more economic crisis – but he read it through. The rest of the front page was taken up with a libel case in which another newspaper was defending itself against an action by a group of pop singers, by producing a string of witnesses to testify to drug-taking and sexual orgies at the leader's house in Hampstead.

He did not hear her come in, but looked up when he heard Betty's voice, saying good morning. She sat in the next chair, smiling. The smile transformed the severity of her face. She looked no more than her age, which was twenty-four, and simple, and, in a strange and touching way, somehow lost. With him, increasingly, he had noticed that she dropped the barrier of coldness and aloofness which she used to keep the world at bay. She had not spoken much about her past life, but he gathered it had been unhappy, in a home where she was physically well cared for but treated as an interloper on a couple content with and absorbed in each other.

The relaxation pleased but also disturbed him. It must lead, he felt, in some way to demands; to a plea for help, support, even love. This was natural, understandable, and he was drawn to it, towards her need and his own. What frightened him was his weakness, the certainty that he must fail any human being who called on him. Failing, he would hurt her bitterly, perhaps more bitterly than she had been hurt already.

'Don't let me interrupt if you're reading,' she said.

Her voice, too, lost its metallic edge; it was warmer, girlish. He shook his head.

'There's nothing in it worth reading.'

'I've given up newspapers: there never is. How did the anniversary dinner go?'

He had mentioned it for something to say, and she had seized on it. The thought of a family, close-knit and mutually affectionate, fascinated her as the exposure of a breast did Price. He said:

'I think they enjoyed it.'

'Where did you go?'

She wanted to know the details – what they had all eaten, the wine they had drunk, who had black coffee and who white. She asked:

'What time did you leave them, then?'

'I didn't. I went back with them, and spent the night at Gostyn.'

She pressed for more, and this time he was conscious of awkwardness and evasion. He did not mention the scene at the house. He knew that was because he was ashamed of his own fear, and unwilling to tell the story without revealing it. Betty did not seem to notice anything. She said:

'I really don't understand …'

'Understand what?'

'Why you live in digs. Your sister lives there, and your parents. I mean, they'd probably be glad to have you with them wouldn't they?'

'I suppose they would.'

'Then why don't you? It's only a few miles. You could come in on your bike.'

He smiled. 'I like being on my own.'

'Surely you'd have more chance of being on your own there than with that landlady breathing down your neck? I mean, it's a big house, isn't it?'

'Yes, it is.'

She recognized his reluctance this time. There was a silence, which he broke at last by speaking about a child they were both interested in, a bright girl who alternated enthusiasm for school with a panicky loathing which made her invent excuses to stay away. The conversation was natural, but behind it, increasingly, his mind was preoccupied with the fact of not mentioning the hooligans who had gate-crashed Stephen's party, and his failure to go in with Rod. Cowardice on top of cowardice, an easy progression. Cowardice, and shame. He had been keeping his hand out of sight again, he realized, even though Betty was not a stranger.

Just before the bell, she said, speaking a little fast:

'There's a recital at the Civic Hall tonight. Elizabethan songs. I don't suppose you ...'

Martin shook his head. 'I can't tonight, I'm afraid.'

'Oh, that's all right. I just thought that if you weren't doing anything ... I only happened to see the poster advertising it on my way to school this morning. I don't know even whether one could get tickets as late as this.'

He made an effort, and said: 'I can't, because I'm going to the Fellowship.'

'Oh ... I see.'

She looked as though she was going to say something else, but did not. She smiled, turning away a little. The bell rang, and she said:

'Back to the joys of arithmetic. I'll take the cups.'

He made another effort, and used his left hand to pass his to her – the hand, with its four nailless stubs of finger, to which thirty years, a lifetime, had not accustomed him.

The rain, which had held off since morning, came down again while he was on his way back from school, in a violent down-pour which soaked him for the second time that day. Mrs Johnson, he was glad to find, was out, and he was able to go to his room and dry himself off without interference. She had starched his robe, as well as ironed it; it was stiff, and cracked open at the folds when he put it on. He stared at himself in the glass, and thought how absurd he looked – the small-featured insignificant face, weak eyes in a pallid skin, above the robe which looked like an old-fashioned night-dress. At least, since it was still raining, he could reasonably wear his mackintosh over it. Another disloyalty, instinctive like all the others. There was no lasting improvement; sometimes, he thought, no improvement at all. His life was made up of small betrayals. In any case, the white skirt beneath the bottom of the raincoat probably made him look more ridiculous than the robe by itself did.

The Fellowship met in the Scouts Hall at Errington Street, twenty minutes' walk from his lodging. He went there through wet and windy streets, under a sky that had grown dark early. There were glances, and occasional derisive comments from boys, but fewer than usual; perhaps people were getting used to the sight of them. Which meant only that contempt was getting the upper hand of curiosity. The Hall was a shack, with a corrugated-iron roof which made it cold in winter, sometimes stiflingly hot in summer. Today, though, it was dank, with a wind blowing through chinks in the walls and the badly-fitting windows. There had been a suggestion of renting the Church Hall nearby, which was bigger and better appointed. They had decided against it, partly because the discomforts were to be accepted, welcomed, but also through a distaste for anything which might connect them, even by association, with organized religion.

They had no belief in being special, no claim to divine revelation. They were merely those who had abandoned hope of the world's material future, who saw mankind passing through disgrace to infamy. They accepted the leadership of Christ, but in no exclusive or excluding spirit. Martin believed in Christ's divinity, in a sorrowful God interacting with the failing flesh of man, but there were others who did not. Spruce, for instance, the chartered accountant's clerk, widowed two years ago after losing his only daughter from leukaemia – Spruce's Christ was a man who had suffered and died, not at the hands of Jews or Romans, but in the torturing grip of an inscrutable, implacable deity. He was fond of quoting Housman's poem:

'Sleep well, and see no morning, son of man.'

The proceedings were very simple. They said the Lord's Prayer together, Spruce with irony, sang the Kyrie in plainchant, prayed or meditated for a space in silence. Then whoever was moved to speak would do so. Some spoke often, some never. Martin had spoken twice, in unwonted flushes of confidence, about his life at school, and the children. Sometimes there was a discussion after that. Then a hymn chosen by the Senior Brother, the Lord's Prayer again, and a clasp of hands all round before departure. They would go on their way refreshed, sustained, to visit the sick and poor and old, to do what little they could to alleviate the misery that festered beneath the flamboyant richness of this land and time.

Martin went to an old-age pensioner, living in squalor in the back room of a terraced house. He took with him a loaf of bread, a tin of corned beef, tea and sugar and a pint of milk, and some boiled sweets. The Brothers spent their own money on these things, but also solicited charity.

The old man was tall and gaunt, the decaying hulk of an infantryman. He had two lines of talk – his Army service and his grievances. The first amounted to a series of incoherent rambling anecdotes, about France in the First War, and India, and somewhere he called Mespot. Without understanding much, Martin found it easy to listen to, even pleasant. The second was a spewed-out bitterness. He claimed he had been entitled to admission to Chelsea Hospital as a Pensioner, but had been deprived of his rights by an old Sergeant-Major of his. This primary resentment was mixed up with others – against the Jews and the Catholics and the blacks who had come to England to live.

This evening, he was glad to find, it was the past which obsessed the old man. He talked of Bombay and Pindi, of battered estaminets frozen in the bloody winter of France, and then, coming to where Martin was sweeping the room, put a bony hand on his shoulder. The general smell of dirt and decay was stronger in his immediate presence. He had given up washing, and had reacted badly once when Martin had offered to help him do so.

'I remember in Mespot,' he said, 'a place where they was digging up buried cities, from thousands of years before Christ. And there was angels, stone angels, with wings. Thousands of years before Christ, I tell you. What do you make of that, eh? Where's your Christianity, when I've seen that with my own eyes? Stone angels, with wings.'

'It sounds very interesting, Mr Benson.'

'Interesting! It was that. I was Corporal then. It was just before I got busted the second time, by that bastard up from the depot. For having a bit of a drink, which there wasn't an NCO in the battalion hadn't had as much or more. I can see it as I stand here: a long trench in the ground and things being lifted up out of it – bits of broken pottery and little statues and such. And stone angels. And no eyes had seen them before mine for thousands and thousands of years. I asked the padre next day how he accounted for it, and he talked a lot of gabble which made no sense. But I'd seen them, as clear as I see you now.'

He broke off, and looked critically at the floor.

'You're not much of a hand at cleaning, are you, son? I'd make a better job of it myself, if it wasn't for this arthritis in my hip.'

'No,' Martin said, 'not much, I'm afraid.'

The old man stared broodingly about him.

'I ought to have been a Pensioner, if I'd had my rights. But they wouldn't take me, and I bloody well know why. He'd got in, all right, that bastard Gunnill. He fixed me, the way he did in Mespot.'

Martin went on cleaning up the room, trying not to listen.

IV

TRAFFIC CAME TO A HALT at the point where Broad Street
ran along a side of Hampton Square. A crowd of young
people had spilled out across the road from the open space in
front of the War Memorial, and half a dozen policemen were
trying to clear them. A lot of Pallister University scarves were
in evidence. Rod shut off his engine, and could hear a chant
coming from the far side, but could not make out what was
being said. He noticed that where the police applied pressure
the crowd obediently melted away, but formed up again behind in a continual flanking movement. There was something
disturbing about this: an impression of seeming pointlessness
combined with purposive method.

There appeared to be no reason why the eddying should not
go on forever. The police were making no real effort to get to
grips with their tormentors. That was understandable, perhaps,
after the recent case in which a London University student had
won damages for assault against two police officers. An empty
taxi had halted beside the Rover. The driver, a man in his fifties,
blue jowled and bald, called across angrily:

'Bloody useless lot. Do what they like, and cheeky with it.
They ought to bring back conscription. Eighteen months in the
Army might do them a bit of good.'

Rod smiled, and shrugged. A change was taking place, the
mob dissolving back in the direction of the War Memorial and
the lawns. It had the look of a planned manoeuvre; the police
followed them awkwardly, like bewildered sheepdogs. After a
while, one of the policemen took over point duty, and cars began to move again. Rod put on his right winker for the turn

which would take him to Gurton Avenue, and the Club.

The steward brought his pink gin to a chair by the window. The only other members in were three whom he did not know very well, noisily playing poker dice. He looked out across the road to the lawns and formal flower beds of Gurton Park. The day was sunny, but a wind ruffled the chestnuts and tossed the pigeons in erratic arcs across the sky.

Footsteps approached, and Bill Lennard took the armchair beside his. The steward arrived almost at once with Lennard's customary Haig and water, and Rod nodded to him.

'On my bill, please. How are things with you, Bill?'

Lennard was one of the people he knew and liked best, within the Club. He had retired from the City in his early fifties, and now did nothing apart from a little dabbling on the Stock Exchange. He was an urbane, easy-going, idle man. Sometimes he passed Rod investment tips; not often, but they had proved worth taking. They were also both members of the same Masonic lodge, the Royal Marine, but outside those two spheres they had little or no contact. At one stage, the Gawfreys had been asked to drinks at the Lennards, and subsequently had had them to dinner at Bridge House. Hilda had found Bill Lennard pleasant enough, but after the second, closer examination in her own home, dismissed his wife as one of the bridge-playing, would-be patronizing nonentities she could not stand. Rod had an impression that the dislike had been reciprocated. They were asked back, but when Hilda got out of it the invitation was not renewed.

They talked about the student demonstration. Lennard's car had been halted by another surge across the road, after the one which had caught Rod. Lennard said:

'I don't envy Maurice in having to deal with this lot. Terribly easy to do the wrong thing.'

Maurice was Masterson, the Chief of Police, also a Club member though he rarely put in an appearance.

Rod said:

'I think the police are adopting the right tactics so far.'

'Do they have any tactics?'

'Letting them run themselves out. They'll get tired of it after a day or two.'

'I wonder. They're very well organized. Did you see Geary on television?'

'I switched it off. I didn't like the look of him.'

'Nor did I. Manchester Grammar at its worst.' Lennard had been at Eton and, like all Etonians, was a little obsessed with the fact and with schools in general. 'But the little sod is bright enough. I thought at first his motivation might be ordinary rancour over being sacked before he took his degree, but I have a feeling I was underestimating him. I think he's going for a career in politics, and he sees the students as a good starting point.'

'I wouldn't have thought they were much of a jumping off point,' Rod said. 'There aren't all that many of them, and they don't even have a vote for the most part.'

'It's precisely the weakness of their position that he's playing on, and cunningly, too. The government is picking on the students because they're the ones who are most vulnerable. If they are tough with them, they stand a better chance of getting away with a tough policy towards the railwaymen and the steel workers.'

'I should think there's some truth in that.'

'Of course, there is. And he's clever enough to bring it out. The government has to carry public opinion with it to some extent. When there's unrest – strikes and so on – sympathy usually moves towards the side of law and order, because people are scared of trouble which might involve them. But it doesn't always happen. It didn't happen with the seamen or the nurses.'

Rod shook his head. 'I don't see how they can give in, after all they've said.'

'Nor do I. Nor does Geary. But the longer he keeps the

pot on the boil, the more personal publicity he gets. And he's championing an underdog, which no-one is frightened of, so he doesn't even get labelled in people's mind as dangerous. He could probably pick up a Conservative seat, if he waited two or three years.'

Rod said: 'The government has got to do something about the economic situation. It looks pretty gloomy at the moment.'

'Gawfrey Constructions feeling the cold east wind? I suppose the increase in Bank Rate didn't help, with the building societies putting up mortgage rates again.'

'It's not just the private housing side. We lost a factory extension contract last week, because they decided they weren't justified in an expansion programme just now.'

Lennard nodded, as though satisfied with the confirmation of a private speculation.

'I wouldn't recommend holding British equities, certainly. I got rid of all of mine I don't need for a tax loss, a month ago. They're all saying that because the market didn't pick up after the last big drop it's soundly based. The answer to that is that it all depends on confidence, and how dear money gets. I think it could get very dear indeed.'

'You're not buying a new car this year, then?'

'I wouldn't, anyway. That's one advantage of a Bentley. Feel like a frame of snooker?'

'If you like.'

The three members were still audible from the billiard room. They had stopped playing dice and were telling dirty stories, laughing uproariously on the punch lines. Unlocking his cue, Lennard jerked his head in the direction of the noise.

'I wouldn't say I'm mad on some of our newer members.'

'Well, you're on the Committee.'

'Yes. And out-voted more often than not. I need support. What about letting your name go forward at the AGM?'

'I'm too junior.'

'Nonsense. Everyone's equal after the first five years.'

'No.' Rod fitted the triangle over the red balls. 'You'll have to count me out, Bill.'

'You give me a black, don't you?' Lennard spun a coin. 'What would that be?'

'Head.'

'Tail it is. You can kick off. I shall come back to you on this one. I'm not taking no for an answer.'

He was in his study after supper, checking accounts, when the bell rang on the extension telephone. It was unlikely that the call would be for him at that hour – more probably it was for Hilda or one of the children – but he lifted the receiver, and said 'Rod Gawfrey'. He could hear the string of rapid pips which showed that he was connected with a public call-box, and he waited patiently for them to clear.

'Mr Gawfrey? Mr Rodney Gawfrey, of Gawfrey Constructions Ltd?'

A youth's voice. He said:

'Speaking. Well? What is it?'

'I hear you've been to the police, Charlie. I hear you've been making a complaint about me.'

Now he knew the voice. He said:

'I'm warning you …'

'No, Charlie. I'm warning you. I don't like coppers coming round to my house, putting the wind up my mum. She's got a weak heart – did you know that?'

'You should have thought of it before you came barging into my house uninvited.'

'You wanted them to prosecute me, didn't you, Charlie? But they can't do that, because I've not done anything wrong. I got invited to a party, that's all.'

'You weren't invited by me, or by my son.'

'You don't check it every time you're asked to a party. Life's too short. I didn't break in or anything. The door was open,

34

and the sign said welcome – until you started throwing your weight about.'

'There was over twenty pounds' worth of damage done by you and your pals.'

'Was there, now? Then why didn't the coppers charge me with it? It's a serious offence, malicious damage. Shall I tell you why, Charlie? Because there's nothing to say it was done by me or my pals.'

'You know damn' well it was!'

'So prove it. It could have been that four-eyed kid of yours, and his mates. You don't want to start slandering people. Having a load of money and a big house doesn't give you the right to get the police throwing a scare into an old woman with a bad heart. You're liable to land yourself in trouble, carrying on like that.'

'Is that a threat?'

'Warning, Charlie. Didn't you hear me the first time? You want to get the wax out of your ears. I'm telling you – you go on behaving anti-social like that, and someone's liable to take a run at you. Someone who's not as easy-going as me. I know a lot of people who are very indignant about the way you acted. They're not quiet, like me. Some of them might get carried away.'

Rod said:

'I can tell you something. If I find you, or any of your half-wit friends, on my property, they're likely to get carried away all right.'

'Clever, aren't we?' The same chuckle. 'Just watch it – that's all.'

He heard the clatter of the receiver being dropped at the other end. He put down his own telephone, and stared at it. He was shivering a little with anger.

He had an appointment in Pallister at nine o'clock, and therefore volunteered to run the children in to school, saving them the bus journey. He had breakfast – his usual boiled egg, toast and strong tea – in his dressing-gown, and bathed, shaved and dressed afterwards. He listened to the news on his portable radio. There had been further demonstrations by students the previous evening. One had occurred during a royal visit to Covent Garden Opera House. They had massed quietly until the arrival of the Queen and Prince Philip, and then broke into a loud, well rehearsed chant:

> 'Summer is i-cumen in
> But we aren't getting fat –
> Please to put a penny in the poor student's hat.
> If you haven't got a penny, a halfpenny will do,
> If you haven't got a halfpenny, then sod you, too.'

Earlier in the evening, Piccadilly Circus underground had been put out of action for half an hour by students with 6d tickets blocking the escalators. In Manchester, the train carrying the Minister of Education had been delayed considerably when students continually climbed in and out of carriages, thus preventing the guard from signalling for the train to start.

The Prime Minister, speaking at a dinner of the Bankers of the City of London, had been loudly applauded when he had referred to the childish activities of a tiny group of undisciplined young men and women, who were prepared to accept the privileges of education at the country's expense, but refused to accept a small sacrifice when the nation was facing hard times. They must be treated with firmness, and with the contempt that they deserved.

Rod was shaving during the local Today programme, when he heard Pallister mentioned. He switched off, to listen. An interview with Professor Walter Staunton, of Pallister University.

Staunton, it appeared, was on the side of the students. They had been let down over and over again, and were now being used as tools in a dirty political game. They had the basic right that any section of the community had to act in concert for the redress of their grievances. It had been suggested, the interviewer said, that Professor Staunton was in fact acting as a leader and organizer of students in the Pallister area: was this true? Individual people, Staunton replied, had sought his advice on specific points; and he had been happy to give it. Then he did not envisage himself in the role of a local Geary? He did not envisage himself in any role at all. Staunton laughed: a deep vulgar laugh, contrasting with the cold precision of his accent of speech. Envisagings were best left to the press and television. The interviewer pursued him: was he in touch with Geary? He had met Mr Geary, Staunton told him. At a student conference in Birmingham a year ago. Not since. Did he not think, the interviewer asked, that his role as 'adviser' to the rebellious students – the vagueness of the term was stressed – conflicted with his position and duties as a senior member of the University?

Staunton paused before replying, but the pause was not of hesitation, but for effect.

'The ancient functions of the teaching profession included the leading, guiding, and *care* of the young people entrusted to their charge. That duty, in my view, is paramount, and the questions of University status and organization are trivial by comparison.'

'The shepherd tending his flock?'

'Except that these aren't sheep. They are intelligent young men and women, who represent the future of this country.'

Rod finished shaving. He had offered to find Jane a position in the firm; secretarial in the first place, but probably executive later on. She was an intelligent woman. Even on the secretarial basis, she would be getting a lot more than Staunton paid her. He thought he would renew the offer, making it a bit more tempting. He had not cared for Staunton when he met him, but had thought him innocuous enough. It put a different complexion on things if he was going to carry on like this. Not the sort of man one would want a member of the family to be associated with.

He went downstairs, and rounded up the children. Linda, as

usual, had lost something at the last minute; in the present case, her satchel. It finally turned up underneath the television set in the sitting room. His irritation with her carelessness did not survive the sight of her, ready at last, in her flushed and hectic beauty. The curve of the fifteen-year-old breasts under the crisp whiteness of her blouse, blonde hair hastily brushed back into casual loveliness, dark eyes warily watching his face but ready, when he smiled, to smile unstintingly back.

She was, he admitted, though only to himself, the special one. Not just because she was the girl, though obviously that came into it. It was more that he saw so much of himself in her. Of the boys, Stephen was intelligent, reticent, a little withdrawn from life; he had friends, but at heart he was a solitary, a realist and a pessimist. Peter was more like Hilda: reliable, conscientious, setting standards that he expected other people, and himself, to live up to. Only Linda had the confidence and vitality which had been his own gift from the gods; and behind those qualities, perhaps, the instability which he had always feared lay at the root of his own nature. He loved her for that, as well.

It had rained during the night, and the Rover's wheels swished through quite large puddles that had collected on the drive. That meant the surface had settled unevenly; he would have to speak to Gage about it. As they went through the gates, Linda said:

'What's that? Something written.'

He saw it in the driving mirror now, and stopped the car. The children got out with him, when he had backed up. The black letters, paint still wet, straggled down the two white columns.

On the left, GAWFREY. On the right, BASTARD.

V

WHEN THE AUTHORITIES BANISHED THEM from the University buildings, committee meetings of the Pallister branch of Students' Emergency Action were transferred to the Snug of a pub called the Golden Keys. The landlord had not been too happy about this at first, but accepted the situation without argument when he realized the alternative was likely to be a boycott: undergraduates made up a good part of his trade. He did not even demur at a sign being put up on the Snug door: NO ADMITTANCE: SEA IN SESSION.

The meetings in fact did not last long, because in general they represented no more than the formal agreement of decisions reached half an hour before in Walter's flat. Jane was present at these, not as Walter's secretary but, in theory, as a co-opted voluntary helper to an unofficial discussion group. Walter had fixed this, assuming her agreement. She prepared notes for the agenda, and kept what would have been minutes if the meeting had been official. She did not mind this. In general, the whole thing was fun. From the sober pinnacle of twenty-eight, she could be amused by and could enjoy their callow youth, and their excitement about their activities. One or two of the boys flirted with her, which was also pleasant.

She was, though, a little concerned for Walter, and remonstrated with him before the meeting called to coincide with the return of Joe Pinkard, the Committee Chief, from London.

He said: 'You worry too much.' He was in high spirits. 'Have a Scotch to settle your nerves.'

'Not now.'

He pulled a shirt on over his hairy chest. 'You can pour me one, anyway.'

Doing it, she said:

'No-one's fooled by this. The fact that you're not supposed to be on the Committee and don't go to the Keys doesn't deceive anyone.'

'It preserves appearances, my love.'

'That won't prevent them sacking you.'

'My appointment was for five years. I've got three to go.'

'Except that it can be terminated by a vote of the Senate on the grounds of scandalous conduct.'

'Two thirds of the members voting aye. They wouldn't get one third.'

With a slight edge to her voice, she said:

'Of course. How could there possibly be a vote of censure on Walter Staunton, that celebrated TV personality and purveyor of potted wisdom? That superiority complex has served you well up to now, but I wouldn't press it too far.'

He grinned at her. 'Calculation, rather than conceit. There would be risk involved, and the overwhelming majority haven't got a brave bone in their bodies. Added to which, I've got nothing to lose. If I gave up teaching, I could live comfortably on television and writing; and the publicity of a dismissal would boost my income still further in those respects. I'm a good teacher, and I want to go on teaching, but only as long as I'm left alone. I'm not going to compromise.'

'Your integrity makes me shiver.'

'I'll only stay a teacher as long as I can feel I'm on the same side as the young. It's being with them, sharing their vitality, that makes the drudgery worth while.'

'Makes you feel younger, too, doesn't it?'

She stared at him, with a little smile. It was a moment or two before he smiled in return.

'*Vinaigre,*' he said, '*mais du vin, pas de la bière.*'

The door bell rang. Jane said:

'Your pep pills have arrived, sir.'

He went to a mirror and ran a comb through his untidy hair, while Jane straightened things up around the flat.

'Quarter of an hour before time,' he said. 'The vitality does get a bit excessive at times.' He grabbed her as she went past and pressed his stubby fingers against her breast. 'Could have been worse, though. They could have been half an hour early.'

During the early part of the session, Jane thought about herself and her situation. She was not much given to introspection but something – Walter's assumption that her time was at his disposal, the hurried and for her unsatisfactory act of sex, temporary boredom with the pseudo-revolutionary chatter of the students and Walter's delight in it – triggered it off now.

The gilded convex glass on the wall opposite showed her the physical assets. Despite the distortion and diminution, it mirrored a good-looking young woman. A face long rather than round, the individual features – nose, mouth, brow, cheekbones – large but in harmony. Good strong teeth, grey eyes, ash-blonde hair which was thick and short and easily groomed. A bust with which she was entirely contented, and long, reasonably shapely legs. She looked at their reflection, emerging from the scarlet hip-shorts. 'Slightly bandy …' The swine was right about that, but it had not put him off, and did not seem to be affecting, except possibly as an attraction, the engineering student who was staring across the room at her with quiet lust. The one female member of the Committee, a dark girl who might have been pretty but for an intense expression and a lack of clothes sense, was watching the watcher with gratifyingly obvious resentment.

In addition, she was sound in wind and limb, and of better than average intelligence. An IQ test, the year she left school, had produced a marking of 122, and she did not think she had deteriorated particularly. Yet here she was, with the thirties in sight, mistress to a married man, her boss, with no prospect of change that she could see. The banality of it was more depressing than the thing itself

Part of the trouble, she thought, was that, like Hilda, she did not question a course of action once she had embarked on it. The charge of superiority complex might well have been tossed back at her by Walter. She had come to work for him three years ago, had been fascinated by his intelligence and energy, touched by his one apparent timidity, and had walked into this with her eyes open. She had asked a few questions first, designed to establish that she was not ruining a good marriage, but the inquiries had not been as exhaustive, she admitted now, as they might have been: she had accepted reassurance halfway. As it turned out, this point had been unimportant, anyway. Far from ruining his marriage, her impression was that she had made no impact on it at all.

Hilda, of course, would never have let it happen because Hilda had principles. One sacrificed one's whims to them immediately and cheerfully; sometimes, Jane thought, with a little too much satisfaction. A girl did not let herself get involved with a married man – the automatic canon of respectable female behaviour. She had subscribed to it herself but, as it so often proved, without conviction.

She toyed with the idea of breaking with Walter. She was not sure whether she had ever been in love with him, in the romantic sense. He had fascinated her, and still did. He irritated her more than he had done, but against that there was the plus of being fond of him, of the appeal, perhaps, to her very latent maternal instinct. She would miss him, possibly a great deal more than she expected, but it was a deprivation, she was sure, that could be borne.

And that would leave her unattached, a still eligible commodity on the marriage market.

She felt the small curl of disgust in her mind. From banality to banality – the bachelor girl who makes a sudden frightened dash to get oil for the lamp which the wiser virgins filled in their early twenties. What should she do? Make out a list of men and get Hilda to invite them to Bridge House … experiment with different scents and hair-dos … what about a discreet subscription to a marriage bureau? It might work, but at least she could live with herself as she was now; she could not with the woman she was envisaging.

Someone had let in Pinkard, who had finally arrived, and Walter was getting up to welcome him. Jane watched him with a renewal of affection. Dear Walter, she thought, my defence against the female cliché.

She was glad to abandon her line of thought to pay attention to what Pinkard had to say. He had come direct from the train which had brought him from a meeting of the central co-ordinating committee, chaired by Geary. He was bubbling over with this, but doing his best to cover it with a mask of matter-of-fact severity – with difficulty because he was a fleshy extrovert youth who laughed easily. He directed his remarks to Walter, who listened, picking his teeth with a cherry stick.

'I saw Geary first, as you suggested, and put your idea up to him. He got it right away. There was some opposition at the meeting, but he pushed it through.' He shook his head, in admiring recollection. 'He goes at things when he puts his mind to them.'

Pinkard had slipped up there; the small frown on Walter's face showed that he was not pleased with him. The others had not been present at the talk the two of them had before Pinkard went to London. He might have assumed that Walter had put them in the picture since then, but it was not the sort of assumption that a canny organizer would make. The girl, Stella Briggis, said:

'Might we know what the idea was?'

The sourness of her tone made itself felt, and Pinkard looked from her to Walter in momentary confusion. He started to say something, but Walter cut in:

'The point is that it was only an idea. There was no point

in talking about it here until it had been put up to the central committee, because it's something that has to be handled on a national level. It wouldn't have done for us to get enthusiastic about it and then have it shot down.'

Pinkard once more had a shot at speaking, but Walter overrode him. There would be a new spokesman soon, Jane thought: Pinkard would be lucky to stay on the committee.

'But since it has been approved, I can explain it now. It's very simple. Our campaign has been carried on with intelligence and hard work, but that's not enough. The reason it's not enough is that students as a body are too few in comparison with the mass of the nation. The things we've managed to do have had a nuisance value, but it's been the nuisance value of a gnat. We'll need vastly to increase the numbers on our side if we're to have a hope of succeeding.'

Someone said: 'Splendid notion, but it's still a nine-month job.'

There was appreciative laughter, in which Walter joined. Stella Briggis said sharply:

'We're not really here to listen to feeble jokes, are we?' She spoke to Walter: 'Is that the idea? It sounds more like a pious hope.'

Walter took the implied rebuke amiably; the old gynophobia at work, Jane thought. He said:

'No, merely the logic of the situation. The question is: where can we go for help? Not to the trade unions – not to the workers at all, in fact. Their interests are not the same as ours, and can't be made to seem the same. That also applies to the middle classes.'

The engineering student said: 'It applies universally, surely.'

'Not quite. It's not just the leader writers in *The Times* and *Telegraph* who would like to see us come to heel. A very large number of people would – the overwhelming majority of the over-thirties. I don't know whether envy or fear is the stronger motivation, but they are opposed to you precisely because you are young. Since that is so, my suggestion was that we should make an all-out attempt to recruit the rest of your age group.'

He paused. After a moment, someone said: 'How?'

'Various ways. Concentrate on the youth-age division in our propaganda, for a start. Start drumming up support in clubs and cafés. The way the gang idea has developed in the past few years should help there. It should be possible to contact particular people who will bring others in automatically. Above all, turn this into a general harassment of authority and the world of the old.'

Douglas Wild said: 'Call up the yobs, you mean?'

He was one of those who flirted with Jane, a soft-voiced, pipe-smoking Aberdonian doing Social Sciences, less garrulous than the others, possibly more mature. Walter said:

'You could put it that way.'

'Do we want that kind of help? It wouldn't exactly advance our image as a responsible intellectual elite.'

Walter said: 'I imagine this was the sort of objection Geary had to face on the central committee.' He looked for confirmation to Pinkard, who nodded, opened his mouth, and closed it again. 'What can't be escaped is that at the moment we are not getting anywhere. Oh yes, we're disrupting traffic to some extent, and getting a few headlines on press and television. But the police are taking care not to be provocative, and the novelty value won't last. You're getting them out in the streets at present, but will you continue to get them out once it's become something of a bore? I may be wrong, but I don't think so. The government is simply sitting tight and waiting for us to collapse. Which we will do, unless we can widen the scope of operations.'

'So we try to bring in gangs of pinheads, in the hope that they'll do the damage we can't do ourselves?' Wild knocked out his pipe in Walter's rock-crystal ashtray. 'I think I'd sooner we lost.'

Stella Briggis said: 'Perhaps you would. It doesn't make a lot of difference to you personally, does it? Others are less fortunate.'

Wild senior, it was known, owned an extensive fishing fleet. He looked at her with disgust, and did not bother to reply. That, Jane realized, was a mistake. His contempt spurred her on, while his silence discouraged those who might have supported him. There was some wrangling, but no other open opposition. Walter let them talk, and then summed up.

'Joe has been authorized to ask for our support of the change in tactics approved by the central committee. I think we could have a vote on it now.'

Walter himself did not vote, of course, any more than Jane did. Wild's was the only hand raised against it. The rest voted in favour, most of them with enthusiasm.

VI

MARTIN AND BETTY had coffees in a place called the Disaster, on the Broadway. He had not been inside before, and did not like it. It was decorated mostly in black, with aspidistras and large artificial lilies in urns, and the walls were hung with black-and-white photographs. Facing them was a blown-up snap of trenches in the First World War; further off he could see a train crash, the blitzed ruins of Monte Cassino, a drawing of the *Titanic* going down. Beneath and between them, people chattered; a small boy whined at his mother for an ice-cream.

The constraint between them had begun earlier. They had gone to the Zoo. It was not a very large or interesting one, and he had thought her silence was due to boredom. When they were looking at the lions, though, she had burst out with it: the sight of caged animals upset her, always had done. Surprised, he had asked her why she had not told him this when he suggested the outing. Her face was tensed up, brows knitted into deep furrows. He had wanted to come … she had not thought it would bother her so much. She had not been to a Zoo since she was a child.

They had talked about it. To Martin, what was important was that the animals were well looked after, fed and watered, protected from disease and natural enemies. The cage was their security. Betty, he gathered, was most upset by the enforced isolation, the deprivation of the animals' rights to enter into relationships. It was a strange, anthropomorphic viewpoint. They were not all isolated, he pointed out; some were coupled. But forced into coupling, she insisted passionately, with chance and volition equally ruled out.

Discussion, which he had thought might ease the strain between them, made it more plain; they had relapsed into silences which were mutually excluding, mutually abrasive. He had hoped that having coffee together would let them get back to the earlier footing, but this place did not help. Betty, though, made an effort, talking about indifferent things – a girl she knew, the concert she had been to the previous evening, even politics – quickly and brightly. He did not think it would work at first, the effort being too obvious, but found himself thawing, the tension disappearing. They drank their coffees, and ordered more. A girl came with pastries on a trolley, and he asked her if she would have something.

'No, thank you.' He shook his head to the girl, and there was a pause. 'What are you doing this evening, Martin?'

The question embarrassed him. 'Nothing much.'

'But what?'

'I have to see someone.'

'Your old people?'

'Well, yes.'

'On a Saturday night?'

'I generally do.' He hesitated. 'I think that's when they feel most lonely.'

She stared at him. 'Doesn't everyone?'

He was confused; aware that something was being asked of him, fearful of it becoming a demand which he could not meet. With the ones he visited, it was different. The demands were simple, superficial – for food, physical aid, a listening ear. There was no involvement.

Silence had dropped between them again. He said, to break it:

'What will you be doing?'

She stared at him, with a little smile, before replying.

'I'll have a bath, I suppose, wash my hair, do my mending. There are all sorts of things to keep one busy, aren't there? But nothing like you, I'm afraid. No good works. Listen to music, perhaps. Tinsel on earth, instead of treasures in Heaven.'

He did not reply. After a moment, she dropped her hand over his, and said:

'I'm sorry. I'm not mocking, truly. I don't know how you do it. Or why. Will you walk me to the bus stop?'

VII

IN THE WAITING ROOM, Rod scanned his *Daily Telegraph.* The left-hand lead story was about the economic situation, and the warning to Britain from the Congress of Swiss Bankers; but the headlines were almost as big for the news of this suicide by a student. The letter he had left was reproduced. It was addressed to a girl, another undergraduate at his college. He had found it impossible to go on, impossible to work for worries about money. He was in debt, and his creditors were pressing. He was sorry about the mess he was leaving behind, but he could see no hope of doing anything about it. He sent her his love, and hoped she would be happy.

Various people had been interviewed: the girl, his tutor, the head of his SEA group. His mother was widowed, an old-age pensioner, and he had been trying to support her as well as himself. According to his tutor, he had been a brilliant young man, with immense potential as a mathematician. Not merely brilliant, but creative also. The country and the world might have lost another Whitehead, perhaps another Einstein. The girl said he had been under strain for a long time; but since the government standstill on students' allowances it had become much worse. He had been withdrawn, despairing.

The head of his SEA group challenged the verdict of the inquest. It was not suicide, but murder. The government, the Prime Minister in particular, stood indicted on that charge.

The girl said: 'Colonel Sherring will see you now, Mr Gawfrey.'

He folded his newspaper, and followed her to the inner room.

Sherring was a fat, rumpled man, with cigarette ash on the front of his blue suit, but with small quick eyes and a precise and confident voice. He offered Rod a cigarette, lit one up himself and, slouching back in his chair, invited him to tell his story. While he listened he looked out of the window, from time to time darting a glance at Rod as though checking the authenticity of a particular remark. When Rod had finished, he sat forward, spilling more ash on his lapels, and made rapid shorthand notes on a pad in front of him, translating or commenting on them as he did so.

'Four incidents so far,' he said, 'five if we include the telephone call. Four incidents involving damage, shall we say? One, the gatecrashing of your son's party. Two, the defacing of the pillars outside your home. Three, the smashing of windows in an estate under construction by your firm. Four, damage to your motor-car while parked, with side panels scored by a nail file or something similar. You are convinced that all four incidents concern the same person, the youth who telephoned you. I don't think one can rule out the possibility of the damage to the car being ordinary motiveless vandalism – there's so much of it these days – but for the rest I imagine you are right. Have you been back to the police on this?'

'Yes.'

'What do they say?'

'The same as they said the first time. They have no way of proving anything, and they haven't the men either to put a permanent watch on the boy concerned or on my property. They've asked the local chap to keep an eye on the house. They said they would be prepared to send someone to see the boy again, but there was nothing they could do, and both parties knew it. If they left him alone, he might get tired of it. If they pestered him, he was more likely – since he had not been cowed by the previous visit – to treat this as provocation and do more damage.'

'And what did you decide?'

'I didn't, then. I said I'd let them know. I realize they can't put a permanent watch on him, especially as things are at present, with this student unrest. But it occurred to me that, although they couldn't do it, there was nothing to stop me paying someone else to observe him and follow him. That's why I came to you.'

Sherring ground out his cigarette, and immediately lit another. He said:

'My secretary, I believe, has told you that the fee for a preliminary consultation is ten guineas. A bill for that amount will be sent to you within the next few days. Some people regard it as high, for a quarter of an hour of my time. The point is that I am not soliciting business.' He smiled, a fat wintry smile. 'The country as a whole may not be booming, but the private inquiry business is. My difficulty does not lie in getting cases, but in finding and training suitable men to handle them. I prefer company stuff, for a number of reasons. As a professional, I dislike having good men, even though you would be paying the top rate, tied down on unnecessary work.

'My best advice is that you do as the police suggest, and write it off as a bit of bad luck. They are almost certainly right in thinking that if you take no further action, the trouble will die down. They get bored quickly, even with malicious activity. Moreover the present climate which makes the police relatively less helpful could actually be to your advantage. If the SEA go through with their notion of calling in the yobs, you are likely to get him off your back that much quicker. There's more fun, and a greater sense of self-importance, in whooping it up in Pallister than in pursuing a feud with someone who ignores you. Do you take my point, Mr Gawfrey?'

'Yes,' Rod said. 'I don't agree with it, though. I don't see why I should submit to this sort of thing as long as there's a chance of doing anything about it. I'd like you to take the job on.'

'One can't be precise at this stage,' Sherring said. 'But it can't possibly cost you less than fifteen pounds a day. I doubt if the damage you are getting would work out as high as that.'

'It's not a purely financial point.'

Sherring shrugged, scattering more ash. 'I see.'

Rod said: 'What I was proposing was to take up the police offer of having them see the boy again. There's nothing they can do to him, of course; he will simply be irritated by it. The chances are that he will try to hit back at me. That's where I want your help.'

'Fair enough,' Sherring said. 'I can have him followed. He may be wary, though. My men are good – better than CID, I would say – but they can't make themselves invisible.'

'There is one thing …'

'Go on.'

'We have a batch of eight houses under construction just this side of Gostyn. They're off the main road, about three-quarters of a mile from it. There's one of our boards pointing the way. And no night watchman.'

'Yes,' Sherring said, 'a very useful point. We could put a man there. We could use a relatively unskilled man, too, which means I could keep the charge down to fifteen bob an hour for that part of it. Three pounds an evening.'

'Money's not the main consideration, as I've said. I object to some half-witted lout trying to terrorize me, and I want to see him stopped. If your man is unskilled … I want evidence on him, do you understand? There could be a half-dozen with him, perhaps more.'

'He can get help, at the right time.'

'There are no telephone lines through to the houses yet.'

'Well, we shall have to use our resources, won't we?' He gave a cackle of laughter. 'A carrier pigeon in each pocket, maybe.'

He told Hilda what he had done that evening, after her parents and the children had gone to bed. Rod took a whisky and sat with her in the kitchen while she heated and drank a glass of milk. She heard him out without saying anything, her silence a disapproval. This was not because the hooliganism had angered her less, but out of her deep-rooted mistrust, stemming from her early childhood in depression-ridden, grimly socialist Tyneside, of the police. They served the enemy, the vicious useless rich. Her acceptance of their own changed circumstances had done nothing to remove that fierce, emotional resentment.

Private inquiry agents were even worse, he knew. They carried the connotation of privilege in law, justice openly purchasable according to the depth of pocket.

As always, her censure, although unspoken, bothered him. This was one way in which their marriage was out of balance: she was not at all concerned when he showed that he disagreed with some action she had taken. He pressed the point. One could not just put up with this. It was not simply a matter of damage to property. There was always a chance of the children being got at. What would she do if …?

She reacted before he had a chance to formulate possibilities.

'If one of the children is so much as threatened, I'll go and beat the bastard to a pulp with my own hands!'

Her vehemence could still confuse him. Recovering, he laughed, partly in amusement at the thought, partly in relief, in the reassurance of her single-mindedness and essential strength. He asked her:

'Do you think I should have beaten him up, anyway?'

'Don't be a fool, Rod! That would be just …' She laughed, relaxing. 'I suppose you've done the right thing. It's just that I don't like …'

'I know.' They were at ease together again. 'By the way, have you spoken to Jane?'

'Not really. I've hardly seen her.'

'This business is getting more and more tricky. Did you see that they're having a national day of mourning for that young student, with memorial parades in all the big cities? Staunton will be behind things in Pallister, which means that Jane is likely to be in the thick of it.'

Her feelings were mixed on this, as well. She was in favour of opposing the State, but disliked the indiscipline and apparent lack of purpose of the contemporary young. She was also influenced by a deep desire for respectability for herself and her family. It was in order to support righteous insurrection, unthinkable to get one's name or, worse, one's picture in the press.

'I will speak to her,' she said. 'I've got to be careful, though, Rod. She can be obstinate, if she thinks she's being coerced.'

'She's not in yet, is she?'

'She said she might not be back tonight.'

'Do you think she's sleeping with Staunton?'

It was surprising, in a way, that he had not put the question to her before; but long ago, before they were married, he had got used to the depth of her instinctive loyalty to her own, which caused her to leap to their defence against any minor criticism, even from him. He admired the quality, and had learned to put up with its minor inconveniences.

But she said now, quite mildly:

'I don't know. I don't think so. She admires him too much.'

He stared at her, and laughed. She said:

'I always think of admiration as something that works from a distance. She stands back, and looks at him. She's not involved.'

'Some women go to bed with men without being involved, in the sense you mean.'

She said with distaste:

'I suppose some do.'

'Not you, though.'

Their eyes met and after a moment she smiled.

'No. Not me.'

The call came through just after half past eight in the evening. Sherring said, with satisfaction:

'Gawfrey. Glad I've managed to get hold of you. We've done better than I expected, a lot better.'

'You mean, you've got something on him?'

'On him, and four others.'

'What?'

'There was nothing to it. I put a chap in on that site you thought they might go for. No results for two nights, but half an hour ago they came in on full throttle. My man got through to us on a walkie-talkie, and we simply tipped off the police. The Inspector has just been through to tell me they're in the bag. Caught in the act, with our fellow as an eye-witness in case they try to wriggle out of the police evidence.'

'That's very good.'

'Very good? It's bloody marvellous. Quick and neat and satisfactory to all parties: the firm, the client, and the police. I wish we had a few more like it.'

'What will they get?'

'Our motor-cycling friends? Assuming it's a first offence – first conviction, rather – probation for a certainty.'

'Not much of a deterrent.'

'I couldn't agree more. But it strengthens the hands of the police remarkably. If they step half an inch out of line now, they'll clobber them. No, you've done your duty as a citizen, and you've got them off your back. You're a shining example in these demoralized times.'

'Well, thank you for ringing to tell me.'

'Part of the service.' He hooted with laughter. 'We aim at efficiency. We'll have your account in the mail first thing in the morning.'

VIII

THE MEMORIAL PROCESSION had been planned to start at the University, wind through the main thoroughfares of the city, and culminate at the Civic Centre. Posters had been plastered in advance, and the word had been spread, individually and through loud-speaker vans, that all young people were invited – urged – to join in, as part of the national protest against the tyranny and mismanagement of the old, particularly against the government which had been responsible for Matthew Marshall's death.

The weather, which could have ruined the enterprise, blessed it. The storms had blown themselves out during the night; the day was clear and bright, hot but not oppressive. At two in the afternoon, when they started, edges were still sharp against the blue; branches of trees moved in a small cooling breeze. A crowd watched while they formed up outside the Senate House. The banners were raised: WHO MURDERED MARSHALL? ... THE SENILE STUFF THEMSELVES WHILE STUDENTS STARVE ... WANTED: EDIBLE TEXTBOOKS ... IF YOU HAVEN'T GOT A HALFPENNY THEN SOD YOU TOO ... IT'S TIME YOUTH MARCHED ...

The crowd was a young one, the overwhelming majority in their teens, a lot of them no more than fourteen or fifteen. Then, as the column moved forward, they fell in with it.

They joined in batches along the way. At first they were fairly quiet, but they became progressively noisier as the procession moved down to the centre of Pallister. The committee had distributed broadsheets during the previous few days, giving the parodies of popular songs and hymns which were to be sung. Judging from the volume, the distribution had been good. The parodies themselves, Jane had thought, were pretty feeble, but they were, to varying degrees, obscene, which clearly made up, as far as the singers were concerned, for any deficiencies in wit. Cardew was the Minister of Education, directly responsible for the freeze on students' grants. They sang:

> 'Old Mother Cardew
> Went to the larder
> To get a poor student a bone
> To get a poor student a bone.
> When she got there
> The cupboard was bare,
> So she lifted up her petticoat
> And this is what she said:
> "Get hold of this – "
> BASH BASH
> "Get hold of that – "
> BASH BASH
> Oh, when there isn't the cash to spend
> You do feel lonely,
> When there isn't the cash to spend
> You're on your only,
> Absolutely on the shelf,
> Nothing to do but play with yourself,
> When there isn't the cash to spend!'

The police were there, lining the busier streets, holding up traffic to let them through, sometimes in knots around radio cars. They made no attempt to interfere, in accordance, Jane knew, with their instructions. Government policy was to play things down as much as possible – put up with the nuisance of the processions and get them over quickly.

The atmosphere stayed good-humoured until they got to the Civic Centre. By that time they numbered several thousand. The leaders, with the microphone and amplifiers, took up their position at the top of the steps, and their followers occupied the lawns and spread out over the ring road that encompassed the municipal buildings. Jane and Walter remained on the fringe, to maintain the appearance of his non-participation, as far as the official side of things were concerned. She had become separated from him during the milling that took place as the procession came to a halt, and was now surrounded by shop-girls in the new hip-briefs, with bare midriffs, and their boy friends in khaki drill, some of them wearing puttees. She looked for Walter, but could not see him. What she did see were mounted police coming up the hill from the station.

Others saw them too. There was a formless shout, followed by particular cries. 'Watch out for the Mounties!' 'The bastards on horses!' The mounted police trotted around the perimeter of the crowd, aloof and remote, apparently disregarding the clamour entirely. On the steps, there were a couple of oscillating howls from the speaker, and it came into action. Somebody – Jane thought it might be Pinkard – spoke, his voice booming distorted across the packed heads.

'We are warning the police. We will not tolerate …' A roar of applause drowned his voice, and he had to wait for it to die down. 'We will not tolerate interference with our democratic right to hold a public meeting in protest against the fascists in Whitehall. We will defend ourselves against any attempt to suppress free speech. The old men in Whitehall are not going to keep the youth of this country under. The men on horseback are not going to cuff us out of the way as though we were peasants. We will …'

The roar swamped his words again, and this time kept up. It was part applause, part high spirits, part anger. The police horses slowed to a walk, but went on round the edge, their riders staring impassively ahead. Through the din, Jane heard an individual voice shout:

'Get the bastards!'

There was a banner nearby, with the words: WE'RE TOO YOUNG TO VOTE BUT WE STILL HAVE TO EAT. Some boys in pseudo-uniforms grabbed it from the girl students who had been holding it. They ripped the cloth away. The sight confused her. A counter-demonstration? Then she found herself pushed and jostled, caught in a bow-wave of humanity as the boys pushed their way to the outside with the bare poles.

They broke through, and she saw what their intention was. As the next policeman came by, mounted on a big chestnut, one of them thrust a pole for the horse's legs. The horse stumbled and reared. Although not a rider – she had wanted to learn as a schoolgirl but it had been one of the things that had come under Hilda's interdict – she had always loved horses, and the thought of this beautiful great beast being tormented, perhaps brought down, maddened her. She flung herself at the boy with the pole, and tried to wrench it from him. Someone – one of his mates, probably – hit her on the side of the head, and she went down. After that, it was all confusion. The crowd, still roaring, was on the move, but in no agreed direction, except that the overall tendency was to flood outwards from the centre. The mounted police were no longer trying to keep up a neutral guard, but were laying about them with truncheons. She could hear what sounded like another loudspeaker, in the opposite direction from the steps of the Town Hall, and guessed it was the police car giving orders; but it was impossible to distinguish anything except the shouts and cries of people immediately surrounding her. She struggled to her feet, and was almost at once knocked over again. She gasped with pain as someone trod heavily on her leg, and tried to cover her head. It was the sort of situation, she realized, in which a person having gone down might be crushed to death. She had a sense of waste, of the pointlessness of her life; and a determination not to accept the futility of such an ending. She fought her way up, felt her hip-shorts rip at the waist, and was carried with the mob, breathless, almost helpless, but more or less on her feet.

There was no doubt now about what was happening. The crowd was scattering and the police were moving up in force.

They worked in batches, with gaps between them through which the more active were encouraged to escape. It was the obvious thing to do, and Jane tried to go with the surge towards the nearest outlet. She was almost there when she tripped on a kerb-stone. The crowd was looser, more fluid, no longer binding her to it. She went down for the third time, and blacked out.

Someone was lifting her roughly, shaking her. Panic came before pain. The crowd ... she was under them, and they would kill her. To die like this – Hilda would ... Pain, then, throbbing at the base of her skull. She gave a small involuntary moan. Light: the sunlight of a summer afternoon. The arm was covered in blue cloth. Blue sky. And no-one pressing in. Empty space. She looked and saw a few huddled bodies, with police moving amongst them. It was a policeman's arm that raised her. She whimpered with a new jolt. He said:

'Hurt yourself, have you? Serves you bloody well right. Your pals killed a mate of mine – do you know that?'

She shook her head, only slightly but it hurt terribly. He said:

'He was doing his job – extra Saturday afternoon duty, when he could have been home seeing to his garden. Because a lot of useless bloody young idiots have got nothing better to do than kick up a row.' His fingers tightened on her arm, viciously, kneading flesh and bone. 'And you're old enough to know better. Look at yourself – at the bloody sight of you. You're disgusting.'

Her hip-shorts had been ripped off completely. From the waist down, she was wearing only her flimsy nylon briefs and one shoe; the other had been lost. Her legs were dirty from being trampled on. Her blouse had been torn, too, so that her bra was exposed. She said:

'Could I have something to cover me?'

'Like hell, you can. I'm not in the ladies' outfitting business. I'm taking you to the van, and if the television cameras get you in close-up on the way there, they're welcome.'

'Please ...'

'You're lucky.' His fingers pinched her cruelly again. 'It's because of them bastards that we've got to show restraint. They'd love to get a bit of police brutality on the news programme. Come on, you dirty bitch. Don't worry. I'll call you Miss if they bring a microphone up.'

He half-carried, half-pushed her to the police van. She was dazed, and saw things in unconnected tableaux. The television news van of which he had spoken, with a figure slowly panning a camera. Pigeons settling on the grass and then, disturbed, flying away in a shimmering cloud. Police bending round a figure, also in blue uniform, on a stretcher. A youth trying to kick himself free as he was dragged along by his arms and legs.

'Right,' he said, 'get up there.'

The van was half-full, mostly of youths but with one or two dishevelled girls. Their faces were either sullen or frightened; they were all silent. Jane had a foot on the step, when a voice said:

'Not this young lady.'

Another policeman. She had an impression of tallness and ugliness, a face that at first glimpse looked puffy and badly shaped. She was afraid of him, and of what she was being reserved for. The man holding her arm said:

'Taking her to the station to be booked, sir. Causing a disturbance.'

'No,' the ugly one said. 'She tried to stop them bringing the horses down. I had the glasses on her. Find her something to cover herself with.'

Someone gave him a police cape, and he put it over her shoulders.

He smiled, and his face looked different.

'You've had a bit of a shaking up,' he said. She liked his voice, she decided: strong, a little rough. 'How do you feel?'

'I don't know.' Her head was hurting, but not so badly. 'A bit better.'

'We'll find you a car to take you home.'

'Thank you.' Staring around, she saw a man being brought in, his face smeared with blood. 'What happened?'

'One of our men was killed. Three deaths altogether, on the first count. God knows how many injuries. I think one of the horses will have to be shot.'

'I mean – how did it happen?'

'Someone collected a lot of dry wood together, someone else poured petrol over it, and a damn' fool struck a match. Nothing unusual.' He showed her how to fasten the cape. 'What's your name?'

'Jane Weston.'

'I like Jane. It was my grandmother's name.'

He led her away from the van towards a police car.

She said: 'The horse – not the chestnut?'

'No, not the chestnut.'

IX

MARTIN'S ROBE was not ready when he came in from school. There had been a minor disaster with the weekly wash – the wind had blown the line down – and although it hadn't really been dirty she had put it through the machine again: she knew he liked to have things clean. She overwhelmed his demurrals on that point while she served him his high tea. This was some sort of fish, pre-cooked, frozen and bread-crumbed in Grimsby. It had a vaguely fishy taste, and was stamped in the shape of a fish, a miniature plaice. Mrs Johnson thought of herself, with some pride, as a good plain cook.

She brought the robe up to his room, freshly ironed, half an hour later. She had had the television set on while she ironed, and was full of the news.

'There's been more riots again,' she told him, 'and in Glasgow they set fire to a big store, and there's dozens burnt alive. And some sort of bomb let off outside Parliament. Isn't it a terrible world? You'd wonder how they do things like that, wouldn't you, young as they are?' She gave him the robe. 'Will it be all right now, then?'

'It's fine, thank you.'

'If there were more like you, Mr Weston – the quiet ones. But that's the way it is. Self, self, self, and let the weak go to the wall. They had a bit of the Prime Minister on, appealing to their better natures. It's not much good appealing. I've not kept you late for your meeting, have I?'

He shook his head. 'I've got time enough.'

The streets through which he walked to the Scouts Hall were drab and quiet as ever. No ripples reached here from the demonstrations and sporadic violence which dominated the centre of Pallister evening after evening. They were, in fact, more quiet than usual. He saw no teen-agers, did not hear the grinding roar of motor-bike engines. The centre of the city was the magnet, drawing them to gape if not to riot.

The continuing hot weather probably did not help. Day followed stuffy day, not always sunny but always oppressive. This evening the sky was a grey weight over the grey houses. In the hut, it was stifling; one drew breath as a conscious act. He did his best to make a prayer of it: an awareness of God sustaining one from breath to breath, instant to instant.

Following the prayer, the Kyrie, the meditation, there was a difference. The Fellowship had started in South Wales, in Cardiff, and a visiting Brother had come from there to speak to them. He was a small man, an apple-cheeked Iberian, his hair strong and wiry though more white now than black, his robe worn and shabby. He spoke with power, and with the lilt of the valleys.

'Brothers, I do not need to tell you of the sickness of our time. Even though you do not pay much attention to the world, you cannot avoid seeing what is before your eyes, or smelling the corruption under your noses. It is a world of violence and self-seeking. The battle sways to and fro, and it makes no difference who wins because no good can come of a victory. They have no sense, any of them, except to achieve their own ends – no compassion, only self-pity. The old say the young are irresponsible and vicious; the young say the old are savage and oppressive. They are both right. What matters is that they are all men, and all have turned their faces away from God.

'In these times, with the gales of evil blowing, it is the more important that we of the Fellowship should tend with care our little lamps of love. And that we should band ourselves more and more closely together, in harmony and in united purpose. God tells us to be fathers to the old and sick and deserted, brothers to one another. And to suffer the time into which

He has called us.'

He paused, a long pause in which his eyes slowly went along their meagre ranks. Martin felt power, and an uplift of courage, when they met his. He spoke again, slowly, with more deliberation:

'It may not always be so, Brothers. God's patience, like His arm, is long, but only God Himself, in His Goodness and Greatness, is infinite. The generation of vipers may flee the wrath to come, but they will not escape it. For lo, one cometh in a raiment of camel's hair, a leathern girdle about his loins, and his meat is locusts and wild honey. The time is not yet, but the time will be.'

He paused again. In the silence, a voice cried out. Spruce, the chartered accountant's clerk, whose Christ was a man, put to death by his God as well as his fellow creatures.

'Amen!' he shouted. 'God is not mocked. His fire will scourge and cleanse!'

Martin hardly heard him. He hugged the courage that had come to him, made dizzy by the blessing. It would not last, but while he kept it he was transformed with hope.

X

S HE WAS BY HERSELF when the telephone rang. Picking it up, she said:

'Professor Staunton's office.'

'This is Police Headquarters. A call for Miss Weston.'

'Speaking.'

'Would you hold the line, please, Miss? Superintendent Jennet wants to speak to you.'

On the telephone, his voice sounded deeper, more stolid.

He said: 'Miss Weston? Hope you don't mind my telephoning. I was wondering how you were getting along.'

'I'm fine, thank you. It was nothing but a few bruises.'

'You were very lucky.'

'Yes, I realize that. But how did you know I'd be at this telephone number?'

He chuckled. 'Not very difficult for a policeman. I'd have rung before but we've had our hands full the past week.'

'Yes, I can imagine. It's very kind of you to inquire. And I haven't thanked you for saving me from being booked. I thought I was going to have to spend a night or two in gaol.'

'That's all right.' He paused. 'There is something you can do for me, though.'

'What's that?'

'I've got an evening off for a change. I was wondering if you'd come out and have a bit of supper with me.'

The question confused her. As she hesitated, he said:

'Policemen do have private and social lives, you know. I hope you can come.'

She felt both pleased and alarmed. Temporizing, she said:

'I'm not sure. I don't … That is, I have to work rather irregular hours. I can't be sure that I'll be free this evening.'

'How soon will you know?'

'By this afternoon.'

'I'll ring again then, and ask you. Will that be all right?'

'Yes. Yes, that will be fine.'

Walter arrived a quarter of an hour after that. He was in one of his manic moods: she heard him singing outside in the corridor, a Mozart aria. He flung the door open, and almost shouted at her:

'It's all over!'

'What is!'

'We've won.' He came to her desk, lifted her, waltzed her out into the room. 'The news has just come through. The government has given in completely. The grant increase will go through on schedule.'

She felt the closeness of his physical presence like a kind of magic, a source not of desire but of strength. A strength which, at this moment, she resented. She said:

'Well, congratulations.'

'We've done it. That little bastard in Downing Street has climbed down.'

'Clever Geary. Clever you.'

'We're taking the committee out to celebrate tonight. Book a table at the Colombe d'Or.'

'You and the committee? That's eight.'

'And you. Nine.'

'I'm afraid I can't. I've got a date.'

'Break it.'

'No.'

'Don't be silly. Put him off. He'll be all the keener. This is an exceptional day.'

'I'm not sure that I want to celebrate, anyway. The death toll from riots was given as over fifty this morning.'

He stared at her fiercely. 'Are we responsible for that? A lot of those were students. The riots didn't start until the police used teargas. They acted like nineteenth-century colonialists, putting down trouble in the native quarter. They were the ones who declared war. What matters is that we've won.'

'Yes.'

His brief flare of anger had gone. He had answered her point, and that disposed of it. That confidence, she thought, continually welling up – where did it all come from? Even when she hated it, she could not help being impressed. He released her, after a quick urgent squeeze of her hips in to his loins, went back to his own desk, and sat down. He leaned back, stretching out his arms and smiling.

'Ask them to lay on that duckling au Chambertin – they need a few hours' notice for it. And lobster mayonnaise before that. They can put a few bottles of Corton Charlemagne to cool, as well.'

Depression really settled on her after he had gone to his lecture. Her annoyance with Walter faded, and was replaced by annoyance with herself. He was as he was, and as she had long known him: overbearing, exasperating, selfish, but at least a whole person, directed towards ends that were meaningful and comprehensible. She was a tattered thing by comparison, not knowing what she wanted; not even sure that there was anything she could whole-heartedly want.

Her policeman, for instance. The impulse to accept his invitation for the sake of thwarting Walter had gone. In any case, nothing thwarted him. He would smile tolerantly at her, and make some casual remark which went deep to the heart of her motivation. Despite the apparent spontaneity, he always had something in reserve. It would probably be a comment on her mistrust of the urge towards stability and security which she had come to suspect in herself. She knew from one or two remarks already made that he had discovered this, as he had discovered so many things about her. His knowledge of her inner self was one of the most important factors in their relationship: she resented it, feared it, and depended on it.

She found she was getting a headache. She prepared to go to lunch, went as far as the door, and came back to the telephone. She got through to Police Headquarters, and asked for Superintendent Jennet. The sergeant said he would check, and she regretted making the call, hoping he would be out. But he answered almost at once.

'Nice to hear from you again.'

'I'm sorry,' she said. 'I find I am going to be busy this evening after all.'

'That's bad luck. I'm tied up tomorrow myself. What about the evening after that?'

'No, I'm afraid not.' She made an effort. 'I do work irregular hours, as I told you.'

He said cheerfully:

'Ah well, can't be helped.' She was preparing to put the telephone down. 'Miss Weston?'

'Yes.'

'I'll ask you again, you know.'

'Please do.'

She was surprised to realize she was smiling.

XI

G ERRARD CAME RIGHT TO THE POINT:

'Those Jap machines are electrically powered. If you take on a dozen, you'll have to have another electrician on maintenance.

Rod said: 'The things are just about fool-proof. Simple routine servicing once a year.'

'I've heard of stuff being fool-proof before now. The fact is, your electricians have got enough on their plates as it is.'

'Look, we both know they're not overworked.'

'No, and they won't be, either. Another man goes with the machines. There's nothing to argue about, Mr Gawfrey.'

Rod commonly got on well with union officials, but Gerrard was something of an exception to this. He was a hard-minded, soft-bodied man. He had replaced a communist and was obsessed with a determination to show that he, as a life-time Labourite, could negotiate as toughly as anyone. Controlling his annoyance, Rod said:

'You're making it impossible. These machines represent a saving, but it's not all that big a one. When you've taken the increased capital cost into account, it isn't enough to pay another skilled electrician, at the present rate of wages.'

'You know more about that than I do.'

'I can show you the figures.'

'You can, but it would make no difference. There's a principle at stake.'

'If we put the machines in ...'

'We want another man on. Otherwise we withdraw labour.' He brought a battered tin from his pocket, drew out a home-made cigarette, and lit it: he had refused the ones Rod offered. 'I'm not mad on anyone buying Jap stuff, any road. My father was a prisoner out there for three years. He died under sixty from it.'

'That's a long time ago.'

'Yes. I've got a good memory.'

'And there's no English machine anywhere like it.'

He took a deep breath, and puffed out smoke with satisfaction.

'You make your mind up, Mr Gawfrey.'

Rod said bitterly: 'It isn't difficult. Under those conditions, I have no option. I won't confirm the order.'

'Fair enough.'

'So I suppose that concludes our business.'

'I suppose it does. By the way, I think I ought to tell you that the union as a whole is putting in a claim for a general increase. We're asking for fifteen per cent, back-dated to the beginning of this month.'

'Haven't you forgotten there's a wage freeze on?'

'There was. If they expect family men to stand for that when a gang of kids get a fifty per cent rise because they've done a bit of marching and shouting, they've got another think coming.'

'You won't get it. The economy …'

'We've heard about the economy long enough. And about the foreign bankers. They should have thought about that before they gave in to the students.'

'It doesn't help to make things worse.'

'God helps them that help themselves. Standing politely to one side doesn't get you anywhere. I know of four other unions that are putting claims in, and I'll tell you something else: the TUC will back strike action to enforce them.'

'It would be illegal, as things stand.'

'And do you think they'll have the guts to put us in gaol, when they didn't have the guts to stand up to teen-agers? So as to impress the foreign bankers? I'll tell you what they can do to impress the foreign bankers: what about a capital levy? We haven't had one since Cripps.'

Rod said:

'I enjoy a political argument, but I'm afraid you'll have to excuse me for the present. I've got to be in court in an hour's time.'

Gerrard put on a crooked grin. 'What's up, then? Failed the Breathalyser?'

'As a witness.'

Understanding came. 'Those yobbos they picked up damaging the houses over at Markham?'

'Yes.'

'I'd like to see them put away, the bloody useless lot. Not in prison, where they get things done for them. On an island, somewhere, where they'd have to work to keep themselves alive, and where they could carve each other up as much as they liked. They'd be no loss, any of them.' He got to his feet. 'It's definite, about those Jap machines?'

'Definite.'

'Fair enough. I won't keep you.'

The presiding magistrate was Coates-Bender, a member of Rod's Club. When the defending counsel began a long discourse on the contrition of the accused, he cut him short.

'I don't want to limit your freedom in any way, Mr Laker, but I never feel these sentiments of regret carry much conviction at second-hand. We have all had the opportunity of witnessing the demeanour of these young men in court, and can form our own opinions on how contrite they are likely to be.'

He placed them all under probation. He also said:

'I should also like to put on record my appreciation of Mr Gawfrey's action in assisting the police. It is true that this was in defence of his own property, but not all citizens, by a long way, are as alert and courageous in that defence as he showed himself to be. And the defence of one's own property: in a legal fashion, is tantamount to a defence of the property of all, of society itself. In my view, he is very much to be commended.'

The boys were not looking at the bench. Their eyes rested, sullen and intent, on Rod.

The usher stopped him as he was going out. Mr Coates-Bender would like to see him in the Magistrate's Chamber. He went there, and found Coates-Bender peering into a mirror, anointing a stye on his eye.

'Ah, there you are, Gawfrey. Damn the thing. Haven't had one of these since I was a schoolboy. It's amazing how irritating they can be. Your young hooligans …'

'Yes.'

'I'd like to have awarded them corrective training, but it wouldn't have stuck. They were all first offenders, in law at least. The press would have played it up: savage reprisals against youthful high spirits, and all that. I'd have been reversed, and they'd have seen themselves as heroes to boot. It just wasn't worth it.'

'No, I see that.'

'Anyway, we've got tabs on them now. I don't think they'll bother you again. I don't think they'll bother anyone for a while. You can give me a lift if you were thinking of going to the Club for a drink. Save re-parking my car.'

PART TWO

A TIME FOR PATIENCE

The latest measures announced by the CHANCELLOR serve to underline two things. The first is the seriousness – one might say desperation – of the country's position. For years we have alternated crises with brief periods of economic buoyancy. Under both Conservative and Labour administrations, we saw the stop-go policy of deflation followed by reflation, of urgent warnings that we stood on the brink of ruin followed by optimistic assertions that this time we should have controlled expansion and continuing prosperity.

In fact, the intervals between crises have been shortening. The tentative reflation embarked on at the beginning of this year had to be halted before it was properly underway, when our balance of payments suddenly and sharply took a turn for the worse. Before it had been loosened a single notch, the belt was re-tightened by two or three. The mood of organized labour was bound to be, in the circumstances, an ugly one.

It was at this juncture, in early summer, that the students' demonstrations, against the proposed abrogation of the previously agreed increase in grants, flared up, and were joined by other teen-agers. By accident or design, the demonstrations turned into riots, with considerable damage to property and accompanying loss of life.

After six days of this, the then government capitulated to the students and reversed their previous decision. This seems now, and was labelled by informed opinion at the time, an act of utter folly, but one can understand the probable motivation. The urgent concern was presumably the avoidance of civil unrest, at a time when unpopular decisions were going to have to be taken in the very near future. It may also have seemed that the concession was of minor importance – a relatively tiny sum of public money was involved – and justifiable in that the earlier rejection had been an act of doubtful faith (and one opposed by influential people inside the Cabinet on those grounds).

What the country saw, though, was weakness and vacillation. Labour was not prepared to accept the new stringencies, and warnings that this was the most desperate peace-time crisis in our long history were disregarded. Wolf, after all, had been cried often enough before, and the house of straw had stood. The coinage of moral exhortation had also been debased. The only thing that impressed the unions was that the devil might well take the hindmost.

So we had the series of strikes in June, possibly encouraged by the un-English generosity of the sun which blazed down day after day and made the garden, the country, the seaside, so attractive an alternative to the factory bench. The government, belatedly facing the challenge it had created, attempted to use the legal powers it had acquired to break the resistance of the unions who had come out. All they succeeded in doing was stiffening the attitude of Labour as a whole. Within a week we had our second General Strike. Within a fortnight, the government had collapsed, the demands of the strikers had been conceded, and Parliament had been dissolved.

The resulting election, and the landslide victory of the previous Opposition, solved nothing. The new PRIME MINISTER'S first act on taking office was a sharp devaluation of the pound. This was merely a recognition of the inevitable, and leads us to the second point emerging from yesterday's pronouncement by the CHANCELLOR. It is quite simply that the present government has no more idea of a positive solution to the country's agony than its predecessor had. We are a ship running before the storm, rudderless, without a scrap of sail.

Forty years ago, a world that believed in the inevitability of affluence was hit by a savage economic blizzard. Then, as now, leaders were helpless as a combination of economic and social factors dragged industry to a near-halt. The answer eventually was provided by Keynes. Deficit spending was the key which would open the door to future prosperity,

and keep it open.

Unfortunately, the comparison fails in one vital particular. The Keynes answer stimulated international trade, and trade solved the depression. But our troubles are our own, and Keynesian urgings are like telling us to lift ourselves by our bootstraps. The rest of the world looks on, apprehensively but so far relatively unscathed by our catastrophe. The only help they can give the sick man of Europe is a pauper's dole of food.

For this we must be grateful. It is true that selfish considerations are not absent from their aid. If barbarism engulfs one country, even a country quarantined by the sea, it may well spread to others: the dying man might still destroy his neighbours. But there is generosity as well, particularly as shown by our friends in America. And without the food ships which come into our ports, unbalanced by exports, we should, quite literally, be starving. As it is, we are on short and unexciting commons. The pauper cannot expect champagne and caviare.

Most of us are resigned to this. Numbed, perhaps, by the suddenness of the collapse, we accept and wait. If we have patience, things will pull round. The ones who are restless are predominantly the young. One must hope they will learn control. We have paid, and are still paying, a heavy price for their insurrection of six months ago.

77

I

THE STREET WAS NOT UNLIKE THOSE in the Gostyn Estate, but older; built not long after the war and, he noticed, shoddily. There were cracks in several houses, including the one at whose door he now stood. The woman who answered his ring was about fifty, bulky, with a large bosom and long neck. She wore a flowered pinafore over an old jersey and skirt. She looked tired and a bit bewildered, but it was a common expression these days.

He said:

'My name's Gawfrey. Buying and selling. This is a buying trip, but if there's anything you want I'll make a note and do what I can for you.'

'Buying, is it?' There was Irish in her voice. 'I find it hard enough to buy the rations, and a bit of coal for the grate.'

'As I said, this is a buying trip. I'm doing the buying. There might be something you want to part with.'

She hesitated. 'Come in, then, out of the draught.' As he followed her into the house, she added: 'My husband's out, looking for work.'

That was a good thing. There was more likely to be trouble when the man of the house was about. The men felt more bitter about having to sell the household bits and pieces and often openly resented his part in it.

He had to listen, as they went, to the usual, wearisomely familiar complaints, about the food, the electricity cuts, all the drawbacks of the way in which they were forced to live now. Her husband had had a senior post with a firm running a chain of supermarkets, and had lost his job when the firm collapsed at the end of summer. He was willing to do any kind of work – labouring, if necessary – but there was no work even for the young men, and he was fifty-two. She did not know how they were to manage – how they would get through the winter, even.

'That painting,' she said in the hall. 'It's an oil painting – I mean, a real oil painting.' It showed a man driving cows over a narrow bridge across a stream in which great leafy trees were reflected. The rural face of thriving Victorian England. 'It's by an RA. We always thought it might be worth something.'

Rod shook his head. 'I'm afraid there's a poor market for art, around here at least.'

'Come on upstairs,' she said. 'I've got something there to show you.' Climbing ahead of him, she went on: 'It was two years ago my younger daughter got married and went away. That left the two of us in the house. He'd worked so hard, and got on so well, starting as a clerk and making his own way, and I knew he'd always wanted to have a study. So I turned Bridget's room into a study for him.'

She threw open the door. It was quite a small room, looking out on their own narrow strip of garden, and the almost identical garden and house beyond. Most of one wall was taken up by a big desk, dark oak with a green leather or imitation-leather top, with an executive's swivel chair in front of it.

'I'd saved money for years on the housekeeping,' she said. 'I wanted him to have something really worth while. But what's the good of it now? What can you give me for it?'

Rod said:

'I don't think it would be practicable for me to make an offer.' He did not want to hurt her feelings. 'I'm single-handed. I wouldn't be able to get it downstairs and out to the cart.'

'I'll gladly help you.'

'Even so …'

'And my husband would help when he's in. He it was that told me to sell it. He doesn't like to look at it now, after all that's happened.'

He was tempted to say something vague about coming back another day, but did not like to think of them waiting vainly for his return. He shook his head.

'I can't buy it.'

'But there must be some sort of an offer you can make. It's good wood. Look at it.'

Rod said harshly:

'Thirty shillings – for them both, desk and chair.'

She stared at him, her face creasing into disbelief.

'They cost me over a hundred and seventy pounds, and less than two years ago.'

'Old pounds.'

'But thirty shillings! It wouldn't pay for a week's rations. I won't sell for that. I'd be as well using it for firewood, with the price of coal what it is.'

He said nothing because there was nothing to say. She had, though she would not believe it herself for a while still, arrived at the truth. He would have lost on the deal. It was worth its weight as kindling, but no more. He turned back in silence to the landing.

Another door was open, and he could see that the room inside was filled with junk. He asked her if he could look. She said apathetically:

'If you want to. It's just lumber we keep in there.'

He thought he had drawn another blank, until he saw them on a table by the wall: a couple of Edwardian oil-lamps. One was missing a shade, but they had not been converted into electric table-lamps. The wicks turned up, in response to the pressure of his finger and thumb on the small winding wheel. One of them seemed to be quite new.

He said: 'I'll give you fifteen shillings each for these.'

He had a customer who had asked him to look for paraffin-lamps against the time which he feared when there would be no more electricity. The fear seemed irrational to Rod, and he thought it likely that if it did happen paraffin would be impossible to come by, but he was willing enough to execute the commission.

The woman looked suspicious, and he realized he had offered too much. She would have been happy at five shillings for the pair. Thirty shillings made her feel that she was being tricked. In fact, he could not ask more than fifty shillings of his client. He realized he still had a lot to learn about his new profession; certain basic principles he doubted if he ever would grasp.

She began to haggle with him, and he merely shook his head and went downstairs. She caught him up outside in the garden, carrying the lamps.

'I'll take it,' she said. 'God knows we need the money.'

He paid her, reading her unspoken thoughts. She was a defenceless woman, her life and her husband's smashed by circumstances beyond their control, at the mercy now of a swindling travelling salesman. He walked away, sick with disgust, to his horse and cart.

Travelling back, he told himself that he was lucky; he had salvaged something at least out of his own collapse. Rusty, the horse, for instance. He did not have enough to buy an animal at present prices, even throwing in Bridge House. Things might have been worse.

The firm, like many others, had collapsed with the devaluation of sterling. The prices might look ridiculously low, but no-one was buying houses. No-one was in the market for construction of any kind. He had acquired Rusty by accident, taking him in part settlement of a debt when his own position did not yet seem too serious. (Linda, like Jane before her, had been thwarted of horse-owning by Hilda's rejection of the concept and what she imagined it stood for. Having the horse on the premises for a few weeks, he thought, might soften her; and anyway he was helping a fellow Mason.) It was only after the crash that he had realized Rusty's utility value, and managed to hold him back when the Rover and the Mini were sold, along with the stocks and shares and insurance policies, to meet what was not covered by the sale of business assets. The days of the Depression were back: they offered nothing to a failed building contractor, but a travelling salesman might keep body and soul together. The editorials in the press still promised an up-turn by Christmas, but he had no faith in them. He knew his business to have been well run and basically sound. The events which had broken it were not likely to find a quick remedy.

They came to traffic lights where the road intersected the main road from Pallister to the west. They turned red in front of him, and he had to rein in. He wondered why the lights were kept operating, now that the private motorists' petrol ration had been abolished completely. For morale purposes? As the lights went green, he moved across. There was a speck in the far distance which was probably a bus, and several figures on bicycles: nothing else. Bicycles, and bicycle parts, fetched a price now. And the buses were full, of course. But people travelled less, too. It was strange how quickly horizons had closed down. The world of the waiting motor-car, of a forty-mile drive to see friends, seemed a lot further than months away.

Rusty jogged on. He had taken his translation from the pampered pet, lovingly braided and ribboned before gymkhanas, to a working horse, very well. He was a young strong beast, a gelding less than four years old. Rod had a fair amount of winter fodder stored for him, and there was still some grass about the house: it had been a mild winter so far. He cropped the lawns, no longer mown. Shoeing had been the main problem. Fortunately Bill Miggs, in the old village of Gostyn, had kept his hand in with pleasure horses, as a side-line to the business of wrought-iron gates, which his father had started in the thirties when a blacksmith's forge had seemed an anachronistic relic. He had made and fitted heavy-duty shoes, replacing the previous light plates, and Rusty had taken the new load on his feet well. But they still wore through too quickly; he needed shoeing again already.

They came in through new Gostyn. A number of the houses were empty, their gardens untended. Most of these would be cases where people had been unable to keep up mortgage payments, and had moved away, doubling up, probably, in the crowded tenements in the city, where a concentration of three or four people to a room was becoming common. Others had been allowed to stay on by finance companies who knew they could not sell the houses in any case. This, like most things in the year's debacle, had been haphazard, with a man in one house being spared while his neighbours on either side were hit. The chance aspect, the being subjected to the whims of a capricious god suddenly revealed as deadly and all-powerful, had been one of the more demoralizing elements in the breakdown.

Through the gates, Bridge House came in sight. It looked very little different; the outside had been painted in the spring, and the front gardens were of a formal nature, mostly bushes and grass, which did not yet show signs of deterioration. They still lived there because there seemed no sensible alternative. The house was on the market, but there had been no offers, even at the absurdly low price he had put on it, and there were no prospects of offers. They had moved into a few rooms near the kitchen, and Hilda was coping uncomplainingly with a situation in which domestic help was cheap again, but not cheap enough for them to afford it. Elke had gone back to Austria, to marry her hotel-keeping fiancé. She wrote to them, saying that it was all terrible, is not, and last week had sent them a food parcel. Smoked ham, butter, real coffee, and chocolate for the children.

Rod took the horse and cart round to what had been called the stables even during the time that motor-cars had been housed there. He unsaddled Rusty, and was preparing to groom him and see to his feed when Linda came round and begged for the job. He surrendered it, and watched her for a while. She was loving it. Children adjusted to things so much more easily and, being without resentments and regrets, could better enjoy what there was. She looked healthy, too. Thank God, he thought, for the US government, and the people who invented fish protein. It was a dull diet they lived on, but there was no immediate sign of starvation, or even malnutrition. Protein, with vitamins added, in a tasteless grey meal.

His mother-in-law was polishing furniture, using elbow grease in lieu of the polish which was both expensive and hard to come by. She was singing as she did so. If anything, she seemed happier, finding herself of more use, in her own eyes, than she had been since the children had grown up. Stephen was lying full length on a settee. There was a book open in front of him, and he was staring at it, but Rod doubted if he were reading. He, in contrast, had reacted worse than the others. Always a watcher and physically idle, he had withdrawn still further, his responses dulling into a lethargy of which Rod disapproved but which he could not altogether condemn. In this transformed world, he was bound to be at a loss. For the adults, it was a matter of picking up the pieces of a shattered life; for the younger children, a question of assimilating things like the disappearance of motor-cars and chocolate, the acceptance of existence on an economy level. Stephen stood between the two. He had wanted to be a civil engineer. Theoretically he was still working, for A-levels and University entrance. But he was too intelligent not to perceive that everything had changed, that his best chance might lie in inheriting the horse and cart.

Hilda was in the kitchen, at the Aga. She had preferred that form of cooking and fortunately had stood firm against his proposal, a couple of years ago, to convert it to oil heating – there was no oil now, and the central heating system stood cold and useless. Fuel for the Aga was not easy, either, but he had managed to store a fair amount. The big pot contained the all too familiar vegetable stew, more potatoes and turnips than anything else. She seasoned it as well as she could, and it was laced with Frotein, but the best cook in the world could not do much with resources as meagre as were available. Fortunately, there was the spice of hunger. He had a better appetite, from his long days, out on the road, than in the time when there had been fancies to tempt him, and Scotch to set the gastric juices flowing.

She asked him how things had gone, and he told her: a mediocre day apart from a silver tea-set which he had picked up at a big house in the old wealthy residential suburb of Pallister: there was a good market still in precious metals.

She asked: 'Did you see any signs of a disturbance?'

'No. Should I have done? It was all very quiet.'

'There was a flash about Pallister on the wireless. A raid on the petrol stores at the refinery.'

'Here, too? Youngsters?'

There had been raids previously in the London area and in Glasgow, followed by night rides through the countryside on the now banned motor-bikes. In Scotland, the police giving chase had been ambushed. Oil had been spread on the road. The bikes had got past it travelling on the verge, but the two police cars had skidded and crashed, one of them bursting into flames. Two policemen had died.

'Yes,' she said. 'Youngsters. I'm glad Stephen doesn't want to go out much these days.'

'I suppose so.'

He felt the strain of accumulated fatigue, of holding depression constantly at bay. Dusk of a December evening. It was something else he tried not to think about, but he could have done with that Scotch.

II

IN THE PERIOD BEFORE BREAK, Martin had to take Price's class as well as his own. According to Moncrieff, who had instructed him to do this, Price had been waylaid the previous evening and beaten up – not too badly, but enough to keep him in bed for a couple of days. He had recognized one of the half-dozen who set on him as a boy who had left Comprehensive school the previous summer. Price had known him and had trouble with him when he was at the Primary school, and was having roughly identical trouble at present with his brother.

Moncrieff said:

'He won't bring charges, though. I think that's a mistake.'

He did not go into the motive for not bringing charges. It was not, as at one time it might have been, the sense of personal failure as a schoolmaster, the stoical determination not to bring in authority to crush where one had botched the moulding. It was, as they both knew, fear: the mistrust of authority's power to protect. Assaults on their elders by groups of the young were common enough these days. The fact that this one had a probable motivation did not make an essential difference.

It was obvious that the children knew what had happened. In general, they were cheekier, more restless, than they had been, but today it was altogether more marked, especially in the neighbourhood of the boy Leigh, whose brother had been concerned in the attack. A dark strong boy, at once sly and aggressive, he got up and asked Martin:

'Where's Mr Price, sir? He's not ill, is he?'

Martin said: 'He'll be away for a couple of days.'

'But what happened to him, sir?'

This was the senior form, the eleven-year-olds who would go on to the Comprehensive next year. Their faces grinned up at him, innocent for the most part, not knowing what it was all about, but in one or two cases, he thought, diabolical. A crony of Leigh's said:

'I heard he slipped and hurt himself in a dark alley.'

Another voice: 'Just outside the Queen's Arms, wasn't it?'

Leigh asked: 'Is that what happened, sir?' His sharp ugly features stared up contemptuously. 'I'm sure it's not true, sir, but I have heard it said he's a fairy.'

Male homosexuality, more and more openly a part of the ordinary scene after its legalization, had become very common since the slump. Learned papers had been written, suggesting that it was caused by a sense of frustration in manhood directly due to the economic shock: men felt that, losing their jobs, they had let down their wives, and turned to each other rather than face the expected reproach. Liaisons of this sort were, at any rate, now taken for granted in levels of society where they had previously been almost unknown. This had also resulted in an increasing number of assaults being caused by – or being claimed to be caused by – homosexual propositions.

There was a general swell of laughter, partly at the sexual reference, partly at Leigh's effrontery in saying this in the presence of a master, one of Price's colleagues. Martin felt himself shivering, and a dryness in his throat. He knew what he should say, the action he should take, but the picture was so vivid in his mind of the dark street at night, the heavy footsteps, fists punching and boots thudding against flesh. And Price had shirked the risk of having it happen a second time. So far he was all right. Sometimes they followed him and jeered or chanted after him, but that was all, and as a member of the Fellowship one expected it. One could accept the humiliation of being a buffoon, and offer it to Christ. But the other ... the different humiliation, above all the pain ...

Ignoring Leigh's remark, he said, above the laughter:

'Let's get on now. Can anyone tell me why King John was reckoned to be a bad king?'

III

JANE TOLD HERSELF HOW HEALTHY cycling was, as she pedalled in to Pallister against a fairly strong and bitterly cold wind. She remembered getting the bicycle, for her thirteenth birthday. It had been a tremendous disappointment, because she had wanted a record player. That was the year after Hilda married Rod. She and Martin still lived with their parents in the poky terraced house in Paisley Street – Rod and Hilda had taken over one of his houses, with central heating and a wonderful big bath, squared and black with a chrome rail at the side – but she knew that more money was coming in than before, and where it came from. She had hinted to Rod about the record player, subtly she thought when Hilda was out of the way, and had thought the hints were bearing fruit. Then she woke up on a grey soggy morning, to the sound of rain dripping down the window, and jumped out of bed and pelted downstairs to the parlour, to find the bicycle.

She knew right away it was Hilda's doing – that Hilda had insisted on the more utilitarian present – and had spent most of that day and intermittent periods during the next six months hating her. It had been a very good bicycle, a great improvement in every way on the old one which she had outgrown and which had been bought second-hand in the first place, but she was determined not to like it. She would not ride it to school, and it languished most of the time in the shed, rusting except when her mother forced her to clean and oil it. It came with them to Bridge House, but by that time it was just a part of the family lumber: Hilda had her own car and Jane was borrowing it freely.

At the time she had seen the logic, or so she thought, of

Hilda's position. Her old bicycle was past it, and she could not very well expect two expensive presents: a new bicycle was the reasonable choice to make. It only occurred to her now, as she dismounted and started the long walk up Meredith Hill, that this had not been all Hilda had in mind. It was very likely that she had noticed her attitude to the new affluence, and felt it necessary to check it. Jane smiled to herself, blinking tears from her eyes as the wind sharpened. That would be typical of Hilda. Stick to your principles even when it hurts – and whoever it hurts.

She was glad of the bicycle now. Rod, who was careful of machines, had greased it before stacking it away in the stable loft, and it had remained in good condition. The inner tubes of the tyres had to be replaced, but the outers were in good condition – just as well in view of what they cost, when you could get them. And she saved herself the bus fare, which almost made the discomfort seem worth while.

After the long haul up Meredith Hill, there was the gentle downward slope of the Broadway, with open parkland on either side. The trees were winter-bare, and she saw solitary figures here and there, possibly aimless but more likely picking up firewood. That did not apply to the group of teen-agers, who milled or huddled together, in one case packing one of the bus shelters. Some of the boys whistled after her, and a couple of them made a pretence of chasing.

Walter had said the office, not the flat, but he was not in when she arrived. Her desk and chair were still there, as were her typewriter, trays, the pencil sharpener Walter had insisted on buying because he had seen one in some exhibition and thought it terribly ingenious … all the paraphernalia of a secretary's domain. Everything, except the secretary. The University continued – Education, the new Prime Minister had said, was more important than ever – but there had to be sacrifices: the fifteen per cent cut in salary to match that in the Civil Service, and the abolition of all ancillary services not vitally necessary. Professors could type their own letters, or send tapes along to the pool.

Walter, of course, did neither. He ignored the letters that he did not like or did not interest him, and had persuaded her to come in from time to time and blitz the ones that mattered, by which he mostly meant his private correspondence. He could scarcely have afforded to pay her: apart from the cut in his official salary, his income from writing and broadcasting had dropped sharply, and he was still keeping the flat on in Pallister, spending more and more time there now that he had no car. It would have been nice, though, if he had made some sort of offer, or, at least, expressed regret for imposing on her. Nice, but improbable.

He was in a bad temper when he came in. The Principal was threatening to suspend one of the students of whom Walter thought very highly, and had refused to give way when Walter protested to him about it.

'What's the reason for suspending him?' Jane asked.

'Because of his exhibition. He's a sculptor.'

'Obscene?'

'That's what the fool says. The boy's got a great deal of artistic talent.'

'What sort of thing are they exactly?'

'He's called it "Excrements". Life-like representations in various media – different textures and colours.'

She made a face. 'It sounds infantile, but I wouldn't have thought it was worth taking seriously.'

'It's not the things themselves so much as the titles he's given them.'

'The titles?'

'He's named the people they're supposed to be excrements *of*. Fairly eminent people, too. Not just as the Prime Minister or Archbishop of Canterbury – full names and honours. Including royalty. That's what Edwards says he's roused about. Actually, it's probably because of his own.'

'He's included the Principal as well?'

'He should be flattered, considering the rest of the company.' His cackling laugh rang out suddenly. 'A set of small, dark pebbly stools: real miser's products. And I'm sure he is constipated.'

She asked him: 'Do you really find it so funny? A bit Third Form, surely.'

'In point of fact, they're extremely penetrating character studies. He's taken his idea from something in those lectures Reilly gave here last year. The point about excretion being the equivalent of creation, and reflecting the intrinsic personality as creation does. It's not at all new, of course, as an idea, but it started him off, and he does quite a lot with it. You ought to see what he does with the royals, for instance.' He laughed again. 'Side by side on gold-painted papier-mâché thrones!'

There had always been what she recognized as silliness, alongside the intelligence, and it had irritated her in the past. Now her feeling was more a weary disgust, her impulse not to hit him but simply to get away – not to have to see him again. She said:

'Shall we get the stuff cleared now?'

'And the PM's,' he said. 'A watery-looking mess. Absolutely him.'

She sat down with her notebook, and he dictated his letters. When he had finished, she started taking the cover off her typewriter, but he came and grasped her arms and pulled her up to him, his hands moving to hold and squeeze her breasts.

She said:

'I won't be in for a couple of days, and you want to get these off, don't you?'

'You'll have plenty of time. I've got a lecture in quarter of an hour, anyway.'

She thought: if he mattered to me at all, that's the sort of remark that would make it impossible to do it. But he did not matter. She went to lock the door, then came back and allowed him his probing and fingering, and the brief pulse of intimacy. Nothing happened with her, but he either did not notice or did not care. It was a long time since anything had happened. He rose from her, and she got up and tidied herself and sat down again at the desk.

From the door, he said: 'Are you sure you can't get in again till Friday?'

She said calmly: 'Quite sure.'

'That's a pity.'

She slipped paper and carbon into the machine, and began typing, not looking up when the door closed behind him.

There was a long queue at the Labour Exchange. It moved forward very slowly. The clerks treated them with triumphant contempt, themselves suddenly part of an elite: the job-holders. For ten minutes at one period, there was only one clerk at the counter, the rest gossiping and drinking tea in the background.

Immediately in front of Jane were a couple of women in their forties, executive secretaries from the same firm: the ball-bearing factory which had been one of Pallister's biggest before it closed down. They carried on a dialogue of nostalgia, about events and personalities from the time when their only financial doubt had been whether the Christmas bonus would be ten per cent or fifteen. It was not poverty which oppressed them so much as the loss of personal importance. They could put up with Frotein and patched clothes far more easily than with the disappearance of their authority over the girls in the General Office, the privilege of coming back ten minutes late from lunch, of eating at a special table in the firm's restaurant.

Four girls behind her were also in a group. They were shop assistants, from the department store which had put up shutters a week before. Their conversation was even more inane, but on the subject of their boy friends, and the acid party they had been to the previous night. Whatever else was in short supply, there seemed to be plenty of LSD going round. She shuffled forward, excruciatingly bored by both lots of chatter, half-stifled by the frowsty atmosphere. It was something, she supposed, that it was warm.

94

It was cold enough outside. She pulled her coat more tightly round her, and was heading for her bicycle which she had padlocked to the railings, when she heard her name called, and recognized Micky's voice. She felt the quick lift in her spirits, the uncompromisingly physical tingle, even before she turned to look. He was in the car, on the other side of the road, waving to her out of the open window.

She hurried across, and said: 'What are you doing here?' A depressing thought struck her. 'You're on duty today after all?'

He shook his head. 'I just thought you could do with a lift. Climb in.'

'In a police car?'

'Does that bother you?'

'I was thinking about you. Mightn't you get into some sort of trouble?'

'I doubt it.' He leaned across and opened the door for her. 'I can always say I'm taking you in for questioning.'

It was warm inside the car. She snuggled back against the yielding leather, savouring the luxury. That, and the wonderful physical thing which happened with him: the sense of relaxation and tension, bound up together, not opposites any more but teamed like trained horses. Entirely physical, she insisted, and very likely exaggerated by all the other physical deprivations. But good.

His flat from outside was not unlike Walter's: two rooms instead of one and in a less elegant area, but in much the same sort of block. It was very different inside, though. There was none of the clutter – the books, journals of proceedings of learned societies, sleeves of chamber music recordings, dirty pipes lying in bone china saucers, no bric-à-brac of small pieces of advanced sculpture, no abstracts on the walls. The atmosphere instead was one of tidiness and neutrality, one could say severity. In the sitting-room-diner, the pale yellow walls were bare except for two Guardi prints: views of Venice on what looked like a cold sunny morning, with a wind whipping foam on to the waters of the Grand Canal. The walls of the bedroom, distempered a light ochre, were completely bare, and the three-quarter bed gave an impression of being squared off, barracks fashion.

He put a Peggy Lee LP on the radiogram, and poured Jane a drink. He still had Scotch, but she had an idea he did not drink it except with her – she had noticed the level of the bottle remained the same from one visit to the next. They kissed, but then sat apart, talking. She did not share as many interests with him as with Walter, but the conversation was easier, all the same. He talked quite a bit about police work, and she liked that.

Things followed the usual routine. Micky poured himself a second drink while she, refusing, took her glass into the kitchen to prepare lunch. He had done the cooking to begin with, but had willingly surrendered the role to her. There was always some titbit, such as canned meat, which was not only expensive but highly pointed on the ration cards. She had thought at first that he might be getting special concessions as a policeman, but realized now that this was like the whisky: saved for the one meal a week which they shared. There was never anything else except basic foods in his larder.

Today, along with the meat, he had put out rice and, of all things, a can of okra. She prepared a dish and put it in the oven before going back to him. They kissed again, and talked again, and she had the drink she had refused before, a small one. He told her of the difficulties they were having with youth gangs. There were certain districts which they could only patrol in groups – like the old stories she remembered her mother telling of the bobbies having to go three in a row down the Scotland Road in Liverpool. He said:

'I think we're going to have to pull out of some parts altogether, if it gets any worse. We haven't got the men for it.'

'I should have thought recruiting would be easier now.'

'With so many out of work? There are snags, though. It's happened so fast, and it takes time to expand training facilities. In fact, the way we're extended, it's just about impossible to spare men to train recruits. We need them on the job. We had a chap half-killed in Mirton only yesterday. He was in a patrol car, and he left the car to check a call they'd had about a suicide. A gang of them got him, and set about his mate when he went to see what had happened. Fortunately he'd called a couple more cars in before he left his own. As it was, some more of them had managed to rip the tyres and put a brick through the windscreen.'

Lunch was ready, and she served it. They had a couple of bottles of beer, another extravagance with the swingeing excise tax imposed in the most recent emergency Budget. No wine was coming in at all, of course. Micky had half a bottle of claret in the kitchen which he was saving, he had told her, for her birthday.

They had a pudding of a few bottled fruits: she had brought him a couple of jars from Hilda's stocks at Bridge House. No coffee, but cups of weak tea, with a little milk and no sugar. Jane took the things out and came back, and this was the kiss which went on.

He had put the electric fire on in the bedroom, so that it was warm in there. They undressed, watching and smiling at each other. There being no distractions to the eye heightened their consciousness of each other. This desire needed no stimulation. Ease and tension again, but above all a sense of peace. She moaned at the shock, anticipated but always strange, of his body. The vision of Walter came to her, and she thought again how unimportant that was, too unimportant for it to matter whether it was done or not.

Micky knew that she still helped Walter out with his work from time to time, but he had never asked about him, never suggested the possibility of anything else. She doubted if the idea would occur to him: he was, in many ways, a rigid, unsubtle man. Walter knew nothing of Micky. When, after that first telephone call of his, following the riot at the memorial march, he had continued to ask her out, she had faced the fact of Walter's ability to destroy any other man's influence in her life, and come to a conscious decision. Before she first said yes, she had made up her mind to keep this thing from him. It had been an act of rebellion against Walter, not a feeling that Micky would be any more important than the others had been.

That, probably, was what had made it so good. It was a part of her life from which Walter was excluded, of which he was ignorant; and this enabled her to relax. That was another reason for continuing to let Walter have his way with her sexually. Refusal or objection would not only frustrate him but arouse his curiosity. He would bring the frightening intensity of his mind to bear on the change in her, and would not rest until he had fathomed the reason and destroyed what he would see – calmly, she thought, without jealousy – as a threat to himself.

She lay there, warm and sweating, and touched Micky's body, the softness and smallness where there had been hardness, domination. If she were in love with him, she supposed, there would be no risk; Walter would not have the power to take anything from her that she really wanted. But what she wanted – dreamed about during the barren days between – was not the man, but this. It was Walter's mind that fascinated her still, for all its lapses into nonsense and puerility, Walter's personality that made Micky's seem that of a minor character in an indifferent novel.

She wondered about Micky's wife. There were no relics in the flat of her time here – of any woman's presence, in fact. It was masculine and negative. But Micky had not avoided talking about her. He had answered her questions with detachment but no reluctance. Pretty, he had said, and fairly intelligent, a woman of charm but no character. She had wanted a man who would make her into something that she was not, and had found him in a publisher's representative: a commercial traveller, Micky explained, but on a higher cultural level. (She had thought that was meant as a witty sneer, and then decided not; it was just one of his factual observations.) There had been a double divorce, and the couple had moved to London. No children: she had been pregnant once, but miscarried.

It all sounded very much like him: an operation that was smoothly and efficiently carried out, with the best made of a bad job, and no recriminations or deep emotions. He was wrong about the wife, probably. It seemed more likely that he had tried to change her, to make her conform to his own pragmatism and self-sufficiency, and that she had rebelled against this. Jane felt that she could sympathize.

What about herself, though? The picture, she decided, was not a pretty one. But was there any reason why it should be? The world had been a casual and pointless enough place before the collapse, and was worse now. Things were real in their own right rather than as part of any universal aspect. At present, the most important thing of all was what took place here, for a few hours at a time, but it was still a separate joy, a satisfaction isolated from the other, less powerful ones.

He moved against her, and she turned to him, a swimmer clinging to a spar after the ship had gone down. But the sea was warm, dotted with floating wreckage, and she felt strong still, and without fear.

IV

B AILEY SAID:
'Good to see you again, Mr Gawfrey. You're looking very well, sir.'

'Pink gin, steward,' Lennard said. 'And the usual Haig for me.' He settled into his chair. 'Lucky thing, Rod, running into you.'

He said to Lennard: 'I'm afraid I'm not a member now. I didn't renew my sub.' He glanced at Lennard, who was his usual immaculate self – a well-cut, carefully valeted blue suit, brightly polished shoes, old-fashioned silk tie, and even at this time of year with a rose in his button-hole – he grew them in his conservatory. 'I can't afford it, Bill.'

Lennard showed none of the embarrassment that he himself felt. He smiled warmly as he took Rod's arm.

'For God's sake, who's to worry about that? You can always sign the Visitor's Book if you want to make it all official. In fact, it's better if you do – saves any trouble over drinks. You'll let me buy you a drink, for the sake of the good times past and the good ones to come.'

Now, stretching himself, Lennard looked round the room. There were more people in it than Rod would have expected, and they had the usual drinks in front of them. But there was only one other, apart from Lennard, whom he had known at all well. As though to emphasize the same point, Lennard said:

'We've had quite a few drop out, of course. And unfortunately the wrong ones, for the most part.' He shook his head. 'It's not the same, coming in here. As you know, there are some who are doing not at all badly out of the depression. I could name half a dozen who have made killings in the black market. In the old days, we'd have had them out, and sharpish, but as things are, what can one do? The Club's struggling to keep going, as it is.'

'I suppose so.'

Bailey brought their drinks. Whisky was now over seven pounds a bottle, even in the depreciated currency, gin almost as much. Out of his reach, as were all drinks except an occasional glass of the specially brewed three per cent beer, which tasted feeble and innocuous and was. He could not resist saying:

'I'm glad you seem to be managing all right, Bill.'

Lennard said:

'Part luck, part foresight. I got into foreign stuff before the Stock Market plunged, and since they were bearer bonds, held abroad, they didn't get me when the devaluation came. In fact, they're worth a hell of a lot more now, from the UK point of view. I'm limited in the amount I can bring in, of course, but they've not been unreasonable about that. And some things have improved. Labour's easier to come by. As you know, I've got a bit of land, and a couple of greenhouses. I've got some stock now – small herd of cattle, few pigs, that sort of thing – and I grow my own vegetables. I'm better than self-sufficient. Something over for selling.'

Rod could imagine the prices. He had extravagantly bought a pound of butter a week before, and paid nearly a pound for it. The derogatory references to black marketeering presumably were meant to exclude farm produce. He sipped his gin, and said:

'Don't you find it a bit difficult getting in here from where you are?'

'Without the Bentley? Not really.' He smiled. 'I get a lift on the tractor to the station at our end, and it's a pleasant walk across town here. I've had the Bentley greased and jacked up. A lot of people are being careless with their motor-cars. One in good condition is going to be worth having when this little trouble's over.'

'How soon do you reckon that will be?'

'I don't know.' He spoke in a tone of measured frankness. 'Not too soon, I'm afraid, and it's going to be worse before it's better. Maybe a lot worse. That's another good thing about the smallholding. We can live on our own, if we have to.'

'The PM has said there are signs of an economic pick-up.'

'He can say what he likes, but I've not gone far wrong in the past by paying no attention to political pronouncements. I prefer my own sources of information.'

'What do they say?'

'They say trouble. Have you seen Maurice Masterson lately?'

'Not lately.'

'He was telling me Glasgow's been under mob rule for the past three days, and since yesterday London south of the river has been almost as bad.'

'There's been nothing on the news.'

'They're keeping it quiet in case it spreads. Or trying to. I think that's a mistake. The rumours that do carry are all the wilder. But I suppose they're hoping to get it under control quickly.'

'What sort of mob? The yobs again?'

'So it seems. They get hold of petrol, get their bikes out, and take off. The police can't stop them. I suppose these empty roads give them a sense of power, and after that …'

'I saw a horde of them in broad daylight yesterday,' Rod said, 'belting down the Broadway.'

'I've seen it twice. They're out of control. It would be time to bring the Army in, if we still had an Army.'

Rod shook his head. 'I don't understand it.'

'Don't you? I understand it very well. They've had years of being allowed to do what they like by their seniors, of being wooed by advertisers for their purchasing power and having their moronic views taken seriously. Pop singers debating the existence of God with elderly deferential bishops on television – girls from behind a Woolworth's counter discussing the merits of the latest batch of idiot records as though they were Mozart scores – psychiatrists praising the frank and fearless honesty of the new generation in the cultural Sunday papers. The goose was laying a continuous stream of golden eggs, and they were all for them. Now everything's changed. They're being asked to do without things, and at the same time are being thrown on the streets all day instead of merely at evenings and weekends. They're bored and deprived, and they're probably scared as well. If the world can do this to them, perhaps they're less important than they thought, and that's a terrible thing to live with. So they go out and break a few windows, burn a few buildings down.'

'What's the answer?'

Lennard shrugged. 'I don't know. Things will probably sort themselves out, but not yet, I fancy.' He pressed the bell for the steward. 'A gloomy prospect. Have the other half, old man.'

'No, I've got work, I'm afraid. Thank you all the same.'

'No time for a game of snooker? Ah well, another time, maybe. Sure you won't change your mind about a quick one?'

He smiled in goodbye, but did not get up from his chair. He had not asked anything about the work Rod was now doing. Tact – or had he, perhaps, spotted him with the horse and cart? He wondered, too, about the gesture of inviting him into the Club for a drink. An act of kindness, for old time's sake? That was the charitable explanation. He let the door of the Club close behind him, and set out across the park. He stopped at a bench and took the packet of sandwiches from his overcoat pocket; he decided that the gin had warmed him enough, and he would economize by skipping the cup of tea. The day, in any case, was mild for the time of year. He realized as he unwrapped the sandwiches and started eating them that he was in view from the Club windows, but was not concerned about that. The sandwich filling was cheese, in extravagantly thick slices. The meat-flavoured Frotein paste was supposed to be as nourishing, and was a good deal cheaper, but Hilda would not accept it. He smiled in the bare winter park, thinking of her with love.

On the way home that evening, a gang of motor-cyclists passed him. There were more than a score of them, doing, he judged, about seventy. The smell of their exhausts lingered on the air like a scent of the forgotten past.

V

M ARTIN'S LAST CALL was on a pensioner couple, the wife bed-ridden with arthritis, the husband a fat silent man who rarely moved from his chair in front of the fire. They lived in the two downstairs rooms of the house, for the most part in the front one where the double bed had been fixed up. The stairs were thickly cobwebbed. Martin had offered to clean them, but had been refused. The woman said she could not think of having strangers upstairs.

She made up for the taciturnity of her husband by talking almost all the time, but on one subject: her own real or imag-ined physical pain. Everything came back to this. She delighted in holding up her misshapen hands, drawing Martin's attention to them and to the agony they caused her. He had to stifle nau-sea at the sight, and at the sound of her voice. The husband sat reading old boys' adventure books – Henty and Ballantyne. There were a couple of dozen of them in the room, and he read them over and over again. The television stood in one corner, a box of polished walnut decked with the false gold of anodized aluminium, its square face blank and blind. The cathode ray tube had gone some weeks before. Even if it had been possible to raise the money for it, it could not have been mended. The factory had closed down, and there were no replacement tubes available.

He came out into a dark but not particularly cold night; the spell of mild weather was continuing. It was good to get the smell of the house out of his nostrils. He felt very tired – he had awakened during the previous night and been unable to get to sleep for hours – and the thought of bed was welcome.

Then he remembered that Mrs Johnson had asked him if he would call in and get her some aspirin from the chemist. She had had a headache all afternoon, she said, and she was out of them.

In fact, she was an aspirin eater by habit. He thought of simply saying he had forgotten the errand, but found himself turning away from the direction that would take him home, and towards the local shopping centre. The chemist stayed open till nine: most small shops did nowadays, making up for the meagreness of their daily trade. It was, he knew, not compassion that moved him, but the old compulsion: he must not fail in small things because of the inevitability of failing in large. To answer small demands meant escape from the possibility of larger ones. He walked on, a few drops of rain hitting his face. Something else embarked on for the wrong reasons, but no more avoidable for that.

He heard the motor-bikes roaring before he came to the light of the shops. They were distant, but sounded as though they were heading straight for him, and he moved in close to the wall. Then their engines revved and cut, somewhere in front. Martin stopped, then continued on his way.

A road of terraced houses, lit by widely spaced lamps, led transversely to Cornish Street where the shops were. There was noise there as well as brightness: shouting and laughing, excited voices. He came to the corner of the street, and paused again to see what was happening.

They were at the chemist's. Motor-bikes were parked outside, taking up the width of the street. Some youngsters were standing about, others milling by the door, more, he guessed, inside. He heard someone cry: 'Do the old bastard!' And the reply: 'Find the acid – that's what counts.' It was a raid for drugs, then. He wondered what reason they had for thinking there would be LSD there, but the answer was simple really. Almost certainly the chemist had been selling it illicitly, and the gang had heard about it and decided to clean out the stocks.

Martin turned away. A beam of light from one of the motor-bikes, which was being moved by its driver, caught him as he did so. A voice called something. He did not want to think it could have anything to do with him, but found himself quickening pace. There was the blare of an engine starting up, followed by a second. It would be a mistake to start running, he told himself. They probably weren't after him at all, but would be if he acted in any way unusually. The racket was louder, and they broadsided round the corner into the road in which he was, their headlights drilling tunnels of white in the darkness. Then he started running.

They caught him easily. One dropped back, while the other, passing him, slewed round to block his path. He stood, blinking, dazzled by the brightness. The one in front said:

'It's a Holy Robey.' He throttled the engine down. 'Who are you spying for, Robey? The police?'

'No.' He was confused. 'I was only going to the chemist.'

'Then what stopped you?'

'I thought …'

'You know what Thought did?' That was the one behind. 'Used his last french letter on a bint on the pill.'

They both laughed. The first said:

'He wants to go to the chemist's, so he goes to the chemist's. Walk along nicely now.'

He went back down the road, with a motor-bike crawling on either side. He must not show fear. It was only one of their stupid jokes. There was nothing to be afraid of. They came into the road with shops. A gang of kids – that was all. They were singing: the song called 'Acidman'.

> 'I go high, I go high,
> The grues stay down but I go high,
> The Mary Jane, I pass it by,
> The acid hits me high, high, high …'

The chemist's shop had been partially wrecked; the glass in the door had been broken, a stand knocked over, the contents of one of the counters swept into a heap on the floor. The chemist was leaning back against that counter, with blood on his face. His wife stood by the door to the living quarters, blanched by panic. Four teen-agers in white leather jackets were picking things up, looking at them, putting them in their pockets or tossing them on the floor. The two escorts got off their motor-bikes and led Martin forward, gripping him hard by the elbows.

'A Robey, Commander. Said he wanted to go to the chemist's. But he was hiding round the corner, seeing what was going on.'

The four came to the door of the shop. There was a crowd outside, some in leather jackets, though black or brown, not white. There were two or three girls, but they were probably not with them – merely local girls who had come out to see the fun. No older people, and the windows round about, apart from the shops, were dark. They would be watching from behind curtains, in darkened rooms. The gangs were brutal with those who got in their way, or looked as though they might.

The one addressed as Commander was a tall, gross youth, black-haired, with rounded babyish features. He put his arm round a sleek blond boy who stood beside him.

'What did you want at the chemist's, Robey? You ran out of pile ointment, maybe?'

There was a titter of approval. Martin said nothing, but he could not stop the sickly grin which he knew was on his face. The Commander said:

'People answer my questions, or else I'm wasting my breath, ain't I? You think I'm wasting my breath?'

Martin said: 'My landlady wanted some aspirins.'

'Pills for the landlady. Hey, so the landlady's on the pill? I am surprised at you, a holy man, too. I really am surprised.'

The baiting went on for some minutes, mainly from this one but with interjections from others. Fear subsided a little. They did not seem to be vicious. They would have beaten up the chemist to make him tell them where the LSD was. He was probably all right as long as he looked a fool, and answered their questions politely. He had a feeling the Commander was getting tired of it, and that he might soon dismiss him. Then the blond boy, his hair brushed back smooth and hard from a small, pointed face, said:

'Believe in God, Robey?'

He hesitated, but it was a case where there was no point in treachery.

He said: 'Yes.'

'Ever see him, this God wonk?'

'No.'

The Commander took over again. 'That's hard. You a creeping Jesus, and you never get to see the big man?' His fingers moved to caress the blond boy, gently stroking along the line of his jaw. 'Sounds like a pretty poor sort of organization to me.'

The blond boy said:

'Maybe we should help him.'

The tone of voice was amiable, but Martin found himself shivering uncontrollably. The Commander said:

'How are we going to do that, Bob?'

'Take him on board. Float him high. I'll bet he's never made a trip. Ever made a trip, Robey?'

'No.'

'He's scared,' the Commander said. 'We oughtn't to scare a Robey, or the God wonk won't like it.'

The blond boy said:

'When I make a trip, it's like mountains and switchbacks, doing a ton and a half on a road that runs across the sky, picking the flowers in a garden full of cocks. But I'm not religious like you are. Maybe you'll see angels, the Pearly Gates, the geezer on the golden throne.' He pressed his head in against his companion's neck. 'What do you think, Commander?'

'I think the God wonk would like that,' the Commander said, 'I think it's a fine idea.'

'Hold him tight,' the blond boy said. 'Sometimes they don't know what's good for them.'

The two who had brought him gripped his arms tightly as the blond boy advanced, feeling in his pocket. He brought out a small plastic box, and opened it. There were small compartments inside, a sugar cube in each. He was conscious, absurdly, of wondering where they had got the cubes; there had been none in the shops for months.

'Open up, Robey,' the blond boy said. 'Put out your tongue and climb on the magic carpet. Train leaves for Heaven from Number One platform.'

The face stared close to his own. He could feel the warmth of the boy's breath. It was not foul smelling, but he hated it … air which had been in another's body heating his skin, entering his lungs. The best thing would be to seem to acquiesce – accept the sugar cube, and get rid of it as soon as they released him. He opened his mouth.

'That's good,' the boy said. 'Few minutes' time, you'll think you're the Pope, Archangel Gabriel, old JC himself, walking on the water.'

Someone called: 'How about the Virgin Mary?'

They laughed, and even the blond boy's tight hard face cracked into a smile. The lump seemed very big in his mouth. He smiled himself, awkwardly. The hands had released his arms, and he turned to walk away.

The blond boy said:

'I didn't tell you to let him go, did I?'

He was spun round and gripped again. He could feel sickly sweetness dissolving into his saliva, the edge crumbling against his tongue. The blond boy said:

'I read a book once, about witches. Used to go into Mass and take the wafer from the priest. Then, as soon as he'd moved past, they'd spit it into their handkerchiefs and keep it for the Black Mass they had later on. I wouldn't like the Robey to do that. Wouldn't like to think of the holy sugar being used by

Robeys at one of their jigs. You just hold him while it melts.'

The Commander said: 'Anything in that Black Mass kick, you think? We might bust a church open and do something like that, maybe.'

The blond boy shook his head. 'Prayers said backwards. Who the hell cares?'

'Orgies, though. They had orgies, didn't they?'

'With women. And kissing a billy-goat's arse. Not my kind of freak-out.'

'Christ, no.'

They went on talking, while the sugar dissolved in his mouth. He felt only numbness, and the nauseating sweetness. It seemed a long time before they let him go, but he was resigned to the waiting, and almost surprised when release came.

The blond boy said:

'We could keep him around – see how it takes him.'

The Commander said: 'Sod that. We got more interesting things.' He put his hand on the blond boy's head, careful not to ruffle the sleek helmet of hair. 'Drop the Robey. We're moving on.'

This was a strange and wonderful place. A canyon whose walls were the squared outlines of terraced houses. He saw things in the light from the street-lamp which he was passing, and stopped so that the seeing should be fuller, stronger. The texture of brick: honeycombed, rubbed by a hundred thousand passers-by over a million different seconds. A place where one day, in a winter's frost, perhaps, or at a moment when a heat-wave was causing tar to blister on the surface of the road, concrete had cracked, leaving this jagged scar, whose depths were mystery. Near the base of the lamp itself, a globule of phlegm, hawked out from some old man's bronchitic chest. He peered to look at it, not with repugnance but with amazement. Its reality and its uniqueness delighted him. Here was the ground of being, the miracle of existence in epitome.

The light itself seemed, as he turned upwards to the lamp, to beat against his face, a radiant intangible rain, but dry, not wet, cold and yet warming, a flowing artifice, made by man, by God-in-man, by man-in-God. Such power everywhere … Power and love. A privet hedge, topping the begrimed brick wall. Each leaf itself. One there, with its edge withered by a patch of blight, the brown and the dark green, never to be repeated. A spider web, barely visible at first and then, under the dominion of his eyes, spun steel and silver, holding at one point a raindrop that was a rounded crystal of worship, a bead of meaning. Power and love. The spider, crouched dark and dreadful, and full of beauty and strength, grasped in each instant by God.

There was nothing to fear; there never had been. The power was God's, and the power was his, also. He thought of the boys in their white leather jackets and laughed, and his laughter, echoing in his ears, was a wonder in itself, a paean of praise and triumph. There was nothing to fear, and never would be.

The power was his. Eyes saw, ears heard, hands could touch and strike. Blood throbbed in his veins, sinews contracted to the impulse of a thought. He walked again, rejoicing in his body. He was exalted, knew himself elect. He held his left hand before his eyes, gazing at the stubs of fingers. His. And so not crippled and misshapen, but glorious. Why had he never understood this before? It was all so clear and irrefutable.

The light of the next street-lamp. The pavement was a world, far below his probing eyes but each detail sharp. A burnt match, a flaw in the flagstone, a small insect travelling slowly across the vastness of steppe between kerb and wall, a scrap of paper shivering in the light breeze. A world, open and defenceless. He watched as the insect traversed its immense and tiny plain, passing near the fluttering paper, skirting the flaw, actually crossing the matchstick. It had done half its journey, three-quarters, come within a foot's breadth of its mighty and meaningless and squalidly ordinary goal. And there, bringing his foot down slowly and precisely, he crushed it.

He went on down the road – the bringer of death, wielder of justice. He thought he heard the noise of motor-bike engines, and laughed again. He wanted them to come, racing towards him through the night, so that he could put up his hand and stop them, send them spinning away to crash, in tangled flesh and metal, against the wall. Not revengefully, but in demonstration. All things balanced: these, and the dead insect.

Then he looked up and, without warning, fell a million million miles.

Cloud covered the sky except for one star. It burned at him and through him, a regarding indifferent eye. He stood in the gloom of the hideous drab canyon, and tried not to be seen. He was small, a dark thing in the dark, a blemish on a blotch, but he was visible and known. His blood bubbled in his sick veins, his bowels creaked and groaned. There was corruption in his nose and his mouth, and the corruption was his own, the effluvia of his festering and repulsive body. To think of it was pain, and the pain a reinforcing proof of weakness and unloveliness. The light shone on him, and he was known.

As he had always been known. The light was cold, abrading. In its harshness he saw himself as others had seen him: this capering squalid creature with its caricature of a hand. A thing which would have been pitiful if its ugliness had not replaced pity with disgust. Moncrieff, Rod, Jane and Hilda, the boys at school … contempt was all they had ever felt for him, all they could ever feel.

And that was not all. He knew he was contemptible but there were worse things, and they were not spared him. He saw the insect once again in its slow progress, avoiding some obstacles, overcoming others, the end approaching of one stage on the thousands of stages between birth and death. And then the darkness darkening further, consciousness snuffing out, a pointless ending to a creature of God's making. His throat tightened, and he screamed aloud, the mind's hell replacing the body's purgatory. He dropped to his knees and half-lay, half-crouched on the pavement. He could neither pray nor move. His suffering was outside time, or time itself had stopped.

Two or three times, he was conscious of the presence of others. Once a man's voice asked questions, before going away. They thought he was drunk, probably. Nothing mattered to him except the agony, which lasted for a hundred years before, slowly, it began to fade. At last he was able to pull himself to his feet, each small movement a directed effort.

He brought his hand up, and looked at his watch. It was after one o'clock. The street was silent and deserted. He started to walk home. His head was not aching exactly, but ringing with emptiness.

VI

THE RIOTING SLACKENED for a couple of days, then flared up again. It was mentioned on television and radio news bulletins now, but the government claimed that everything was well in hand. A few unruly elements were causing trouble, but the police would deal with them. Law-abiding citizens, the overwhelming majority of the country's population, could best help by keeping off the streets where there was trouble.

This was a morning on which Jane was to cycle into Pallister to see Micky. She was cleaning her shoes in the kitchen when she heard the front door-bell ring, and a little later Hilda came through.

'A Superintendent Jennet,' she said. 'He says he knows you.'

Her voice was disapproving, Jane said:

'Thanks. Be a love, and give these a polish.'

Taking the shoes, she said: 'I didn't know you knew any policemen.'

Jane ignored that, and went to the door. He was in uniform, and there was a car outside with a Sergeant in the driver's seat. She checked her movement towards him, and said in a neutral voice:

'This is an unexpected pleasure.'

'Your telephone's out of order. I tried to get through and couldn't.'

'Oh … I suppose we'd better report it.'

'I've done that. They'll send an engineer when they can. I'm on duty today, after all.'

'I guessed that.' It was a strain not showing anything because of the possibly watching Sergeant. 'You needn't have come specially. I've got to go in to draw my money. You could have left a note at the flat.'

'That's why I came. I don't want you to go in there today at all.'

'Why?'

'Things have turned nasty. Nastier, I should say. That's why we're all on duty. And there's something else. We're having arms issued.'

'As bad as that?'

'Someone thinks so. I think it's a mistake myself. Guns won't help much, and they could do a lot of harm. But that's not my pigeon.'

She said: 'Look after yourself.'

'Don't worry.'

He moved slightly so that he stood between her and the car. His hand came forward, and she took it. The firmness, dryness, warmth of flesh, the strength of bone beneath it. She was aware of this not with desire, but as something that protected and sustained her. Knowing that there was to be only this brief contact produced a feeling of weakness, not resentment. She said:

'Will you get in touch?'

He nodded. 'I'd better go now. I had an excuse for the trip – plausible, but only just plausible.'

She closed the door as he walked towards the car, but slipped through into the green sitting room and watched, surreptitiously, from a window. When it had disappeared through the distant gates, she braced herself and went back to the kitchen. Hilda said:

'Will these do?' She handed Jane the shoes. 'I suppose it was a private visit, not official? He didn't sound as though he wanted you on anything official.'

'We were supposed to have lunch together, but he's on duty. Did you know the telephone was out of order?'

'Is it? I got through to Mary Ann half an hour ago.'

'Must be incoming calls only. He happened to be round here on some job, so he dropped in to tell me.' She looked at the shoes. 'Thanks. You always get a better polish than I do. I won't need them today, but it will keep.'

'But aren't you going in for … other things?'

'To draw my dole, you mean?' Hilda always avoided using the expression. She was proud of her socialism and her working-class background, but this, nevertheless, was a dirty word. 'He advised me to keep out. There's more trouble, apparently.'

Hilda nodded, without much interest. Even a person with a strong social conscience grew accustomed to the sound of distant battle. Rod was not in Pallister that day, but on a country round. Hilda said:

'How long have you known him?'

Her curiosity must have been strongly roused for her to put the direct question. Jane said:

'Oh, a few months.'

'I should think he's very different from your Professor.'

'Very different.'

'I wouldn't have thought … quite your sort of person.' Jane did not reply to that. 'Less intellectual, surely.'

'I suppose you could say that.'

'He's not married?'

'No.'

Jane carried her shoes up to her room. Hilda, for some reason, was taking Micky seriously in a way she had never, for instance, taken Walter. She wondered why. She understood her sister's strongly rooted if irrational police phobia; but was surprised that she should attach so much weight to someone who was apparently no more than a casual acquaintance. Something in herself, perhaps, not in him? Hilda was a good mind- and gesture-reader where the family were concerned.

She walked to her dressing table and, bending down, stared in the glass. The lineaments of ungratified desire? Not, surely, in so wary an old campaigner as she was, both in the lists of love and family. There was nothing to see there.

But enough to feel. Physical longing came now, with image and remembered sensation, less a hunger than a bursting urge to draw breath, a sense of her whole being as frustrated and incomplete. The intensity of it shocked her, and she sat down on her stool. She was trembling slightly. This was weakness again, but a different weakness.

Linda, who had been sitting reading, dropped her book and rocketed out of the room when the telephone rang in the hall. She was always quick off the mark – she loved telephoning and being telephoned – but the way she moved indicated she was hoping for her newly acquired boy friend rather than one of her girl friends. She came back slowly, looking fed up, and said:

'It's for you, Jane.'

The telephone engineers had been round earlier in the morning. She had a conviction that it must be Micky, confirming that she could be reached, possibly ready to fix a time for their next meeting. She found herself smiling.

Walter said:

'Jane?' He sounded irritated. 'I've been trying to get through to you.'

She stared across the hall at a Utrillo print of a frozen snow scene.

'The line's been out of order.'

'No-one told me. Anyway, I've got you. I want you to come in this afternoon.'

'I'm not coming in to Pallister at present.'

'What do you mean? Why aren't you?'

'I've heard there's been some pretty bad rioting.'

'Who told you that?'

'Someone in Gostyn who had been in.'

'Nonsense. The whole thing's exaggerated. A slight uproar yesterday, but it's all calm again now. I'd like you to get here by three. The flat, not the office.'

She told herself he had no way of compelling her, not even, as happened with love-making, through her own fear of arousing his suspicions: it was perfectly reasonable that she should not want to expose herself to the risk of being involved in the disturbances. (She disregarded his picture of the Pallister scene; he was a man of accuracy, but not at the expense of self-interest.) All she had to do was say no, and put the telephone down.

And all that meant was branding herself to him as a coward. She said, with a cold anger that was partly directed against herself:

'By three? I'll be there.'

'Good. Have you drawn your chocolate ration, by the way?'

'Yes. I'll bring it to you. 'Bye, Walter.'

The town was quiet as she cycled through, though there were signs of violence not long past – broken windows, gutted buildings, partly dismantled barricades. She got to the flat at five minutes to three, and Walter said:

'I thought you'd be here before this.'

'You said three.'

He turned from her to the other person who was there: Morrison, who had taken over the local leadership of SEA after Pinkard had been eased out. He had a talent for flattering Walter with intelligence and irony, and had been very much his blue-eyed boy. It was not apparent this afternoon, though. Walter picked at him mercilessly. When there was a reference to something that he could have done and, in Walter's view, ought to have done on his way to the flat, it was accompanied by the peevish comment that he had been told half past three, anyway. Jane got the point then. The programme as planned by Walter had included half an hour for her and him alone together before whatever was scheduled to take place, and therefore the usual quick copulation. Once she knew the reason, his irritation amused her.

Morrison handled him well, she was forced to admit, staying cool and showing neither resentment nor obsequiousness. He fed him with the sort of remarks that were likely to lead him into channels where his intellectual interest would be stimulated, and Walter did in fact gradually calm down. Jane tidied the living room and went in to tackle the kitchen, which was its usual unsightly mess. There was a dirty plate bearing a strip of fat cut from what had plainly been a large steak. At a rough guess, three new pounds on the black market. His gluttony, which had once amused her, as a child's might, aroused faint disgust.

She had gathered that this meeting was the precursor of a larger one: she had assumed of the SEA committee. They were still in existence, still a little flushed by their victory of the early summer. To most people their brief notoriety had been eclipsed by the General Strike and the economic slump, but their self-assessment remained Napoleonic. Listening, though not closely, to the conversation in the next room, she realized, however, that other people than SEA were involved. She began paying more attention when Morrison, in his mocking North-country voice, said:

'What I'm saying is that there could be an *attempt* to construe it as trying to set up a civil authority in opposition to the legal one.'

Walter said:

'Don't be bloody silly. No-one's talking about setting up an authority.'

'*I* know that, but …'

'The thing is, there is no authority worth talking about. You saw what happened yesterday. The place was in the hands of a mob, with the police completely helpless. And the trouble started with those two gangs fighting each other. If we can get them to see reason …'

Gradually she fitted the pieces together. Walter had repeated his earlier manoeuvre of establishing contact with the leaders of the four or five main gangs in the city, but this time, instead of inviting them to join a student demonstration, he had asked them to come along to the flat to see him. They were to arrive between half past three and four. Walter wanted to persuade them to do two things: abandon their increasingly violent mutual warfare, and act in support of order rather than against it.

It struck her as hare-brained in the extreme. She could see that the leaders might welcome the idea of a conference. It would give them something to occupy their small pointed heads, and would probably strike them as flattering – the sort of thing which happened in the old films about Chicago in the Twenties which were a current vogue. But it was absurd to imagine that anything could come of it. There was no reason on earth why they should abandon their fighting or rally round the tottering establishment. To do so would be to expose them even further to the boredom which was chiefly responsible for sparking off their lunatic antics. All Walter could succeed in doing was to make himself look ridiculous. She felt a vague distaste for the thought; it would be an embarrassing spectacle to watch. She listened to him talking to Morrison:

'What is important and valuable about the present situation is precisely the fact that it is an insurrection by youth. Youth's role in the past has been to support revolutions organized by middle-aged and old men for objectives which were only partially and incidentally connected with youth's own needs and aspirations. In any culture, the young represent the dynamism of the society, its creativity. If that can be released, channelled …'

There had been a time, she knew, and not all that long ago, when, without having any view for or against, she would have listened with pleasure to this sort of thing, enjoying the quickness of his mind, the flow of vigour. She let it go, and drifted into a reverie. She was in Micky's bed, and in his arms. Naked. She examined the word in her mind, and found it lovely.

Walter had to call her twice. He wanted her to put the kettle on, and get things ready to give the boys tea.

They had brought their bodyguards, of course, but had been willing to leave them outside in the corridor. Jane wondered what the other tenants of the block would make of them. Presumably they were something like the six who had come in and who lounged in the chairs and on the divan. They all had white leather jackets, ornamented and caparisoned in different ways. One had a number of what seemed to be genuine gold chains across his chest, sewn to the leather. Another was wearing a blue velvet cap, with red stones winking in it. Could they possibly be rubies? All but one had piebald cheeks and chins, their beards sprouting in tufts of different shapes and sizes, with patches of shaved skin between. The exception was a stocky youth with a particularly vigorous growth of hair. His hairline centred on a monstrous brown moustache and ran back on either side to the top of his ears; below these two demarcation lines he was clean shaven.

She was surprised to find that they seemed genuinely impressed by Walter who, for his part, was entirely at ease. He was, of course, something off the telly, a face remembered from the – to them – ancient pre-pubertal days when they were told to sit quiet and not fidget because Father wanted to see this programme. There was a magic there. Also, he succeeded in conveying the genuineness of his conviction of their importance. They were becoming used to elder people propitiating them, and they knew the ingratiation concealed fear and dislike. This was entirely different. Moreover, his account of their importance was couched in terms which, although they did not fully understand them, they recognized as stemming from a real intellectual power. That was flattering, too.

He, for his part, was in his element. His public figure had always been a good one, and always seen to its best with a young audience. But the young before had been students, preconditioned to an acceptance of his intellectual leadership, easily moved by small academic jokes. These were different: the raw brashness of youth, brought up on the telly, strip cartoons, the jukebox. Compared with the others, they presented a challenge. He was finding that he could meet it, and the realization was intoxicating. There was not much of Hamlet in his make-up, but what there was represented, to him, a slightly shameful weakness. His favoured self-image was Fortinbras, and in this scene he could indulge it.

Jane took minutes, not paying much attention to what they constituted. An agreement of a sort was drawn up, with specific demarcations of territory lines. Certain rights and privileges, as between particular gangs, were outlined and agreed. Provision was made for dealing with members who might infringe the rules agreed by the leaders. The leaders themselves were to meet regularly in congress.

One of them, the beardless one with the bushy moustache and hairy cheeks, said:

'We'll have to have someone running it.'

They studied each other warily. Another said:

'I reckon it ought to be the Professor.'

Walter said:

'I'm afraid that's not possible.'

There was a brief, considering silence. Velvet Cap said:

'It has to be him, or none of this will work. I mean, it's got to be somebody from outside. I mean …'

He trailed off into inarticulateness, but others took it up. If one of them, at the beginning, had proposed another leader as generalissimo, it would probably have been accepted readily enough. But Walter's domination of things had made this unlikely; and as the discussion became general their suspicions and mistrust of each other had a chance to emerge and develop. It was obvious that the general agreement, enthusiastically entered into only a matter of minutes before, was in danger of being rejected.

Walter said:

'Look. I can't do this officially, for all sorts of reasons.' He grinned at them. 'You don't want me to lose my job, do you?' They grinned back. 'But I'll sit in with you on the meetings, and I'm prepared to give advice as and when you need it. There's nothing to stop you deciding among yourselves that you'll regard my advice as binding on you.'

Hairy Cheeks said: 'That will do as far as I'm concerned. We take an oath that we do as the Professor says.'

Walter said:

'No need for oaths. You can pass a resolution to that effect, or just agree informally. I think that's the best way.'

'We'll do it what way you say.'

The oath idea, Jane thought, would have been a bit difficult in any case. You really needed something to believe in, outside yourself.

She got away, to her surprise, fairly easily. Walter was to be escorted on a round of the various headquarters, sitting pillion on a motor-bike. He said something about her coming along, too, but it was not well received. Even where they were not overtly homosexual, the gangs were very much male-dominated and it would not do for a woman to appear on what was something of a ceremonial occasion. Walter did not press the matter. He was going to be chaperoned, anyway. And this, plainly, meant more to him than sex.

She cycled round to Micky's flat, getting in with the key he had given her. He was not there, and there was no message. She stayed for half an hour, and then began the long trek back to Gostyn through the dark.

VII

A GREEDY MAN, Rod thought, but a circumspect one. He examined the bits of silver with care, turning them over slowly in his hands and peering at the hallmarks. Since the last visit, he had picked up from somewhere a book on the metal, and he checked the marks against it.

He was ponderous, slightly stooped, with an ugly face, pale despite his profession, and big white hands. He farmed with the assistance of two men and a boy, and had had the forethought to go back to horses. Diesel for the tractors was still available in theory, but increasingly difficult to come by, the supply likely to be disrupted by trouble at the ports. One of the men was married, and the wife came in to clean and cook; otherwise he lived alone in the drab but very solid Jacobean farmhouse, two miles from the main road and hidden behind a small copse of birch and ash. His own wife had died a few years before.

'I'm not sure I should go on buying by weight,' he said. 'Value comes into it more. A small christening cup can be worth a sight more than a big pair of candlesticks.'

Rod said:

'I don't know anything about silver.'

'Well, I'm picking up a bit. You're not thinking I'd twist you, are you?'

Almost certainly he would. Rod said:

'No, I'm thinking of the problem at my end. I have to buy it by weight because I don't know any better. I can hardly change the system on the selling side.'

He did not like the man, but it was important to keep in with him. He was the best contact he had found since extending his operations to the country: close-mouthed, and with an insatiable hunger for silverware. He bought everything that was offered, and paid, at an agreed rate, in eggs, cream and butter, poultry, salt beef and pork. While Rod was there, he put the silver ornaments up in his living room; but by the next visit they had gone. He almost certainly had a treasure-house hidden away somewhere. Like almost all farmers, he had entirely lost faith in currency, and his imagination did not rise to gold or precious stones. It was silver that would make him a rich man, when the troubles were over.

Shrugging now, he said:

'Just as you want. More than likely, it's swings and roundabouts. You want to pick the stuff up now?'

Visits were timed for him to be alone in the house, with the woman away at her cottage beyond the copse and the men working up in the fields. He helped Rod with the stacking, lifting a leg of pork as easily as Rod lifted a chicken. They got it into the false bottom of the cart, and stacked the non-rationed roots and vegetables on top. Rod doubted if this would pass any sort of official inspection, but it might be enough to deceive the yobs. It was not likely, for that matter, that the police would have inspection patrols out at present – they were too badly needed in the city.

They went back to the house for the glass of home-brewed ale which always came out at this stage. Rod was asked if he would like anything to eat, but refused. He could have eaten, but would not do so here. The completion of the transaction invariably made Lyddell amiable, but today it seemed more marked. He talked, in a high good humour, about the latest government pronouncement, which Rod had not heard. It appeared that the ban on motor-bikes, which in recent weeks had become a dead letter, was to be strictly enforced.

'They ought to have done that right from the beginning,' Lyddell said. 'They broke into the stores and pinched petrol, and they've been allowed to get away with it. That's what makes them feel big, being able to roar round the roads while everyone else is forced to walk, or go by bus or train.'

Rod said:

'So long as they *can* enforce it.'

'That was something else on the news. Not with it, you understand, but straight after it, so you could work out what the connection was. They'd decided against making a general order to arm the police, but this was still at the discretion of Chief Constables, and Chief Constables were closely in touch with Whitehall. They'll stop this nonsense now, all right.'

'I hope you're right.'

Lyddell said:

'Get the yobs sorted out, and there'll be some chance of getting things moving again. It's a bit of discipline that's needed. I don't like having to deal the way you and I do, but a man's got to make the best of the way he's forced to live. If you don't look after Number One, there's no-one that'll do it for you.'

Rod finished his drink, and prepared to leave. Lyddell said:

'One thing you can do for me.'

'What's that?'

'You get around a bit – in the city, and all. You might know of someone who'd like to come and work out here, in the house that is.'

'A woman?'

'I was thinking of a young girl, more.' His white face stared at Rod. 'Someone to see to things in the evening when Mrs Smith isn't here. Get my supper, warm my slippers, put a bottle in my bed.'

'Isn't there a girl from the village who would come in?'

'I wouldn't fancy anyone local.' A greedy man, but a circumspect one. 'I thought if someone came in from the city they could pass as a niece of mine. I've always kept my affairs to myself. She'd be able to see that her folks were looked after, as far as food went.'

Rod could imagine what Hilda would have said. He would have not liked to say it for her. But this was the best contact he had, and you could not pick and choose the men you did business with. He said:

'I don't know of anyone, but if anything turns up ... I'll see what I can do.'

Lyddell called after him: 'She doesn't have to be spirited. A quiet one will serve well enough.'

Rod took the cart into the stables, unhitched Rusty, and saw to him for the night. He was surprised that Linda had not come out to lend a hand, but assumed that she had too much home-work and Hilda had insisted on her finishing it. She accepted Rusty quite well, as a workaday animal, but was still suspicious of any signs of horsiness in Linda, and quick to check them.

He did not unload the cart, simply making sure there was no way of rats getting at the food. He never unloaded on the premises. It was unlikely that Hilda would come out unexpect-edly, but he preferred not to take a chance.

He had not told Hilda that he was dealing in food now. Her reaction was all too predictable, and would have been emphatic. She tolerated the purchase of black market food, on a limited scale, for the family's use, but would not have stood for making a profit out of it. To buy a bit of cheese or bacon, a dozen eggs, was all right. One belonged to the exploited, and could be resentful about it in good company. On the other side was all the monstrous company of exploiters, back to the corn factors of ancient Egypt.

Normally Rod consulted his wife's prejudices. He did not have many strong ones himself and was willing to accept hers. This was only partly in order to have an easier life, and not have to face her disapproval – generally silent but no less evident for that. It was more because, in a way, her prejudices warmed him, creating blacks and whites out of his own greys, a world more entrancing, if more illogical, than the one in which he would otherwise have lived. He liked living in hers.

In this case, though, there were overriding considerations. It had started when he had gone to a man running a smallholding just outside Gostyn, in order to buy eggs. He had offered money, but the man had spotted a bicycle pump on the cart, which he had picked up that morning, and wanted that. The rate was much better, and Rod made the deal. Later he thought about it, as a general policy. There were strict penalties for illicit trading in food, but it was obvious that no serious attempt was being made to enforce them. It was worth what risk there was, when one thought of the far higher profitability. He said nothing to Hilda, but began branching out more into the country. Most of the food he sold, putting only as much into the household supplies as would not make her suspicious.

It meant positive as well as tacit untruthfulness. She asked him sometimes about his trading, out of interest, and he had to paper the gaps when, as today, his time had been largely taken up with people like Lyddell. He was working out a story as he went into the house, but it was not necessary. She was too concerned with other things.

Linda had come home distressed. There was a ten minute walk from school to the bus stop, through a quiet residential area. This afternoon, she and three other girls had been chased by a gang of boys. She herself, and another of the girls, had got away, but two had been caught. They had found some men who had gone back there. The boys had scattered, and they found the girls all right, except for being bruised a bit and partially undressed – one down to her bra and knickers.

Rod said:

'I'll get on to the Headmistress in the morning. If necessary, they'll have to put some sort of escort on as far as the bus.'

'They can't do that,' Hilda said. 'Would it be much good, if they could? They were lucky to find men who would go back, and lucky the boys scattered – there can't have been many of them. If you put schoolgirls under an escort, the big gangs are likely to get interested.'

He saw the logic of it. It was a bad idea to draw their attention to anything: curiosity was the strongest stimulant they had. He said:

'Then …'

'I'm going to keep her at home,' Hilda said. 'The boys, too.'

'The boys?'

'Until this mess is cleared up. They're not getting much work done at school, as it is. They can work here as well, if they bring their books back. I'll supervise them, and Jane will lend a hand.'

'Can we keep them at home?'

'I'm not going to ask.'

The idea seemed better the more clearly he grasped it. They would all be here in Bridge House, safe and together. There was no reason for any of the gangs to penetrate into this backwater – nothing to bring them here. He thought: I'll start laying up stocks of food, just in case things get worse. The government could threaten firm action, but it might not be so easy to enforce it.

VIII

Astonishingly a dozen children had come to school. So had Betty and, of course, Moncrieff. He looked very solemn and controlled and gripped his pipe masterfully between his teeth. In fact, he seemed to be in a state of shock. He sat in the common room, staring out of the window, and asked Martin what he thought they ought to do.

Martin said:

'Close down, I should say. I'm surprised there hasn't been an instruction.'

'I've tried to get through to the CEO. There's nobody there before nine, of course.'

Fighting between the police and the gangs had broken out the previous day, and had continued through the night. One could still hear occasional shooting. A distant shot served as a full stop to Moncrieff's remark. There had been a broadcast announcement proclaiming martial law in various places, including Pallister. Martin had thought that this automatically involved the closing down of schools, but had come in to make sure.

Betty said:

'There may not be anyone in at all. The part round the Civic Centre's the worst of all.'

Moncrieff said:

'I don't know his home telephone number. It's the sort of thing one ought to have. I can't think why someone didn't think of that.'

He sounded peevish. Martin said:

'I think we ought to get the children home.'

'One accepts responsibility,' Moncrieff said. 'One doesn't argue about that. But there's no point in taking on more than one has to. We've had nothing at all from the CEO on what to do in an emergency of this kind. If martial law implies closing all schools, I ought to have been told that. As it is ... They talk about using initiative, but they're quick enough to smack you down if you do something that turns out to be not official policy.'

'It's the safety of the children that counts,' Martin said.

'Yes, Weston. I don't need to have that pointed out. At the same time, it's rather easier for you, isn't it? You don't have to carry a can back.'

Betty said:

'Once the school's closed down, the children are their parents' concern. If anything happened to them while they were at school ...'

Moncrieff sighed. 'I'll have one more shot at getting hold of someone.' He got up reluctantly and went, pausing at the door. 'Round them up, will you?'

She said, as the door closed:

'He's disgusting, isn't he?'

'I don't suppose he can help it.'

She picked up the potted plant Miss Garside had brought in to brighten the room, and stared at the pointed scarlet blossoms among the dark glossy leaves.

'You're very good at making excuses for people, aren't you, Martin? For everybody. Because you despise us all equally?'

'No,' he said truthfully. 'If I make excuses, that's not the reason.'

'What is it, then? The aid and comfort of the Holy Ghost?'

He shook his head. 'We'd better get the children together, in case he decides to close down.'

She said indifferently:

'He's decided already. He got the message: he's not answerable for the children once he's sent them home. And he can run to his own bolt-hole.'

Although the children had come on their own, Moncrieff decided they should be escorted back. He had things to do in the school, he said, and he asked Martin to take on the job. Betty said she wanted to share it, and he agreed to let her be responsible for those living in the school's immediate area. Martin set off with the rest, on a circuit planned to cover their various homes while keeping away from the trouble areas.

The last boy lived in flats near the railway station, just below the Civic Centre. The morning was cold but clear, and the white clock tower was silhouetted against blue. Martin had heard firing after they set out from school, but nothing for the last quarter of an hour. He hesitated, and then started up the hill. The road was empty, and he knew there was a place at the top where one could watch from cover. He was surprised, nevertheless, that his curiosity should be stronger than fear.

Fear, it was true, had little to justify it. This was a familiar place on a bright winter's day, this road the one down which he had bicycled as a schoolboy when briefly in the grips of train-spotting fever. There was no sound of shots or shouting, but the city was not ominously silent. A train came out of the tunnel on the London line and braked, screeching, into the station. He could hear faraway music – a popular sung. Pigeons' wings beat the air as they fluttered heavily across towards their favourite pitch on the lawns. No traffic sounds, but one had grown accustomed to their absence. The trouble must be over, he guessed, at least for the time being. If it were, poor Moncrieff would be in a tizzy, wondering if he had acted prematurely, and therefore unwisely, in closing down.

He reached the brow of the hill. There was a wall here which offered the cover he had thought of; it was not very high but one could crouch behind it if necessary. The need did not seem to exist, though. Rubbish was littered on the lawns and the steps of the Civic Hall, and there was a great area of discoloration on the side of the building where there must have been a fire, but otherwise it was all peaceful. There were figures out there, but they were not fighting. They were ordinary civilians, satisfying their curiosity as he was doing, though more openly. Above their heads the clock in the tower rang its peal of bells: the carillon for the half-hour.

The noise of a car approached from the direction of the Broadway. A police car, he guessed, and a few moments later confirmed that. It came from behind the cluster of buildings, a sedate black saloon with POLICE in blue letters in front. People turned their heads to look at it.

It was travelling very slowly and in an odd fashion, swinging from side to side across the width of the road. There was another noise, mixed with the sound of the engine: voices shouting and singing. He saw that the windows were wound down, and that figures inside were leaning out, and waving. Not policemen. The yobs must have captured a car, and were having the effrontery to drive it, as a trophy, through the heart of the town. Martin crouched down behind the wall. He was afraid now.

The road ringed the lawns and the Civic Centre. The car was travelling towards him, but not directly. He saw that they had heaped something on the bonnet. It was blue. A pile of police uniforms? Could they possibly have raided the police station?

It was not until the car was almost abreast of his post that he made out what it was. One uniform only, but not just a uniform. A young constable stretched across the bonnet of the car, his hands trailing almost to brush the ground. His head had fallen back, and his throat was gashed and bloody.

IX

TELEVISION HAD SNAPPED OFF in the middle of a travel programme, flickering whiteness replacing a scene of pygmies
travelling across the Kalahari desert, their recorded guttural
song giving way to the whine of the carrier signal and then to
ordinary mains hum. The local radio station had disappeared at
the same time. Later London had gone, but was back on the air
the following morning with an apology and no explanation. It
went again, a few hours later, and returned with a voice talking
in cockney, introducing pop gramophone records. There was
no news at one o'clock, or any other time. In the afternoon,
the frequency once more went dead.

Jane found a French station, which gabbled about the revolt
in England having become a revolution. The announcer spoke
fast, outstripping her comprehension. Rod came back early,
and said that things were rumoured to be very bad in Pallister: the police had opened fire on the yobs, and the yobs were
fighting back. It seemed they had got hold of arms from somewhere. The telephone had been dead all day. She tried it again,
but there was nothing there.

She did not sleep well that night. In the morning she could
not find anyone on the air speaking English, and the French station was little more informative than it had been before. There
had been considerable bloodshed, and London was thought to
be completely in the hands of Les Jeunes. Troops were being
rushed back to England from Cyprus. The last of the legions,
said the announcer, being called home, but the barbarians were
already sitting in the Forum.

She did not speak to Hilda or Rod because she knew it would

only lead to an argument, and there was nothing to argue about. She wrote a note, saying that she was going in to Pallister but not to worry: she would keep away from the part where there was trouble – she would be all right. Then, leaving the note where Hilda would find it when she came in from the garden, she slipped out of the house and got her bicycle.

She had thought the road into Pallister might be choked with people going the opposite way, making their escape from the chaos of the city, but this was not so. There were relatively few people, and they did not seem particularly frightened or disturbed. In the outskirts of the town, life appeared to be going on much as usual. Further in, there were signs of damage and past fighting, but nothing very much out of the ordinary until she came through from Broadway to the High Street. Ahead of her, in the direction of Pallister Wall, there were probably as many as a hundred motor-bikes, some parked and others being driven up and down, with the riders cat-calling and chanting above the noise of the engines. It scared her that there was no sign of police – that they were behaving like this, unchecked and with every indication of triumph, She turned away, and took the path through Gunter Park, to avoid them.

The lift was not working at Micky's block of flats. She felt a constriction in her chest as she toiled up the three flights of drab and rather dirty stairs, a physical result of the tug-of-war in her mind between anticipation and crippling anxiety. She looked at the door for a long moment before pressing the bell. Anxiety took the upper hand as she heard it ring inside with no response of footsteps, and she had to lean against the wall to draw breath.

She found the key, and let herself in. The flat was as usual: tidy, not very welcoming. Going through to the kitchen, she found breakfast dishes standing in the rack on the draining board, and was elated. If he had had breakfast then he must have been all right this morning, a few hours ago. Her elation faded, as she saw that the dishes were quite dry. They could easily have been there since yesterday.

She wished she had got a cigarette. The craving, which she thought she had overcome entirely, mixed with the anxiety, the wanting, and became an agony. She walked restlessly round the flat, trying to think of what to do. The telephone, when she tried it, was as dead as the one at home had been. She wanted to go and look for him, to have something positive to do, but had no notion where to start. As she went out of the main entrance of the block, he might be coming in by one of the side-entrances. The thought depressed and confused her. She went into the bedroom, and stared at the precisely made bed, the sheets straight-edged and tightly drawn in under the mattress.

Kicking her shoes off, she lay down. The bed yielded a little under her body; it was hard in comparison with her own bed at home. She felt cold – she had switched on the electric fire but nothing had happened – and she pulled back the top blanket and snuggled under it. It was the first time she had lain here except to make love. The thought reinforced her feeling of desolation and then, oddly, comforted her. That and weariness sent her to sleep.

It was dark when she woke, with night filling the window. Her watch told her it was a quarter past six – she must have slept for over seven hours. She was ravenously hungry. These thoughts occurred to her before she thought of Micky, but when she did her stomach sickened with fear. He had not come back. Something must have happened to him.

There was no electricity supply still, but he was a man who planned for emergencies: there was a torch, she knew, on the shelf above the bed, and candles and matches in the kitchen. She lit a couple and set them up in the sitting room, another in the kitchen. She found packets of the Frotein-enriched dried vegetable mix which was the latest example of American bounty, and put water on to make a stew. He had a gas cooker, and fortunately the gas supply had not been cut off. While waiting for the water to boil, she rummaged in the larder and found a tin of salmon and one of kidneys, stored against their next lunch together. The sight of them was a last straw; she stood and howled in the bare clean kitchen.

Later she dried her eyes and, with the water bubbling in the pan, added the green and brown flaky mess to it. She felt weak, but uninterested in her weakness. The hunger, too, though still there, was something remote. She stood and watched the stew seethe in the pan, in dull detachment. Then the doorbell rang. For a moment she stood still, disbelieving; then raced to answer it.

There was no light, of course, in the corridor, but she would have been able to see anyone standing there by the candle light behind her and what came in from the night outside. No-one. This frightened her. She wondered if she could have imagined the bell, but knew it had been real. She stepped fully into the corridor, and said:

'Who is it?'

'It's me.'

Micky's voice. She turned towards it, to the shadows further up the corridor, opening her arms, and he came into them.

She was shocked by the sight of him. One side of his face was caked with dried blood, its normal ugliness made worse by a growth of dirty beard and a bruise puffing his left eye. He was not wearing the jacket of his uniform. The shirt was smeared with dust and blood, and the trousers were torn at the knee. He was shivering with cold. She led him to a chair, sat him down, and brought a blanket from the bedroom to cover his shoulders. He sighed, and drew it round him.

'That's good.'

'What happened?'

'A lot.' He shivered again, convulsively. 'I've been hiding up till dark. I ditched the jacket, but they could still recognize me as a policeman.'

'Wait,' she said. 'The stew's ready. I'll bring it in.'

She poured it all for him, but he would not accept that, and made her bring a dish for herself. She ate, watching him, astonished by his existence. When they had finished, she brought a bowl of warm water, and washed him, carefully and gently. The blood came mostly from a gash in the side of his head, just above the hairline. She soaked it, and cleaned it. It was not as bad as she had feared, though it should have been stitched. She cut as much of the hair as possible away, and drew the edges of the wound together with pieces of Band-Aid. He went silent while she was doing that, but did not wince.

The rest of the time, he talked. The details confused her, but she got a general picture. The police, in accordance with instructions, had gone after a gang of yobs who were driving their motor-bikes up and down the Broadway and the High Street. The yobs had stood at bay, around Pallister Wall. Bricks had been thrown at first. He was not sure how the firing had started, but when it did it was clear that both sides were armed. And there were more of them in the upper windows of nearby shops. The police had been forced to retreat northwards, and came under enfilading fire as they did so.

After that, there had been no stopping them. They were everywhere, some of them boys of thirteen or fourteen but still capable of throwing stones from behind any piece of cover. The ordinary citizens of Pallister had kept out of it, and gone back to their homes in the hope of watching things, from their armchairs, on television later. A battalion of troops had been brought in, during the afternoon. He did not know what had happened, but he had seen some youngsters, in Army uniform, with the yobs; presumably they had gone over to them. He said that partly with astonishment, partly with pride. His own force had stood up to things better.

The yobs had moved from running warfare to all-out assault. Police stations were the obvious targets for attack. He thought that, when the seriousness of the situation was realized, they should have abandoned the outlying stations, but they had been defended piecemeal and overrun piecemeal. The result was that when they moved against the main headquarters, the defence was inadequate, both in men and materials.

He added wrily:

'Also, that place was built, a couple of years ago, for housing computers and for show. It was not expected to stand siege. It would have been easier in the old building.'

It had fallen, to all intents, during the night, but until morning there was confusion, with both sides holding parts of it. In the dawn, the gangs had consolidated their victory. Micky had been hit by half a bottle during the storming of his block, and knocked out. They must have thought he was dead. When he came to, they had moved on, and were burning files and desks, anything flammable, in a huge bonfire down in the courtyard. He saw three of his colleagues, who had been taken prisoner, killed by having their throats cut.

She said, in horror:

'But why?'

He considered it as though it were an academic point.

'They were carried away, I suppose. They probably never expected to come out on top. When they found they had actually done it, that they were holding police headquarters, they would go wild. And I imagine they were pretty well hopped up. During the fighting, some of them obviously were. I saw one walk slowly forward into gunfire, singing, with his head in the air, almost like a choir boy. Finally, there must have been the question of safeguarding themselves against future punishment.'

'By murdering their prisoners?'

'By eliminating possible witnesses. When other police came in from outside and order was re-established … they had gone too far to have any hope of getting away with probation. Any Pallister policeman who remained alive might send dozens of them down for ten years or more. They didn't like the idea of that.'

Micky had managed to get out of the building, unobserved,

and had headed for the flat. He had taken the precaution of ditching his jacket, but even so he was spotted later, and chased. The part of the city he was in was full of groups of yobs, celebrating and looting. Everyone else was keeping off the streets, so that a lone figure was conspicuous. He decided the only thing to do was lie up until dark, and he did this under the counter of a wrecked shop. He had made his way back, slowly and painfully, had seen the light in the window of the flat, and had rung and then hidden in case it was not she there but someone else – one of the yobs, perhaps. Telling her that, he hobbled to the window and drew the curtains.

'A light might attract a visitor – most places are dark tonight.'

She asked him: 'How long will it be?'

'Will what be?'

'Before order *is* re-established.'

Micky picked up a candle and carried it over to the mirror on the wall. He said, rubbing his chin with the other hand:

'I think I'll get some hot water to shave.'

Jane got up. 'I'll do that.'

He followed her to the kitchen. 'Good job I never took to dry shavers. Re-establish order? I said they were afraid of that, but I wish I could think they were right to be afraid. Pallister wasn't the first place to go, by a long chalk. It started in London, and we'd had nothing through from Liverpool, Sheffield – several other cities.'

She tried to take this in, but found that it did not mean very much. Other nearer considerations were more pressing. She said:

'Gas hot water, as well as a gas cooker. We are lucky. I'll run you a bath while you shave. We're safe here for the night?'

'I should think so. I don't know about the future. They may call the hunt off – get bored with it, or regard the job as finished. But one couldn't be sure, and I'm fairly well known round here. I doubt if it would be wise to stay.'

'Of course you're not staying.' She went to the bathroom, and turned on the taps. Over the noise, she called to him: 'We'll set off first thing in the morning. You'll be all right at Gostyn. You're not known there.'

She lay against the length of his body, aware of its warmth and firmness, of the smell that was him mixed with the smell of soap, of her own softness beside his hardness. After her long sleep earlier, she was not tired, but he was. He put an arm round her waist, a palm against the small of her back, and fell asleep. She lay awake a long time, not moving until he himself, still sleeping, shifted and turned away from her.

The thought came to her as she grew drowsy herself: I really am sleeping with a man, for the first time. She smiled, and fell asleep.

X

FOR FOUR DAYS, Rod did not go out with the cart. It was a confused and uncertain time, but not an unhappy one. The supply of electricity was cut off, returned for a little over twelve hours, and went again. They put on all the heaters they could during that time, trying to warm the house, and afterwards reverted to dressing themselves as warmly as possible, wearing overcoats indoors when they were not doing anything strenuous. There were hard frosts at night, and the surface of the ground only thawed during the hour or two of the sun's zenith. These were cold blue days, with a sharp wind from the northwest.

They had no batteries for the portable radios, but the children searched the bands on the mains radiogram while the power was on. They found one English station operating regularly, apparently from Birmingham. It played pop music and gave news bulletins which were concerned with local affairs only, and chiefly to do with places and times for collecting rations. There was another station, also plainly local, which urged citizens to report to certain places, to be enrolled as auxiliary police. When Stephen tried to find it half an hour later, the frequency was dead.

Some rumours came in from people on the Gostyn Estate, but they were either fantastic – like the one which said there was organized cannibalism in Pallister, with men and women being roasted on spits over great fires in the streets – or pointless. All that was clear was that an attempt was being made at keeping essential services going. The buses had stopped running, but trucks brought food supplies to an emergency ration centre in Gostyn village, where there was also a street market. Gas supplies appeared to be unaffected, and there were even ir-regular postal deliveries. There had been no rioting or fighting out here, and the atmosphere remained quiet: odd and strained, but peaceful. Rod was told that the local police were still about, though they wore civilian clothes and kept clear of the station. He mentioned this to Micky Jennet, who said:

'They may get away with it. I think they're taking a chance, though.'

Hilda knew Micky's identity, and had told Rod. They had kept it from the others, saying merely that he was a friend of Jane's whose home had been burnt during the disturbances and who had therefore come to live at Bridge House. The chil-dren might say something outside, without thinking, and there was no point in disturbing the old folk unnecessarily. Emma scarcely seemed to have noticed what had happened – she talked, as garrulously as ever, on her usual subject, the life, above and below stairs, in the great houses where she had been in service as a girl. Jack, on the other hand, had been badly shocked by what he had heard, and scarcely spoke now, except to Peter. He had given up his old habit of walking round the grounds in the morning, and for the most part stayed huddled in his armchair, staring out of the window.

Rod did not quite know what to make of Micky. He imag-ined that the fact of her having brought him here meant that Jane was taking him more seriously than she had other men friends in the past. Like Hilda, he was a bit surprised by this. He seemed too self-contained, too much a policeman. Rod doubted if they would have many interests in common, ei-ther. Jane had played some of her favourite gramophone records while the power was on – Mozart and Berlioz – and he had lis-tened intently, but without comment.

In himself, he recognized a mild dislike. The irritation stem-med from his actual arrival, and Jane's plea for what amounted to refuge. He could accept the facts of what had happened in

Pallister – of the fighting, even the subsequent killing of police prisoners, but he found it more difficult to accept the implication of the man's flight: that this was not an ordinary mob frenzy which would be over and forgotten in a day or two, but an absolute turning point, from which there was no going back. If he had lain low for twenty-four hours, it would probably have been all right. Other police had very likely done that, and might now be trying to re-establish order. It was unthinkable that order should not be re-established, and the yobs could not do it on their own.

Meanwhile, though, he felt they had plenty to be thankful for. Stocks of food were fairly high, and there was fuel for the Aga. They were all together – the whole family, apart from Martin. His family, by creation and adoption. He was prepared to tolerate Micky because Jane was obviously made happy by his presence. And it would soon be over, things back to normal.

At eleven the following morning, lights glowed in the bulbs which they had left on. It was Linda who spotted them, called excitedly: 'Power's back again!', and rushed to switch on the fires. She went from that to the telephone, but returned disconsolately with the news that the line was still dead. Stephen had found a station broadcasting pop music, though, on the old Home Service frequency. They left it on, and at twelve there was a news bulletin. The announcer had the familiar BBC accent and suavity. He said:

'It is officially stated from Downing Street that the immediate crisis is now past. All citizens are urged to co-operate in overcoming the remaining difficulties by showing patience and mutual good will. Essential services will be maintained, and extended as rapidly as possible. There is no basic food problem. The American government has guaranteed supplies for the next three months, and has, in order to encourage the revival of British industry and trade, dropped all tariffs on British goods.

Minor difficulties may occur in distribution, but these will not last long.

'The Prime Minister has also announced the formation of a special advisory and consultative committee, which will work directly with him. It has the following members: Mr Michael Geary, Mr Brendan Bone, Mr Stephen Le Tissier and Mr Andrew Parkinson. Mr Bone will be speaking on this station at seven o'clock this evening.

'A bus-jet aeroplane crashed this morning while taking off from Orly Airport, Paris …'

At the end of the bulletin, Rod said: 'It looks as though the worst is over.'

Micky said:

'Do you think so? It all sounded very vague to me. Except that bit about the special committee, the members of it. Geary, who organized the student riots last summer. Bone's the lead vocalist of the group called the Battered Objects, isn't he? The one that got off on that heroin charge about a year ago. And Le Tissier's a disk jockey. I don't know about Parkinson.'

Stephen said:

'Big Carnaby Street man. He started spot beards.'

Rod said:

'The government's riddled with committees. I shouldn't think one more would make any difference. A sop to the kids.'

Hilda said:

'I'm surprised there wasn't something about the Prime Minister speaking. It's what people expect at a time like this.'

'We get Brendan Bone instead,' Micky said.

'Something to keep them quiet,' Rod said. 'And help to bring round the ones who are still being awkward. His job will be to pacify them. After all, it's to his own interest to co-operate with the authorities. The fact that they once had a go at him for drug-taking is less important than the fact that he's reckoned to be a millionaire. And, as you say, he got away with the drug charge.'

Hilda said: 'You're probably right. I don't trust this government, though.'

'They've got to pull things round,' Rod said. 'The country's as down as it can get. As far as I'm concerned, I think I can take the cart out again tomorrow morning.'

'I should wait a few days,' Hilda said.

'I want to get some chicks I was promised. There aren't many who will part with chicks now, and this chap might not hold them for me. Much better having our own hens than buying eggs. Even if we're on the turn, it will take a time to get properly straightened out.'

Rod had a good day with the cart. In the morning he went buying, round the northern outskirts of Pallister, and did well. People seemed to feel, as he did, that the really bad time was over. The electricity supply had stayed on, though with voltage drops at peak periods of use, and the buses were operating again. And there was the radio, of course. Even though the news did not tell them anything much, it relieved them of the sense of isolation, of having been deserted by the world outside the street in which they lived. The rumours were less macabre. The most common one was that the Queen had abdicated in favour of Prince Charles. He heard no-one mention this with disapproval, and several spoke warmly in favour.

Where resentment was expressed against the yobs, it was done so half-heartedly, with the main blame reserved for the government who had got things into such a mess. About the massacre of the police they spoke very little, and reluctantly. They did not want to know about it, or remember it. It was over. What mattered was that the fighting was over, too. People, they said, ought to get on with things, with the business of living. In their own cases, mostly, it meant the men signing on for dole, the women queuing for welfare rations. The most bitter complaint was that television broadcasting had not been resumed yet. He heard the almost identical comment from three different women: 'I'd like to hear what Cliff Michelmore makes of it.'

His afternoon trip, into the country, was also successful. He did not go to Lyddell's farm, not having collected enough silver to make it worth while, but had a good haul elsewhere. There was less reluctance to part with things, less suspicion that any trade must be for the worse. The man with the chicks had only half-promised them, and Rod had anticipated some difficulty in persuading him to go through with the deal, but there was none.

Once, as Rusty was plodding along the road, he heard a familiar faint sound to the east, rapidly growing as spinning tyres ate up the distance between. He wondered about pulling off, but there was no lay-by or turning. All he could do was coax the horse over to the verge, and leave as much road clear for them as was possible.

They came through fast – well over seventy, he judged, their engines screaming in advance, exhausts coughing behind them. There must have been at least forty of them. They passed him like Prussian cavalry overtaking a civilian. A couple came so close that he thought they were bound to hit the cart, but they did not. All in the acid-bleached white leather jackets, with black crash helmets. He watched them disappear into the westering winter sun, and listened to the silence that spread back over the empty fields. He was as indifferent to them as they to him. It had been a good day, and he was on his way home, to his family.

He was halfway along the drive before, getting clear of the evergreens, he saw the motor-bikes. They were parked in well-defined rows, with an almost military precision, in front of the house. He urged Rusty into something like a trot, and felt all the fears and anxieties that he had put aside sweep back to stifle him. Jumping off the cart, he ran up the steps and opened the front door with his key.

There were two yobs in the hall, smoking cigarettes. From the door on the left he could hear voices laughing, and the radiogram, full blast, playing what sounded like a jazzed-up version of a Sousa march. The two came towards him. He said:

'What are you doing here? Where's my ...'

'Come and talk to the Commander,' one of them said. He looked quite pleasant – fresh-faced, a country lad – and his manner was not aggressive. 'The Commander wants to see you.'

'My wife?'

'She's all right. Follow along, Pop.'

He was taken to his own study. There were three yobs there. One was standing by the bookshelf with his back to the door, one sitting smoking, the third, a boy about five feet four with freckles and bright red hair, was leafing through papers from one of his drawers which had been pulled out and laid on the desk top. The escorts left, closing the door, but the ones in the room paid no attention to him. He thought the one smoking, a lanky youth with his spot beard dyed grey, might be the leader, and spoke to him. He tried to tread a line between civility and obsequiousness.

'What do you want here?'

The boy inhaled before replying. 'It's like this. The Commander decides where we pitch HQ. We got a new Commander since the fighting, and he chooses this. So we move in.'

'Why here?'

The boy shrugged. 'The Commander says so.'

Rod controlled his anger. There was no sense in provoking them. There were others to think of, apart from himself. He said:

'You want us to get out?'

'That's for the Commander to say.'

'But what does he say?' There was silence. 'All right. We'll pack and go.'

The one by the bookcase turned round. 'No,' he said, 'you stay. I insist you stay.'

The spot beard was new, covering his thin jaw with tufts of black.

But the glossy black hair, hollow cheeks, long nose with flaring nostrils were familiar, and the pallid skin. He said:

'Remember me, Charlie?'

PART THREE

A GENIUS FOR COMPROMISE

The English, someone once said, have a hundred talents but only one genius: that of compromise. We do not take things to extremes; we see more greys than either blacks or whites. Hence our comparative immunity from civil strife. Hence, in political terms, the development of the two-party system. It has led foreigners to charge us with perfidy and hypocrisy. But it has saved us, over and over again, from bitter continuing struggles, and bloodshed.

We find it exemplified in the situation which confronts us today. The government has wisely abandoned those attempts to repress the young of the nation, which led, inevitably, to counter-action, to loss of life and damage to property. Youth has thrown up its own leaders, and the government turns to them, for help and advice. This is entirely proper, in fact unavoidable. Politics, as Bismarck said, is no exact science. It is rather an art – the art of the possible, of the expedient.

The times in which we live are strange, particularly for older people. To those who can recall childhood in Edwardian England, there may be bitter confusion. Long ago, the great battleships, those symbols of an imperial rule, went from our seas. Now the bobby on the beat has gone, too, and it may seem that what is left is anarchy, a wilder more chaotic anarchy even than that which overtook our ex-colonies when, far-called, our navies melted away. There are some who talk of barbarism.

But to do so is to indulge in the pessimism of the senile mind which, having lost all power of assimilation, can only reject and deny. *Der Geist, der stets verneint!* Law springs from the will of the people, and requires the consent of the people. That consent was withdrawn from the old system, and goes out to the new. The fact that the youth of the nation have brought it about only emphasizes the value of the revolution.

It is true that the new society is not yet organized in any tight and cohesive pattern. It might be said that two societies march side by side. Economics, industry, health, foreign affairs – all these remain in the care of Parliament and the government. Law is in the hands of the young, and is no longer national but local.

It is not necessarily the less effective or the less just for that. There may be minor excesses – it would be surprising if there were not – but these must be seen in the perspective of a nation striving to return to dignity, and content to place itself meanwhile in the charge of its younger people. We ask only that this trust should be respected. We are confident that it will.

I

TWICE, ON HIS WAY to the Scouts Hall, Martin saw a rat. The first was only at the end of the road from his lodging, a greyish streak scuttling along the side of a house. He had a clearer view of the second. It looked like an old buck, and was crouched under the light of a street lamp, worrying something in its mouth. It moved as he approached, but not quickly, crossing the road with a hunched hopping gait. Why was that so hateful, Martin wondered? One of God's creatures, after all, made and loved by its Creator. And since God loved it, there must be a way for man to love it also.

There were more of them about lately, or at least they were more in evidence. It was probably something to do with the haphazard and disjointed way in which the city contrived to go on living. Dustbins, for instance, were no longer always emptied on the same day, and might stand out for as long as a week. Or perhaps cats had lost their will to hunt and destroy their old enemy. When man lost courage and perverted his instincts, why should brutes fare any better? A different Revelation: not the lion lying down with the lamb, but the cat turning away from the rat.

The street lamps dimmed, surged back to brightness, dimmed a second time, and went. It was a dark night – the day had gone early under a massive bank of cloud which did not keep the cold out: he thought it might be freezing. He stood for a moment or two, accustoming his eyes to the blackness before going on. While he was doing so, the familiar roar grew out of silence somewhere to his left, swelled and became visible in headlight beams scouring the main road a hundred yards ahead. They went, and the sound went, too, dying slowly. He thought of the rat. One needed to be able to love man first, before making the attempt on the rest of creation.

He groped his way forward. The lamps came on again, before he reached the Scouts Hall. There was never a complete breakdown. In some ways, it would be better if there were.

It was an ordinary meeting, and Martin took part in a state of depression. There was no one causative factor for this. It stemmed from small things, like the ugliness of the rat and the lights blinking out, larger things like the confusion of a night lit by headlight beams, riven by the blare of engines – and out of the cold which, in this tin-roofed shack, bit deep into the flesh and numbed the mind. 'Our Father,' he said, 'Thy Will be done,' but the Will, for whose intention he tried to pray, was something even more remote than usual, less comprehensible. The Kyrie, following, was not an arm, sustaining and uplifting, but a dull pattern of harmonies, during which, surreptitiously, he rubbed his hands together, trying to chafe warmth into his fingers.

The cold bothered him in the meditation, as well. It struck into his knees from the hard floor and lanced at his crippled hand: he tucked the nailless fingers under his right arm, pressing them in. He begged for warmth – not physical warmth, but the warmth of knowing that he was not alone in the cold, the warmth of knowing his small plea was heard, even if denied.

The meditation seemed to go on for a long time. He wondered if it were his discomfort that dragged out the minutes, or whether the others were as drained and unready as himself, There had always been someone to speak, breaking the silence of their individual devotions. Perhaps he should do so – he had not spoken for ... how long? Months, he thought. But he could not now. He had nothing to tell except a discouragement which hung on the very edge of despair.

Then a voice said:

'Lord, we are your poor servants. Unworthy. But hear us, help us.'

They got to their feet, and settled down on the benches. The voice was new to him, and his eyes searched for the one who would remain standing, the one who had spoken and would speak. It was a strange voice as well as unfamiliar, harsh and astringent. A newcomer. There were those who came once or twice, and did not return. This, he now saw, was one who had been present at the last two meetings, but silent. A small dark man, probably in his thirties, nondescript in appearance. No power there, to match the power in the voice. On previous visits he had worn a suit; now he was dressed in the robe of the Fellowship. It did not fit very well, being too big. He looked feeble in it, his head wizened. Martin felt the cold in his bones, and shivered.

He spoke the identification:

'A humble servant of God, by His grace one of the Fellowship, your Brother James. I speak at God's will.'

The voice was strong, though, and bitter. With the others, Martin said:

'Speak, Brother.'

He looked round at them. His eyes were small, peering. Martin thought he might possibly have worn spectacles at some time. He left a silence, of perhaps half a minute, from which he said, his voice softer, in tone as well as volume:

'How do we know if we do God's will?'

It was a true question, not rhetorical. Someone said:

'By listening to God in our hearts.'

'Yes, Brother. I was a sinner, a man given over to Self, to excesses of the body, exigencies of the soul, wickedness of the mind. God spoke, reproving, and through His grace and goodness, I heard Him. Conscience will tell a man when he is doing wrong, if only he will listen. But what of the man who does no evil, but does less good than he might? That is a harder thing to know. Then, when God speaks, it is no more than a whisper, easily drowned by complacency and vanity. The Samaritan can turn into a Pharisee. The man to whom God gave ten talents, returned twenty. He had no cause to praise himself for that. He could have returned thirty, fifty, a hundred. There are no limits to man's power when he does God's work.'

Inside the harshness of the voice, there were nuances, gradations: a strident instrument, but nobly played. Listening, Martin felt his own dullness stripped away. A voice cried:

'Amen!'

James said:

'What do we do, Brothers?' He paused, but only briefly. 'We meet, and pray together, and go out and help the poor and sick, the old and infirm. And do we tell ourselves that we do enough? Do we preen ourselves, returning our twenty talents? There is more to do.'

'What more?'

That was Sam Gilliatt, the grocer, who had helped found the centre in Pallister. He was a frequent speaker – a big square-shouldered man, who had been a sailor.

James said: 'The Lord said: feed my sheep.'

'We do what we can.'

Gilliatt provided food for the poor at cost price from his shop, and also gave much away. James said:

'And the Lord said: man does not live by bread alone. It was the food of the spirit which the flock lacked – which they lack now. That was the commandment.'

Gilliatt said:

'We pray for them. We pray with them, if so be they wish it. But we have never forced our beliefs down the throats of those we aided. We don't hold with soup-kitchen religion, Brother.'

'One thing, Brother.' The voice had softened again, only to call out with a trumpet's rawness: 'Do we believe that Christ was the Son of God?'

They shouted their assent, Gilliatt's voice booming, Martin among them. James cried:

'Then, believing that, who dares talk about soup-kitchen religion? Shall we hide the Truth, like the man who buried his talent in the ground? Is there any food of the body, any help, we can give God's paupers that compares with the gift of His Holy Word? Is there, Brothers? Is there?'

The voice transformed them, and James with them. Instead of being insignificant and nondescript, he blazed with meaning and passion. Gilliatt, and one or two others, were silent, but the rest cried:

'No!'

Martin heard himself call: 'Nothing compares.'

James let the tumult die, and went on, starting quietly:

'This was Caesar's world, Brothers, and we rendered unto Caesar. We ministered unto the bodies of the poor, and washed our hands of their souls. We could deceive ourselves then. But now Caesar is dead, and his world is given over to the devils of his corruption. The lambs cry out in hunger. It is we, and we alone, who can lead them to the crystal springs, the meadows of sweet grass. Shall we fail in this? Shall the lambs starve, for want of the shepherd's care?'

Silence again. The eyes, no longer weak but full of fire, searched their faces. Gilliatt said, reluctant but half convinced:

'There are few of us.'

'Few! I count more than there were apostles. We are few, but will be many. The Lord said: "Go out into the highways and hedges, and compel them to come in." We have but to seek and we shall find those who will help us to carry the burden – the burden which is joy to the spirit.'

Not Gilliatt this time, but Len Pearce, the ironmonger:

'We've kept to ourselves. We've always kept to ourselves.'

This time James did not answer. He stared at Pearce and let the silence grow round him and the words he had spoken. The silence was like a light, showing up their pettiness and futility. It lasted for minutes, and it was not James who ended it. Gilliatt shouted:

'A hymn, Brothers! "Onward Christian Soldiers". Sing, Brothers.'

They sang, in rough unison. Martin felt none of the self-consciousness which normally overcame him, only a carefree, intoxicated happiness. He was aware of the discomfort of the cold, the pain of it in his bad fingers, but differently. Like the martyrs, he thought, accepting pain as joy, degradation as glory. Only the beginnings of what they must have felt, but the beginning was a triumph in itself. He looked at James, who was not singing but staring at them all, exalted.

'Forward into battle,' he sang, 'see His banners go!'

Spruce took him by the arm as they went out.

'I believe,' he said. 'Brother Martin, I believe.'

His pessimism, lately, had been even more acute, his cynicism unchecked. This was Armageddon, and God was watching from a far galaxy, with divine mirth.

'I believe,' Spruce said. The fingers tightened on Martin's arm. 'Christ was God. And Christ is risen!'

II

R OD SAID:
'I'll get out later, when they've gone to bed.'

'And the guard?' Jane asked.

'If there is one, I don't imagine it will be very hard to get past him.'

'When you get out, what then?'

'I'll get help from somewhere.' Jane looked at him. 'They're only a set of young thugs. If a few people band together ...'

'A few? There are over forty in this gang.'

'Well, my God, there must be sixty or seventy able-bodied men in the estate, without going further afield.'

Micky said:

'Able-bodied, but poor-spirited.'

'We don't know that till we try, do we?'

'You may not,' Micky said. 'I do.'

'It's in defence of their own interests.'

'They had their chance to defend their own interests when the fighting was on. They preferred to sit quiet at home, and hope they would get away with it.'

Rod said:

'You might be a bit prejudiced about that.'

'I might be, but I don't think I am. There was no army, and they allowed the police to get cut up. After that there aren't any defences.'

'They can still defend themselves by defending each other. The yobs are a very small minority of the population at large.'

'The whites are in a minority in southern Africa.'

'It's not the same.'

'Not the same, but similar. There are dozens of cases in history of a minority ruling a majority that could crush them in a few hours if they would only stand up and fight. They won't do it. Spartacus was one of the very few who managed to get them going, and the only reason he could was because he started with gladiators – men who had been used to fighting. And the reason he lost was because not enough slaves would come in with him, even when their own army was in the field and beating the Romans. They needed a bit of courage to win – no more than that.'

'Are you trying to say that we're slaves?' Jane asked. 'To the yobs? It's ridiculous.'

'We were conditioned to slavery before it happened. People's lives regulated by the government. Security the watchword.'

'There's a big difference between security and slavery.'

'No, not as much as you think.'

Annoyed, she said:

'Surely your own particular organization was a thing that really was regulated. Discipline, and blue uniforms.'

'Discipline is a form of conditioning, but it has a particular purpose. You do as you're told because that makes you operate more effectively, not just because you want an easy life.'

Rod said:

'You don't seem to have operated all that effectively.'

'No, not very. But there's a limit to what you can take on without some support.'

Jane said:

'It's what to do now that matters.'

She was, Rod saw, regretting having been stung into her earlier remarks, and was trying to turn the conversation. She was plainly fond of the man, and it was true that his experiences must have shocked him: one needed to make allowances. That did not mean, though, that one had to accept defeatism. He said:

'Yes, it's the present that concerns us, not the past. I'm going out tonight to try to round up men who will take them on.' He looked at Micky. 'Will you come with me?'

'It will do no good.'

He felt a quick charge of anger. They had taken him in, and were protecting him by keeping his identity secret. A word to the yobs, and his life wasn't worth tuppence. He demanded:

'Will you come with me?'

Micky shrugged. 'Yes, I'll come.'

The Commander had allowed them to keep the two rooms which Hilda's parents had had, plus a room across the landing previously used for lumber. Hilda's decision had been that the old people should be left in undisturbed possession of their bedroom, while the other two rooms were, as far as sleeping was concerned, divided between the sexes. Rod, Micky and the boys had the sitting room, where they all lived during the day, while Jane, Linda and Hilda herself took over the lumber room. They had no beds, but there were enough blankets to go round. This was one of the things Hilda had stocked up on, and there was no demand from the yobs. They had their own, brought with the rest of their gear in a truck from wherever they had been last. What they offloaded was a queer mixture of basic essentials and whimsicalities. The latter included a Japanese ceremonial sword, a couple of large paintings of nudes by Russell Flint, a collection of cactus plants, and a stuffed black bear presenting an umbrella stand with its right paw. It had been taken into Rod's office, where the Commander now held court, and had a flag stuck in the stand. Very colourful: it showed a green crescent with a red star on a blue background. They had probably picked it up from some consulate in Pallister: several of the African republics had had them there.

Rod's first and sharpest apprehensions had been allayed during the twenty-four hours that followed the take-over. The attitude of the yobs to the family seemed largely one of indifference.

As long as they kept out of their way, they did not bother about them.

Their organization and code of living probably had a lot to do with this. The basis was military, with the Commander apparently holding absolute power. He was the only one who had a room to himself – a bed had been brought in to the office. The others slept on folding camp-beds, as many as eight to a room. They showed a weird combination of laxness and discipline. The former was the surface impression – the guards sat about, smoking, while on duty – but Rod noticed that the Commander and his two chief buddies were obeyed immediately and without argument.

During the first evening, the bikes roared off, returning a couple of hours later with pillion passengers. These were young girls, wearing hip-shorts under looted furs, and, clearly, familiar camp-followers. They cleaned and cooked for the yobs, and in addition supplied their sexual needs. But they were treated with contempt, and the whole thing operated on a mass basis. The girls – about twenty of them – were given a couple of big rooms at the end of the house, and called for, individually or in groups, as they were needed.

This gang, in fact, although not physically homosexual like some of the others, was entirely male-centred. The girls were chattels: a necessity, but to be kept down in case they proved a threat to the masculinity and cohesiveness of the group. As far as could be seen, they accepted this without resentment, and with a feeling of being honoured in having been chosen. It was necessary, Rod reminded himself, to realize how things looked from the standpoint of their generation. To people like himself, these were yobs – packs of delinquents who had taken advantage of a breakdown in society to strut and bully briefly on the world's stage. But they saw themselves as the overthrowers, destroyers of an old system, knights of the new establishment. They did not practise chivalry, but chivalry, he remembered reading, was something that came late, when long generations of civilized life had given women position and power. The Round Table, if it had ever existed, had almost certainly been composed of young bullies just like this. Their women would have been much the same, also – despised and kicked, and kissing the foot that kicked them.

They had plenty of food. The truck went out with a screaming motor-cycle escort and returned with fresh meat, exacted as tribute from the farmers, which the girls unloaded. There were some exotic tinned foods brought in, too, either from the previous headquarters or from some central store dump to which they had access. The girls cooked for them on the Aga. Hilda and Jane prepared Frotein stews for the family on the little electric cooker which had been put in to permit her mother to do small snacks when the old people wanted to keep out of the way. The power cuts made it difficult, but she managed. The smell of roasting meat that came up through the house did not help: they had not dared to go to the stores which Rod had hidden in the loft over the stables.

Rod was still unsure how he himself stood with the Commander. Several times he was called down to the office and humiliated in small ways – by being forced to stand waiting for half an hour while the Commander, ignoring him, chatted to his companions, by being ordered to pick up the Commander's solid gold fountain pen which he had dropped on the carpet, polish the surface of the desk which the Commander's boots had marked. But apart from that he, like the others, was left alone.

He was a symbol of the Commander's triumph – that, after all, was why he had brought the gang out to Bridge House, when there must have been dozens of more suitable and more convenient places he could have picked. So far, that in itself seemed to satisfy him, but it was impossible to tell what the future held. The Commander might get bored with things and move his company on – they were essentially nomadic. Or he might decide that dispossession and the small humiliations were not enough – that he needed something else to demonstrate the change in their positions since that morning in the magistrate's court.

But he was not prepared to take a chance on it being the former. It was better to act first.

They got out easily by the back way, made a wide circuit of the house, and headed for the gates, keeping as far as possible in the cover of the evergreens. The night was dark, and bitterly cold; the grass crunched with frost under their feet. Looking back, Rod could see the lights on all along the front of the house, and thought about his electricity bill. It was just about due. He wondered if the Board would dare cut the supply off if he failed to pay. Probably not, as long as the yobs stayed in possession.

The street lamps were on in the estate, though dimmer than usual. One saw lights in the houses, too – those that were still occupied. An ordinary suburban scene on a winter's night. He was reminded, as they turned in at a garden gate, of the time Hilda had got him to go canvassing with her on behalf of the Labour candidate at an election. The results had been discouraging: Gostyn, new as well as old, was a staunchly Conservative preserve. How pointless that distinction seemed now.

The first door was opened by a small man, bespectacled, in shirt sleeves who, before Rod had much chance to say anything, stammered a lack of interest and shut the door in their faces. Facing the night again, Rod said:

'He wouldn't have been much use, anyway, I shouldn't think.' Micky said:

'No, not much. The next place looks empty.'

'We'll try the one after that. I know the people there slightly.'

Their name was Windle, and he was a local government officer – therefore still in work. Mrs Windle asked them in, and offered cups of tea which they refused. She was a pleasant-seeming woman with a high colour, and a look of capability and intelligence; in her middle thirties. He was a few years older, moon-faced, sandy-moustached, hair receding in two vees, smoking some herbal mixture in a curved black pipe. They listened attentively while Rod outlined what had happened. Windle took his pipe out of his mouth to say:

'Bit of bad luck, Mr Gawfrey. If I were you, I should leave them to it. Move into one of the empty houses here, perhaps. You can sort things out later on.'

'I can't do that.'

'Why not?'

Rod explained. He saw the change in expression on Windle's face, as he realized that bad luck did not cover the situation – that he was, to whatever extent, marked by the yobs as a victim. He went straight into the plea he had prepared. He happened to have been the immediate target, but if this sort of thing were not stopped there was no telling who would be next. Windle said:

'Well, not us, I fancy.' He smiled apologetically. 'We haven't got anything here that would interest them.'

'It isn't just a matter of taking over people's houses. They're running loose, unchallenged now that the police are out of action. They might do anything.'

'Things will sort themselves out. My feeling is, the government's letting them have a run while they – well, build up. I've heard it said they're forming a kind of Army, at Salisbury.'

Micky said:

'Do you know of anyone who's gone to join it? Would you go?'

He made a negative shrug to the first question, and said:

'I couldn't, anyway. I've got my job. Someone's got to keep it all ticking over.'

'For whose benefit? The yobs?'

Windle shook his head. 'It won't last. They'll fight among themselves. They have been doing. You've got to take the long view.'

'We could do something about it now,' Rod said. 'There are enough of us here in Gostyn to deal with this bunch.'

'They're armed, aren't they?'

'They've got some guns. We could get hold of some, ourselves. I know where to lay hands on a couple of shotguns, for a start.'

Windle fiddled with his pipe, not looking up. 'I couldn't do that ... get mixed up with weapons. I mean, as a local government officer ...'

Rod asked:

'Is it more important not to get mixed up with weapons than to help protect the community in which you live from being terrorized by a gang of thugs?'

'It's not the way I look at it, Mr Gawfrey,' Windle said. 'No-one around here is being terrorized at the moment, anyway, apart from you. It will clear itself up.' He finally looked at Rod. 'If the police couldn't stop them, what do you expect us to do?'

'There are more of us.'

'I'm sorry.'

'You won't help?'

He did not answer, but after a few moments, Mrs Windle said: 'There is something else, Mr Gawfrey.'

'What?'

'They don't like being crossed. Over at Frenshott ... some people caused trouble. The yobs burnt all their houses. An old woman was killed because she didn't manage to get out in time.' Her glance went to the ceiling. 'We've got two children upstairs.'

'Yes,' Rod said, 'I see.'

At the next house they tackled, although there was a light visible inside, no-one would come to the door. They went on, to find a garrulous and bellicose-seeming Scotch woman, who inveighed equally against the yobs and the weakness of the Southerners who had permitted this state of affairs to come about. She had her son living with her, a tall unmarried man in his thirties, who listened and nodded. Rod asked if he could count on him for help, and he blinked uneasily. The mother said:

'Indeed, you cannot! He has his mother to think of, and it's no concern of his. It does not lie with us to put the English to rights. Let them tend to their own messes.'

She spoke with a conviction and sudden hostility that brooked no argument, and opened the door for them to leave. It slammed shut after them. They were at a corner. Micky said:

'Which way now?'

Rod said:

'Right, I think.' The cold was intense, dispiriting. 'There's someone along there who might be a bit more use.'

They plodded their way through the estate. Some people refused to open up, some gave them short shrift at the door, others had them in and allowed Rod to talk. From over thirty houses tried, they got only two positive responses. One of these, a short chunky wild-eyed man who had been a commercial traveller until his firm folded up, wanted to go out right away and launch a mass movement against the yobs. He was more than a little unbalanced, likely to be a hindrance rather than a help. When Rod dissuaded him, he turned sullen.

It was nearly eleven, Rod saw: they had been two and a half hours out here. He said to Micky:

'We'll have to jack it in for now.'

Micky nodded. They were standing in the light from a street-lamp, with the houses nearly all dark about them. People went to bed earlier these days. He said:

'As you like. You get a poor welcome at this time of night.'

He had accompanied Rod with few interventions and no comment. Rod said:

'I'll try up in the village tomorrow. They may not be so gut-less.'

'Maybe.' They started walking back in the direction of Bridge House. 'I'm used to this sort of thing.'

'This sort of thing?'

'Endless interviews with little or no result.'

Rod was going to reply to that when he heard the sound in the distance ahead of them. Micky heard it, too. They stopped and watched. The sound grew and there was the glow of moving lights. The glow stiffened into beams, crossing the intersection. They were quiet until they had gone.

Rod said:

'A night exercise.'

'Yes.'

They could still hear the roar of bike engines, though more distant. The street lamps went out, as they walked on; it would be eleven. It was a cold black world, with the engine noise running round its rim like a fringe. Fading, far off. And then nearer. Not in front, but behind them. Rod said:

'They're circling the estate. Why would they be doing that? There's nowhere to go in that direction.'

'Nowhere except here.'

'Do you think …?'

Micky said:

'It was always a possibility. They could work it out: even though they turned you down, the people next door, in the next street, might not. And when the yobs hit back, they probably wouldn't discriminate between the innocent and the guilty. The only way to be sure of being in the clear would be to go along to the house and tell them what was happening.'

'Who?'

'The lady from Edinburgh, perhaps. Or Mrs Windle with two children upstairs. Or the commercial traveller, who wanted action – any kind of action. Does it matter?'

The noise was nearer, but lower in register; they had throttled down and were crawling. There were lights in the sky again. Rod said:

'Should we run for it?'

'I imagine that's what they want us to do. They're enjoying this.'

He was glad of the solidity of the man beside him, ashamed of his earlier resentment. He said:

'If you thought this might happen, why didn't you say something?'

'It was a possibility. You have to take some chances. That's what is wrong with this lot: they won't take any. It's a matter of calculation, and you can't always get the calculation right.'

They had continued to walk forward, their progress made a little easier by the shifting reflections of the headlights of the bikes.

Rod said:

'Well, thanks, anyway.'

He checked, as the night dazzled round him. Beams from behind answered by beams ahead where, unknown to them, bikes had been drawn up across the road, completing a cordon. They walked on, into the glare.

III

JANE GOT PERMISSION to see the Commander in the afternoon. A guard escorted her to Rod's old office. The Commander was lying on the bed in the corner of the room, and two others were sitting smoking in armchairs. They glanced at her as she came into the room, but none of them got up. There was a lot of smoke in the room, which partly nauseated her and partly induced craving for a cigarette herself.

She asked:

'Do you mind if I sit down?'

The Commander said:

'Help yourself, sweetie.' He stretched and yawned. 'What can I do for you?'

'How long are we going to be kept under guard up there?'

'Till the trial.'

'The trial?'

'Well, there has to be a trial, doesn't there? Your brother-in-law and that boy friend of yours have been up to mischief, haven't they? Trying to cause trouble. Behaviour calculated to lead to a breach of the peace. Have I got that right, Cha-Cha?'

The lanky one, with the grey spot beard, said:

'I reckon.'

'We have to keep the peace, don't we?' the Commander said. 'A responsibility, you might say. You understand that, don't you, sweetie?'

She understood that she was being toyed with, and resisted the urge to plead for Micky and Rod. It would do no good. She said:

'I want to know if I can go out, to the village.'

'What for?'

'To get food. We've practically nothing left up there.'

The Commander shook his head slowly. An angry red spot, she saw, was forming on the side of his long white nose.

'I don't think that would do. I mean, you're a witness, kind of. I reckon you'd better all stay where you are till the trial.'

'Will it be today?'

'Maybe. Or tomorrow. Or some time after that.'

'Without food?'

'No, we wouldn't do that. I'll have some sent up. You see to it, Ape.'

That was the short one with red hair, and clean-shaven. He nodded silently. He opened his mouth to pick his teeth, and she saw that the teeth were crooked, and looked green. The disgust she felt for the other two was intensified with this one. She turned away, and out of the corner of her vision saw him noting her aversion. Wanting to get out of the room, she said:

'Thank you. Then I won't keep you.'

'Won't keep us!' The Commander gave a short harsh laugh, and swung his legs down off the bed. 'I like the way she says that. Don't you, Ape?'

The red-head said:

'Yes. She's a nice talker.'

His voice was thin and reedy, but hard. It made her nerves crawl. The Commander said:

'I thought you might be wanting to say something about that brother-in-law of yours – sort of justify him. You'd want to put in a good word for him, wouldn't you? I mean, him being charged with a serious offence, and all that.'

She said, despite her resolution: 'They didn't mean any harm. They just …'

The Commander's laughter cut her short. Cha-Cha joined in, but Ape continued an impassive probing of his teeth.

The Commander said:

'You know what's funny, sweetie? That's what my counsel said in court that time. Exactly that. High spirits, he said. But they did us for it, all the same.'

'I wouldn't call being put on probation a heavy sentence.'

'Wouldn't you? It's a conviction, though. Goes in your record. My old mum was very upset about it.' He paused and watched her, but she said nothing. 'And I'd say this was much more serious, wouldn't you? Stirring up trouble against the government. You might almost say it was treason.'

She met his stare, but said nothing. She was not going to help him in prolonging this farce. He picked up a packet of Perfectos, took one out, lit it, and made as though to toss it back on the table that stood by the bed. Instead, he held it out towards her.

'Fag, sweetie?'

She almost shivered with desire for the taste of smoke in her mouth. She said blankly: 'No, thank you.'

He gazed at her, shrugged, and threw the packet down.

'All right, then, push off. Come down again later, if you feel like it. Always willing to have a chat.'

Night closed in again. About six, two of the girls brought food up – a large tray with lamb chops, roast potatoes, and French beans. Some of the chops were burnt black, the vegetables were out of cans, and the whole lot was mixed together and almost cold. They ate it hungrily, all the same. They had tea left, but no milk, and Hilda went to put a kettle on the little cooker. Jane said, to the men:

'Look, I've been thinking. You ought to make a break for it tonight.'

Rod shook his head. 'It's not on.'

'There's only the one guard. I'll bet I could get him in here, and you could lay him out. Then down the back stairs and off.'

'It wouldn't work.'

'At any rate, you can try!'

Micky said:

'Forget it, Jane.'

Her anger was stirred. She said:

'*You* can say that. It's Rod he's after. He as good as said so this afternoon. He doesn't give a damn about you, but he's got it in for Rod.'

Hilda had come back while she was talking. She interrupted to collect Linda and Peter: she wanted them to play cards with their grand-parents. When they had gone, and the door was closed, Rod said:

'It's like last night: he wants me to try and make a break. They get bored, and a man-hunt would provide a pleasant change. He hasn't had me down in the office all day. The idea is that I should sweat it out. That's why he won't put a time to his so-called trial. A little war of nerves.'

'Well, he's winning, if you just sit back and do nothing.' She stared at Rod, angry at him, too. 'Don't try to tell me you're not scared.'

Rod said:

'No, I wouldn't try to tell you that.'

Micky said:

'You say there's only the one guard. I should think that's probably deliberate, too.'

Stephen said:

'There's somebody sitting in that next room along, with the door just open. I saw his leg when I went along to the bathroom.'

'All right!' Jane said. 'It may need more planning. But you can think of something. We could make a rope of sheets and get you out through the window.'

Hilda said, in a flat voice:

'I can't see Mum and Dad getting down a rope of sheets.'

She had been quieter than usual all day. Her intervention now infuriated Jane even more than her earlier silence had done. She said: 'Who's talking about Mum and Dad? It's Rod who's in trouble. Your husband. They cut the throats of the policemen in Pallister – have you forgotten that?'

Hilda did not reply. Micky said:

'Shut up.'

'I won't shut up! It's different for you – as long as we protect you by keeping quiet. You're not the one they're interested in.'

Rod said:

'Just be quiet.'

She turned to Hilda. 'I don't understand you. I just don't.'

'Don't you?' Micky asked. 'Because you don't think as far ahead as she does, maybe. What happens if we do manage to get clear?'

'What do you mean – what happens?'

'There are nine of us,' Micky said. 'Two in their middle seventies, one a boy of thirteen. We can't all escape, and if we don't, they can take it out on those who are left behind. Don't think they wouldn't.'

'So we're to do nothing?' No-one said anything. 'Just like the people on the estate?'

She tried to hold back the tears, and succeeded for a time. Then the defence went, and she put her head down on the table. Her body shuddered with sobs. Micky came over and put an arm on her shoulders. She felt the weight of it, but no comfort.

In the morning, breakfast was brought up: fried bread in unwieldy chunks and bacon either undercooked or frizzled out of recognition; and once again, cold. They ate it, and the day dragged by. In the middle of the day a big saucepan arrived, containing a greasy stew, which at least was warm. They sat about, talking little. Jane tried to read, but could not. The book was about the fortunes of an elegant Austrian family in the first decade of the century: its fantasy did not command belief. She thought of the yobs, of the scene in the office, and was tempted to go down there again. The Commander might offer her a cigarette. She would take it, this time. Her mind dizzied with the imagined smell, taste, feel of it.

Hilda came through from the other room. She asked:

'Where's Pete?'

'I thought he was in with the grand-parents,' Rod said. 'No?'

Hilda shook her head. Stephen looked up from playing patience.

'May have gone to the bathroom.'

'Go and see, will you?'

It was the fact that they were so crowded, Jane realized, that made it difficult to realize just who was where. In this not very large room there were six of them – five now as Stephen went out on to the landing. Being crowded, and the feeling of pointlessness and apprehension. She wondered if the yobs would do anything at all about Rod and Micky. Perhaps not; perhaps it would just drift on like this. Something must happen some time, she knew: the world could not go on forever confined to a couple of rooms, with nothing to do but brood and eat and sleep. It was just that she could not believe that it would change.

Stephen came back. 'No, he's not there.'

Hilda said:

'Did you check the other bathroom? Someone might have been using that one.'

'We're not supposed to go any further, are we?'

'I don't suppose they'd bother about Pete. Never mind. I'll go and see.'

Jane said:

'I'll come with you.'

The guard on duty was a thin spotty youth, with bouffant fair hair and diamanté spectacles. He waved his automatic in their direction.

'Where are you going, then?'

'To look for my son,' Hilda said. 'Have you seen him?'

'The kid? He went downstairs.' As Hilda went to pass him, he said: 'You're not allowed.'

'But he did.'

'That's different.'

Hilda looked at him. 'You can't stop me.'

His eyes went to the gun, and back to her. He said:

'I'll get someone to find out where he's got to. You go back inside. Right?'

She nodded. 'I'll give you five minutes.'

'I told you I'll get someone.' He was irritated and also defensive. 'Go back in.'

They did as they were told. Jane saw that Hilda was nervous, but keeping, as always, an iron control. She could not really sympathize with either. If she were worried about Peter, she should show that. It was a hardness like the hardness over Rod. But in this case there was nothing to worry about. He had wandered off – they would not concern themselves with a boy, as Hilda had said. It was hard enough for the rest of them to put up with the confinement, with not being able to do anything – much worse for a thirteen-year-old boy. Rod made conversation, talking about the horse, which the yobs had said they would see to. It was to soothe Hilda, Jane saw. The thought of this, of his goodness, made her want to cry again, and she turned to look out of the window. The sky was dull grey, the grass, even in mid-afternoon, streaked with frost – one more in the succession of iron days.

Hilda said, cutting through Rod's words:

'It's five minutes. I'm going to see.'

Outside the guard said:

'The kid's all right.'

'Where is he?'

'Someone's bringing him back up.'

'Why haven't they?'

'I tell you, he's all right.'

Hilda said:

'I'm going down to see.'

'Hang on. No, I mean it. They're here now.'

They came along the landing from the stairs, half a dozen of them in their white leather jackets, with white pointed shoes. Peter was not with them. Hilda said:

'Where's my son?'

'Downstairs, Ma.' A big fat one, about nineteen, with an unformed child's face, his spot beard thin and drooping. 'Go and help yourself. We've come for the criminals.'

'You mean ...'

'The Commander says it's time for the trial.'

'Peter ...'

'I told you, Ma. He's downstairs. No reason why you shouldn't come, so long as you don't get in the way.'

The four of them went down, shepherded by the yobs. Jane's feelings were confused. There was apprehension again for what might happen to the two men, and the transmitted echo of Hilda's nervousness about Peter. But also relief that something was happening at last. They couldn't do anything, anyway. The pudgy face with the inadequate beard, walking beside her ... they were only children, really.

They were led into the green sitting room. Chairs and tables had been brought in from other parts of the house, to create something roughly like a court-room. Rod and Micky were led away to the dock. The Commander and his two cronies were sitting together behind a kitchen table, like magistrates.

Hilda cried:

'Where's my son?'

The Commander said:

'He's all right, lady. You've got my word for that. But we want to get this over first. You sit quiet, and he'll be all right.'

They sat down where they were shown. On the Commander's instruction, one of the yobs read an indictment. It was done with pseudo-solemnity in legal-sounding language, and they all obviously found it very funny. The only one not grinning was the one called Ape, who was picking his teeth again and staring blankly at the two women.

'How do you plead?' the yob asked Rod and Micky. They did not reply. He looked up at the Commander. 'What does that mean, m'Lud?'

'Call it Not Guilty. Get on with it, Nipper. What about defence counsel? Got to give him every advantage. Defence counsel all prepared? Bring him in then.'

He came in through the door at the back, with a yob on either side. They were holding him, but not tightly. It was Peter, dressed as a parody of a barrister. A black gown much too big for him – Martin's old graduation gown, found in some cupboard? – and a wig contrived from cotton wool. They had put a pair of spectacles on his nose, too: the heavy-sided black ones which Rod used for reading and writing. The yobs were laughing as he came towards the centre of the room, stumbling over his feet.

That would be the spectacles, she thought; of course he could not see properly through them. But if this were all – just a stupid joke – there was nothing to worry about. They could not mean to do anything much to Rod and Micky. Peter was probably taking it all as a joke; he quite enjoyed dressing up.

The Commander said:

'Counsel for the Defence. Don't say we're not giving you a fair trial.'

He broke off, into the general laughter that started up again as Peter, staring muzzily about him, tripped over the hem of the gown and fell. The escorts helped him up, not roughly. The Commander said:

'Upsy-daisy. Looks as though Counsel's been on the juice.'

Peter doubled up forward, broke clear, and started to make a wavering way back towards the door. The escorts did not attempt to stop him. Halfway there, though, his head came forward again, and he vomited. The audience laughed. They went on laughing as Hilda ran to him, to hold his head. Jane followed her. The boy retched uncontrollably for some minutes. Then he straightened up, white-faced, and Hilda wiped his face with a handkerchief. The laughter continued.

Hilda said:

'Look after him, Jane.'

She walked, not quickly but deliberately, to where the Commander sat. Her hand came round as he turned his head to look at her, still laughing, and cracked against the side of his face. Jane said involuntarily: 'Oh, no!' She saw Rod start to move across the room. The laughter had cut, with the slap, to shocked silence.

'You bastard,' Hilda said. Her voice was clear, but shaking. 'I don't give a damn what piggish tricks you lousy little sods get up to, but leave my children alone, understand? You've poured whisky into him, haven't you? You think it's funny to make a thirteen-year-old boy drunk? I've heard of a child being killed like that. If you'd killed Peter, I'd have killed you. Do you understand that, you cheap pimply little bully? I'd have killed you, as I will if any of my children are touched again – either by you or your rotten friends. Have you got that clear in your idiot's head?'

The Commander did not move, but looked up at her. Rod had come to stand beside her. The Commander's white face was flushing where she had hit him. The one called Ape, on his left, got to his feet. He said:

'We're going to fix you, you old cow. You're going to regret that. You're going to lick all our boots before we've finished with you. We're going to start by …'

The Commander said:

'Shut up.'

'I'm just telling her …'

'Shut up.' He rubbed his cheek with his right hand. 'You've got some strength in your arm, missus. I thought my bleeding head was coming off. Christ, you can hit harder than my old mum can. Brought bloody tears to my eyes, you have.'

Hilda watched him, tensed, and said nothing. The look he returned was half-angry, half-admiring. He said:

'All right, joke's over. Take him upstairs and put him to bed. Take the others, too.' He rubbed his face again. 'Like a bleeding sledgehammer, it was.'

IV

THE COLD SPELL BROKE, following a heavy fall of snow. The streets of Pallister looked slimy from a distance, and there were patches of deliquescent snow, stained brown and black and grey, heaped in gutters and against walls. It was not raining at the moment, but had been; and more threatened. Martin tried to avoid puddles, but already his feet were wet inside his leaky shoes. He felt it as discomfort first, and then as something to rejoice in, a welcomed mortification of the flesh.

Spruce's flat lay between Mrs Johnson's and the Civic Centre, so he called there to pick him up. Spruce was ready and waiting, and they stepped out together cheerfully. On Spruce's suggestion, they sang a hymn as they walked: 'A Safe Stronghold our God is Still'. Spruce sang bits of it in German – he had visited Germany several times with his wife and thought Goethe a nobler mind than Shakespeare though perhaps not so good a writer. People in the street stared at them, and some laughed. Martin remembered what it had been like when he had been ashamed of them poking fun at him. It was like remembering a childhood scene by looking at an old photograph. One saw it, and knew that it existed, but marvelled that it could have been real.

Spruce wanted to accost the people who were laughing. They could be won over, he insisted. Where mockery was greatest, so was potential belief. All things were possible with God's aid. All it required was faith, and mountains could not only be moved, but sent spinning in dazzling orbits, round the earth and moon and sun. They laughed together at the conceit, but Martin would not agree to stop. One made a plan, and stuck to it. In purposiveness, man came closer to God; in aimlessness, to the Devil.

'I agree,' Spruce said. 'I do agree, Brother Martin. We'll go on. And those two things enter life at every point – life and death. My memories of Clare, for instance.'

Clare was the wife, whose death, following closely on that of Marion, their only child, had flung him to the hell of seeing God and the Devil as one – the hell from which, with Brother James' aid, he had made his joyous escape.

'Every morning I thought of her,' he said, 'and every night. And still do. But then the thoughts were aimless and destructive, while now they have purpose: the purpose of prayer to God, who gave her to me once and will give her to me again, in the day of glory.'

He laughed again, as light rain swept into their faces, and Martin laughed with him. A pack of yobs swept along the street ahead of them, as they came within sight of Pallister Wall. Martin prayed for them, and knew Spruce was also praying. God's Will would be done. That was certain, and one must bide the time between in patience and love. And do God's work, shirking nothing, welcoming everything.

Most of the shops along the High Street were open, though they were not doing much in the way of trade. The only ones with customers seemed to be those which had changed over to Exchange Marts, and the three pawnbrokers, replacing what Martin remembered had been a jeweller's and a sweet shop: he could not recall the third. The cinemas were open, showing old films. The Odeon had a sign outside: 'Admission Prices Slashed'. The commissionaire was standing in the entrance, calling 'Seats at all prices' to the passers-by. The film showing was 'The Sound of Music', with 'My Fair Lady' offered for the week to follow. They wanted escape, he thought, into the easy romantic past, not seeing the glory surrounding them here and now.

Turn but a stone, and start a wing.

'Tis ye, and your estrangèd faces,

That miss the many-splendoured thing ...

He pitied them, and prayed for them.

They reached the Civic Centre and the rain stopped again. He thanked God for that – not for the cessation of his own discomfort, but because people were less likely to come out in the rain, and therefore less likely to have the chance, which Spruce and he offered, through God, of learning the truth, which could make them free as it had already freed him.

They stood on the steps above the car park, and sang. It was perhaps ten minutes before anyone paused near them. In that time, Martin saw the sky clearing in the west, over the railway station, and praised God for His handiwork. The thought came to him that if, instead of wisps of blue appearing among the grey, the horizon had shown the threatening black of cumulonimbus, that would still have been God's doing, still a fit subject for praise. He smiled, singing, and held back laughter which would have broken up the hymn. How silly was all human speculation, and yet how wonderful. For there was no paradox. One praised God for His excellences and for their opposites – all contradictions were reconciled in Him.

Singly and in twos and threes, they drifted in to listen – to mock sometimes, but to listen. Some were regulars; he had noticed the old woman with the green shopping bag on previous occasions, the man with the pipe that had no tobacco in it, the pretty girl who looked frightened, the fat man with the small emaciated woman to whom he kept glancing for some kind of reassurance. The man with the pipe shouted obscenities at intervals. The old woman shifted from foot to aching foot. The fat man demanded scriptural reference for everything that was said. Another man came to stand near the girl, and she moved away, scared, to a different part of the circle. They were all human, all beloved by God. He thought, with bursting heart: as

I am, as I am!

Spruce and he took it in turns to speak, and to answer questions, but in no formal pattern. There were times when he said: 'May I speak to that, Brother Henry?', and Spruce nodded and smiled and gave way – times when it happened the other way round. One man, a newcomer, was persistent in his objections. How could there be a loving God, operating in a world like this? It was not just that there was no evidence in favour: the evidence was against. Life was streaked with pain and misery, and ended in death. What room did that leave for a God of Love?

Spruce cried:

'All the room there is!' He looked out at them, his thin face bright, Martin knew, with the memories of his dead. 'In God's love, all is transformed. Pain and misery and death itself. All transformed!'

The man was strong-looking, big, firm-jawed, his body well muscled and his voice decisive. A little while ago, Martin would have envied him and feared him; now he felt pity and love. The man said:

'Fool yourselves, if you want to, but don't try to fool the rest of us. When there's order, one might believe in an Orderer. Not with the mess we live in today. I'll tell you what the universe is: chaos, emerging from chaos and moving towards chaos.'

'Listen,' Spruce said, 'and you will hear! Look, and you will see! Heaven has no gates!'

He turned and strode away across the car park. Martin watched him go. There was hope there, a soul that had begun to seek. He corrected himself: there was hope everywhere. The man with the pipe threw another obscenity, and he rejoiced in that, too.

A grey-haired man with a twisted face asked:

'What about the yobs? Will God do something about them?'

'Forget them,' Spruce said. 'They are unimportant.'

'They bust up my shop,' the man said. 'They took my son. Do you call that unimportant?'

'Nothing valuable is lost,' Spruce shouted. His words rang against the sky, where there was more blue and the edges of the grey were turning white with the brightness of the hidden sun. 'What God gives, He gives forever. Praise Him, praise Him!'

V

FOR SEVERAL DAYS, Rod was expecting something to happen – the trial to be resumed or a punishment awarded. Gradually, he realized that the whole business had been dropped. The guard had been taken away from the landing, and, as far as could be seen, they were at liberty to go and come as they pleased, both inside the house and out.

It was Hilda, and her outburst, which were responsible for the change. This was apparent in the way she personally was dealt with by the Commander. The rest were ignored – he did not resume the habit of having Rod brought down to the office and baiting him – but she was treated with a semi-impertinent affection. The Commander addressed her as Mum, and the rest of the yobs, except for Ape, followed suit.

Lukewarm or cold food continued to be sent up to them from the kitchen, but after a dish of sausages, both cold and undercooked, had appeared, Hilda spoke to the Commander about it. She asked if she and Jane could use the kitchen to cook their own food – it was difficult on the tiny electric cooker, even apart from the continuous power cuts. He agreed readily, and made some contemptuous remarks about the girls, asking if she could not smarten their ideas up. They were given good stuff, but there wasn't one of them who could boil an egg.

Hilda went back to the kitchen, and organized things. There was opposition from the girls at first; the majority were lazy and slovenly and, while subservient as far as the yobs were concerned, objected to taking orders from a middle-aged woman. One in particular, a thin dark spitfire who was proud of the fact that she was called to serve the Commander's sexual needs far more often than any of the others, was as awkward as possible and at last refused point blank to help with the potato peeling Hilda had laid on. There were plenty of canned potatoes, she said, and she was growing her finger-nails.

The next morning, though, showed a great change. She was ready to do whatever she was told, and kept her eyes down. Her face was swollen with crying. Hilda asked her if anything was wrong, and got no sensible reply. Other girls were equally reluctant to talk about it, though they, too, were entirely obedient now. She did not want to press them until the dark girl, being touched accidentally by one of the others, cried out with pain. Then, on Hilda's insistence, she was told. One of the yobs had overheard the impudence and refusal, and told the Commander. There had been a public whipping that night.

Hilda had the girl's back bared, and looked at it. It was horrifying enough – marked with great weals which had bled in several places, one of them bleeding afresh where she had been knocked. She bathed it, and dressed it, and told the girl to go to bed for the day. She had remained silent up to that point, although the dressing of her back must have been painful, but now became voluble. She begged to be allowed to stay at work; otherwise it would mean another beating.

Leaving her weeping, Hilda went to tackle the Commander about it. He was pleased to see her, but indifferent to the subject of her mission. The girl deserved what she had got, and would get more of the same unless she mended her ways. She was nothing, a pair of legs. They could pick up a hundred like her in half an hour in Pallister. He accepted Hilda's angry reproaches, grinning. She was not to worry over that sort of thing. It would have been old Ape that cut her about a bit. He'd made himself a fancy whip, with knots in it. Ape stared at them silently, busy with his teeth. Regular devil old Ape was, the Commander said, when he got going. Didn't know his own strength. As for the girl … he shrugged. If Hilda wanted to give her a day off, that was all right, too. It was her department, and he didn't interfere.

She could tell the girl he had said so.

Hilda told Rod about this in the linen room, leading off the kitchen, which had become her preserve. It gave them the chance of a little privacy, impossible in the crowded conditions upstairs. Rod said:

'Did she go off?'

Hilda nodded. She looked tired. Her face was drawn, and he realized that she was older and thinner in appearance than she should be. All this strain. She said:

'When I told her it was the Master's command, she went. If you'd seen her back …'

'She'll be all right, with rest.' It was Hilda who needed rest, he thought, but knew there was no point in bringing that up. 'Don't worry about her.'

She said:

'Part of the time I persuade myself that they're just kids, play-acting, and then you suddenly get brutality, like this.'

'Kids can be brutal, when there's nothing to check them. We're lucky.'

'Lucky?'

'That he's got absolute authority, and that you remind him of his old Mum. You saved my bacon, love.'

She looked at him. There was an expression of concentration on her face, almost of pain.

'It was Peter. Well, you know that. As far as you were concerned … I didn't think there was anything I could do. I watched it happening. I think I would have gone on watching. But with Peter, I just didn't think – and, as it happened, it worked. But I didn't do anything for you, did I? I don't like myself very much, Rod.'

'You're a mother. I wouldn't have it different.'

'I'm a wife, too. At least, I thought I was.'

'So you are. The best.'

She shook her head, and repeated:

'I don't like myself.'

'You can't be strong, without having priorities. You're a lot stronger than I am.'

She came to lean against him. 'No.'

'In the ways that count.'

'I don't think so.'

He held her, and was conscious again of how thin she was. One did not notice changes in people one saw every day, people as familiar and necessary as the air one breathed. Her head lay against his chest, and he could see the wrinkles in her neck, the small slow scars of time. The words were there, in his mind, as certain as ever, but the years of living together, raising a family, put a barrier between thought and speech. It was the wrinkles that enabled him to force them through. He said, remembering how it had been to be young and callow:

'Love you, Hilda.'

She moved swiftly in his arms, straining to him.

'Rod, I love you! More than the children – so much more. It's just that …' She clung to him, helplessly. 'You know, don't you?'

'Yes, I know.' He caressed her arms. 'There's something else I know: you've not been feeding properly.'

She looked up at him, crying and smiling. 'I can do with dieting.'

'No, you can't. You'll do something about that? Promise me. There's no excuse for looking under-nourished now you're the Commander's housekeeper.'

'I suppose there isn't.' She dried her eyes on her apron. 'I'd hate the little sod to find me crying – any of them. You're the only one I don't mind.'

'I mind, though. Spoils your beauty.'

'Went ages ago.'

He pulled her in for answer, but she broke away.

'No! He drops in on me at all hours, and they've never heard of knocking.' She patted her hair into place. 'I wonder what's become of her.'

'Who?'

'The real Mum. He may have admired her, but as far as I can see, he never goes to visit her.'

'He probably daren't. She'd very likely beat him up.'

'He could do with it. He's a nasty little swine. Not as nasty as Ape, but nasty enough.'

'Keep your voice down,' Rod advised her. 'Some of them listen outside doors, and there are limits even to Mum's privileges.'

As the situation became static and they all got used to it, Rod thought about going out on the road again, with the horse and cart. Hilda persuaded him out of this. There was no particular need, since they were living on the bounty of the yobs, and it was silly to take any risks unnecessarily. He protested that there were no risks – from all accounts, life outside, in both town and country, was largely peaceful. The buses ran, rations were distributed, the electricity functioned on and off, and so did the telephone. She did not argue that point, but asked him not to go: she wanted him with her. So he stayed at home, and busied himself with various repair jobs. There were enough of these. The yobs strewed their path with breakages, some through carelessness, others for simple joy in the sound of breaking glass or splintering wood. Micky helped out with the work. He was less dextrous than Rod would have expected a policeman to be, but willing.

He got Stephen and Peter helping too, where possible. It was better than having them hanging around the yobs, which was the most likely alternative. Stephen had started growing a spot beard, until Hilda made him shave it off. And Rod had seen him talking earnestly to one of the girls one day. He had made himself known, and the boy went away sheepishly. He did not say anything to Hilda about that. She understood many things, but he doubted if she had much insight into adolescence in the male. And there was no sense in worrying her.

The yobs continued to go about their own business, which consisted in idling, punctuated by bursts of activity when they went off on their bikes, sometimes for an hour or two, sometimes for the whole day. Evenings, when they were in the house, they drank a lot, and kicked up a good deal of noise. This particular gang did not use drugs – he gathered from chance conversations that they had a puritanical contempt for those who did – but they appeared to have an inexhaustible supply of whisky. They invented or adopted games, which they would play over and over, with undiminished enthusiasm, for days; and then quite suddenly drop. There was a craze on Monopoly, and another on poker dice. Once some of them brought back a bow and arrows, which they had found in a looted sports store, and they constructed a target and set it up on the lawn in front of the house. For two days, the daylight hours were taken up with this. On the third morning, it rained, and Rod heard them grumbling about not being able to go out and shoot. The afternoon was fine, warm for the time of year, but by that time they had started their own version of contract bridge, and they did not move from the tables.

It was all pointless, apparently innocuous, the sense of menace fading out of the situation as the family grew accustomed to it. One could not think of it as anything like normal life, but it seemed that one had the measure of the abnormality, and could tolerate it.

But the innocuousness could not be taken for granted: they were not tame. They came back in high spirits late one afternoon from a foray into the country. It was a food-hunting expedition, with the bikes escorting the three-ton truck that held the supplies. Rod was fixing a window in the green sitting room, using glass from one of the outside sheds, when they burst into it. They ignored him, as usual, but were full of the day's work. They had found a farm where the farmer had foolishly tried to put them off by pretending that another gang had cleared him out the day before.

So they had amused themselves with him. They had adopted one of their simpler devices and tied him by his thumbs to a beam. He had yelled a lot, but had still insisted that there was nothing on the premises. Then Ape had had the idea of starting a fire under his feet as they swung eighteen inches off the floor. That had brought results, all right. He told them to go to a place, a couple of fields away, and they would find the stuff. As they were going, he begged them to cut him down, but Ape had said he could swing and smoulder there till they checked that this time he was telling the truth.

And he had been. The cunning old devil had built pigsties and a chicken run half a mile from the farmhouse, in the middle of nowhere. It was by a ruined old cottage, and there were two cows in one room and produce stacked in the other. It would have meant a lot of work carrying it back if they hadn't been able to get the truck up there, across the fields.

They had gone back to the farmhouse after that. The fire they had lit under him had gone out – it was only a few sticks, to scare him. The farmer was still hanging there, and they cut him down. Ape was going to put the leather in, to show him that lying was a bad policy, but there was no point because he was dead. He must have had a heart attack, they thought.

Before they went, they ransacked the house – he was living alone – and had a real find. The old bugger had got a hide-away under the stairs – concealed, but Cha-Cha had spotted it. Full of gear he'd stashed away. Through black market dealing, obviously, so he'd only got what was coming to him. They had shared out on the spot, throwing dice for what was left over.

'Four aces and a king, first throw!' one of them said. 'That was throwing, mate. I've always fancied a silver goblet to drink out of.'

It was a christening cup. Rod remembered the woman he had bought it from, a thin elderly spinster living alone in a big house next to a church. Lyddell had been particularly pleased with it. He finished the window, and was glad to get out.

VI

SOON AFTER THE TELEPHONE came back into service, Jane was called by Walter. One of the yobs told her she was wanted. The courtesy surprised her at first, but she soon realized, from the feeble jokes and innuendoes about boy friends, that he was doing it for his own amusement. He took up a position a couple of yards from her as she picked up the instrument, and listened in with undisguised interest.

Walter said:

'That's you, then. What have you been getting up to, for God's sake?'

His voice had the boisterousness, with a slightly peevish under-current, that she knew so well. She said, watching the yob who was grinning at her:

'Nothing much.'

'I've been expecting you to come in here.'

'That hasn't been possible.'

'Why not?'

She stared at the yob. 'We have guests.'

'What do you mean, guests? What the hell are you talking about? Why haven't you come in to see me?'

The thought had more than once crossed her mind that Walter, if he had any influence at all with the gangs in Pallister, might be able to help them. At first, though, they had all been under guard; and after the trial it had seemed less important. Not sufficiently so, certainly, to justify going in to Pallister as a matter of urgency. So far, during the present conversation, she had been temporizing as a form of discretion, but that suddenly seemed pointless, too. She said:

'We've been taken over – the house, that is. By one of the gangs.' Her listener grinned at her: yob was the word one must not use – gang they rather liked. 'We're living in three rooms upstairs.'

Walter said:

'Which gang is it? I mean, who's in charge? I might be able to do something.'

'He's called the Commander.'

'They all are.' There was a trace of petulance in his voice. 'Don't you know his name?'

'No. I think Rod does. He was one of those Rod was … involved with, last summer.'

'You mean, the take-over was deliberate – not just something casual?'

'No, not casual.'

He did not reply at once. When he did, there was a wariness in his tone. He said:

'Well, I should think you'll be all right. They haven't bothered you, have they?' That sentence was gabbled, and he rushed on before she could say anything: 'They'll probably move on in a few days. They don't generally stay too long in any one place. Look, why don't you come in, anyway? We can talk about things.'

Jane got the message. If all this had been haphazard, he might have been willing to try to help, but he was not going to get involved in anything serious. Even the invitation to come and see him had become perfunctory. It told her nothing new about Walter, but something about his position in relation to the gangs. It was just as well that she had not been depending on him.

She said:

'Yes, I'll think about that, Walter. 'Bye now.'

The yob eased himself away from the wall as she replaced the receiver. She tried to pass him and he got in her way, doing it again when she moved in the opposite direction. On the second tack, their bodies met. He grinned idiotically into her face.

'Funny how this sort of thing happens, isn't it?' he said.

His hand came into clumsy contact with her breast, and stayed there, pressing and grasping. She pushed him away with a single decisive thrust of her palm against his chest. He said:

'You don't want to be unfriendly.'

'Don't I?' She stared blankly at him. 'Will you let me pass? My sister's expecting me.'

He moved reluctantly out of her path. Fortunately, they were not under sexual tension: the girls took care of that. She heard him whistle after her as she headed for the stairs. It was not only the girls she could be thankful for. Hilda's ascendancy over the Commander helped, too.

She had never been very good at household tasks, or liked them, but she concentrated on them now – helping Hilda in the kitchen, washing and ironing clothes for the family, mending and cleaning. She was aware of her own maladroitness, and infuriated by it and by the fact that she scarcely seemed to improve with practice, but she persisted, taking a perverse satisfaction in it and in the tiredness which swamped her each evening. It took her mind off things, off Micky in particular.

The first impulse towards this had been physical frustration. The days between his coming to Bridge House and the arrival of the yobs had been suffused with erotic happiness. In so large a house, there was always an opportunity of being alone together. In addition, there was the assurance that he would come to her bed at night; she had put him in a room just across the landing from hers which made his journey easy. She had not thought she could get more joy from their lovemaking, but, deliriously, found herself proved wrong. She had felt her body blooming from day to day, hour to hour. She was dizzy with delight, and with the certainty of its renewal. Her body moved, automatically and irresistibly, in response to his. She remembered a girl she had known at University who had landed herself with a pregnancy. She had said to Jane: 'It's no good – I'm determined not to, but the moment he puts his hand on me, I'm finished.' Jane had despised her for that, as one might despise an alcoholic or a drug addict, a person dominated by their own weakness. Now it was her past self she pitied, for her callowness and coldness. She had taken her pills carefully and consistently during the years with Walter. She was shocked to realize one day that she had missed that morning's; more shocked still to find that she really did not care.

Frustration came with the yobs. During the day, there were nine of them, in two rooms. At night, she slept on the floor between Hilda and Linda. She could see Micky, perhaps find an excuse for touching him – no more. Doing nothing, she brooded on this. Work did, at least, give her something else to think about.

It was all intensified after the two men had gone out to try to get help, and had been caught and brought back. There was the guard on the landing, dropping in on them whenever he felt like it. There was also the threat of what might happen to Micky and Rod at the trial. To start with, she was more concerned for Micky and, for that reason, felt guilty. He had not been much help to Rod – had only accompanied him reluctantly – and seemed likely to get away with it, anyway, since Rod was plainly the Commander's target. Rod had been a mainstay of her life since her childhood, a sort of cross between brother and father, giving her treats, paying for her education and secretarial training, a background figure of generosity and strength.

It disgusted her that her sexual infatuation should make her more concerned for another man's safety, and the disgust coloured everything. She still wanted Micky, but hated herself and him for the wanting. Instead of trying to touch him, as a promise of the renewal of that other deeper closeness, she avoided him. She thought he might show some sign of surprise or resentment, but he did not. They addressed each other with the ordinary civility they had previously shown as a mask for their involvement. She did not know for what it was a mask now.

Going back to their room after the telephone call, she found herself, for the first time in days, alone with him. He looked at her as she came in, and she stared back silently. The physical pull was still there, but to yield to it, in even the slightest degree, was unthinkable. She almost wanted him to make an approach to her, knowing how easy the rebuff would be.

He said:

'What was the telephone? Anything important?'

She went back to the mending she had left. Shirts for the boys – buttons to sew on, and a jagged tear down the front to be repaired.

'No,' she said. 'Not very important.'

She was aware of the extra edge of steel in her voice. He said: 'Poor old Jane.'

Her head snapped up, and she looked at him suspiciously.

'What do you mean?'

'Nothing. Only that things aren't easy. For any of us.'

She said: 'I've been thinking. As far as you are concerned, it might be better for you to move on. We're not far from Pallister. There's always the chance of your being identified as ex-police.'

'I'm surprised I haven't been,' he said. 'I know one of those downstairs. I booked him once for a faulty silencer.'

'Then it would be better if you went, surely. Safer.' He did not reply, and she went on: 'Don't you think so?'

'If I'm bothering you.'

She said coldly:

'You're not bothering me at all.'

'Then in that case, I'll stay.' He went towards the door. 'I'm going to lend Rod a hand with the gutters.'

The door closed after him. She was sorry he had not given her a chance to demonstrate her freedom of him. She was also a little ashamed of her relief at his answer.

VII

Moncrieff sucked on his empty pipe. He had made a feeble joke about it one day in the common room, to the effect that he could not afford tobacco at current prices and that it did not matter anyway, since he only needed the pipe as part of his image. Which was probably, Martin thought, the simple truth. How strange that he had once been nervous in Moncrieff's presence – afraid of this creature of fear.

'I think I can say, Weston, that we've been very – well, understanding over your – your private interests.' He paused to let Martin reply, but had to go on: 'A schoolmaster is a public figure. One is entitled to one's own religious beliefs, but going round the town dressed as a sort of monk is rather a different thing. We could have made an issue of that.'

He could hardly have forgotten the harangues, the scarcely veiled threats. Martin himself remembered them very well, and his own nervous sweating before and after. But it might have meant trouble – publicity – to ask the Committee to terminate his appointment, and the supply of teachers, in those days of affluence and a seam-bursting economy, had not been easy.

'To behave in this way,' Moncrieff said, 'and at a time like this in particular … We're beginning to get back to normal, learning to live with a difficult situation. We need loyalty, co-operation, a willingness to buckle to and sacrifice ourselves to the common good. There are the children to think of. More than ever, they need the help of those of us who are in a position of authority and trust.'

'Not much authority,' Martin said. 'They only come to school if they like, or their parents send them.'

'But they come,' Moncrieff said, 'or, at least, a lot of them do. And you would be letting them down, Weston.'

'God's work comes first.'

'If one believed in a God, surely one would say that this is God's work.'

'There are priorities. In any case, you have the same number of staff as you used to, with only half the number of children. You can easily rearrange things to fill the gap I leave.'

Moncrieff said petulantly: 'I don't understand you, Weston. You seem level-headed and sensible, and yet you do things like this.' Again, Martin did not trouble to answer. 'And you want to leave right away? You do realize that under your contract you are required to give us a full term's notice?'

'I'm leaving today.'

'But the contract …'

'No contracts are enforceable any more. You know that.'

'But why today? What's the urgency?'

'All God's work is urgent.'

'Urgent today, but not yesterday?'

'Until the call comes, one waits.'

In exasperation, Moncrieff twisted the pipe between his hands. He said:

'You realize there is no going back from this sort of decision, I hope?'

'No,' Martin said. 'No going back.'

Betty found him getting his things together in the common room. She called to him, and he looked up.

'Is it true?'

'That I'm leaving? Yes.'

'But why? Why?'

'To preach.'

'You're already spending all your evenings and your weekends preaching. Isn't that enough?'

'No.'

She said angrily:

'What good do you think you will do? What possible good?'

'I don't know.'

'In that case, how can you justify it?'

'I haven't got any answers to questions, only to imperatives. One imperative.'

She said: 'That's very clever. What about money? How are you going to live?'

He smiled at her. 'The ravens fed Elijah, didn't they?' He saw that there was more hurt and unhappiness than anger in her face, and said gently: 'Don't worry, Betty. People will give me food. And shelter. There is goodness in the world, as well as evil.'

'Will I …?' Her voice was small, trailing off. She looked at him. 'Will I see you at all?'

'Very likely. I'll be preaching at the Civic Centre most days.'

'Yes.' She hesitated; then, coming forward quickly, kissed him on the cheek. 'God bless you, Martin.'

He was surprised to find a crowd in the car-park when he got there. He wondered if someone else were preaching there already, but they seemed to be watching rather than listening, and he heard jeering and laughter. He went to a place, on the opposite side from the Civic Hall, where there was a gap, and looked through. Stocks had been set up in the centre of the car-park – three of them side by side. The contrast between their mediaeval shape, remembered from History primers, and the new white wood was strange, shocking in itself. Only the centre one was occupied, showing imprisoned feet and hands, and a man's dirty face above.

There had been talk about this happening. The rumour had leaked out from the most recent meeting of gang leaders. They dispensed a kind of justice, punishing crime (apart from their own) wherever they encountered it or had it brought to their notice; and increasingly people were willing to take complaints to them, having no other remedy. Punishments had varied from death, in extreme cases, to various bizarre penalties according to the whim of the particular leader. The stocks had been agreed as a general way of disposing of minor offences – better than reintroducing prisons because so much easier to administer. And more colourful; it appealed to their stunted but avid imaginations.

Half a dozen yobs stood at the front of the crowd, which gave them room. They had a tin bath, full of filthy water, and a couple of small buckets. They dipped the buckets into the water, and threw the contents over the man. He made helpless attempts to dodge, and they feinted with the bucket, making two or three false throws before the real one. The other people were watching, some amused, some seemingly disgusted, most with a terrifying blankness.

At that moment, one of the yobs, either accidentally or by design, let go of his bucket. It travelled in an arc, and a bottom edge caught the man high up on the head. He lolled back and to one side, held upright only by his hands in their wooden cuffs.

Martin pushed through, and went to him. Blood was pouring from the cut, though it did not seem a deep one. He folded his handkerchief over it, tying it at the back. The man was coming round. Martin supported his head for a moment, and then felt hands on his shoulders. He had heard what sounded like threats from behind, but paid no attention. The hands tightened, pulling him away from the man in the stocks, and throwing him violently to the ground. One of the yobs stood over him, and kicked him painfully in the side.

The cries were clearer.

'Give him the leather, Mack!'

'Slot him!'

'Put the Robey in the stocks …'

He got to his feet, and went back to the man he had bandaged. There was a roar of anger. Two of them came at him, and he was knocked down a second time. When he made another attempt to get up, they pinioned him. One of the empty stocks was opened. They forced him roughly into it, and slammed down the top. In his confusion he was conscious of the fact that the work looked professional – the edges of the planks had been rounded and smoothed so as not to chafe the skin. They must have got a carpenter to do it.

The first bucketful took him by surprise, and made him gasp. It was cold, as well as being indescribably filthy; it stank on his clothes. He started singing, then: 'To Be a Pilgrim'.

> 'There's no discouragement
> Shall make him once relent …'

The next lot caught him with open mouth, and he was stopped, choking and spluttering. The yobs howled with laughter. One or two in the crowd were laughing also, but not many, he thought. He spat out the foul liquid, and sang on.

They carried on for a quarter of an hour or more, but what support they may have had was ebbing long before that. People moved away, one or two at first, then in driblets; finally with the decisiveness of a mass exodus. Martin sang on, shivering with cold. It was plain that they were getting less and less fun out of it. Finally, one of the yobs said:

'The bloody Robey's barmy. I vote moving on.'

He was let out at dusk, but not by the same ones. They paid little attention to him, but cuffed the other man quite a bit. It appeared that he had been accused of molesting small boys. Next time, they told him, it would be the chopper. They simply told Martin to bugger off and not make a nuisance of himself.

He walked away through the shadows, cold, stiff and exhausted. But full of joy.

VIII

HILDA COLLAPSED while she was working in the kitchen, and the Commander had her carried to the bed in his room. Cha-Cha and a couple of other yobs were there when Rod and Jane came down. The girl who had called them looked as though she were preparing to stay, but the Commander shouted at her to leave.

Hilda said:

'Could I be left … just with my sister and my husband for a while?'

'All right, Mum.' The Commander was restless, and looked worried. 'I'll call your doctor from the other 'phone. Bennett, isn't it?'

Rod nodded. As the door closed, he said:

'What happened, love?'

'It's nothing.' Her face was very white. 'Rod, would you go for a bit, too? I'd like Jane to help me. I'm in a mess. I'm afraid I've haemorrhaged. '

He knew her fastidiousness and modesty, and only said:

'Be all right if I just go to the other side of the room?'

Jane said:

'I'll get warm water and stuff. Won't be long.'

He held Hilda's hand while she was gone. They did not say anything. He wanted to tell her not to be frightened, but was afraid that this itself might alarm her. He did not look at it, but had seen the stain on her dress. Pressing her fingers, he tried to control his own fear. Then he had to go and look out of the window, while Jane washed and tidied her, putting on a clean dress. There was quite a lot of blue in the sky, and a shaft of sunlight striking the grass over towards the gates, but it was also snowing a little, a thin flurry falling slantwise from bulky clouds, white at the edges but darkening towards their centres. It could not be serious, he told himself. Just a woman's thing. The beginning of the menopause, perhaps.

A couple of motor-bikes kicked into life outside, and roared off. There was a knock at the door, and Jane told them to wait. In a few minutes she had finished what she was doing, and told Rod he could let whoever it was in. The Commander stood in the doorway, looking awkward.

'I sent a couple of the boys for him – make sure the bastard comes. They try to give people the run-around, just because they know which pills to stuff in you. Can I stay now, Mum?'

Hilda nodded. 'If you want to.'

He knew she would rather have been left alone with them. She was agreeing because she thought it important not to offend the lout, for the good of the family. Rod did not look at him, but pulled a chair up to the bed and sat by her. He could hear the Commander moving about the room. Now and then he made pointless remarks. 'Soon get you fixed up, Mum.' 'Be all right when that bloody doctor gets here.' 'Don't you worry, Mum, you'll be fine.' Then, with a note of relief: 'That's them back now, and they've got him.'

Doctors had been given petrol for their cars; at first by the civil authorities and later by the gangs. Bennett's Humber drove up with the motor-bikes stationed in front and behind, presumably to ensure that he did not make a break for it en route. It was the sort of pointless idiocy which usually infuriated Rod, but he was too anxious to be concerned with that. Bennett strode in, obviously angry. He dared not refuse a summons from the Commander, but felt his position was strong enough to let his resentment show. He asked curtly that they should all leave the room, while he examined the patient.

They waited outside the door. The Commander was whistling off-key through his teeth, snatches of the same tune over and over again. It got on Rod's nerves. He had to fight the urge to tell him to shut up. It was becoming unbearable when the doctor came out.

The Commander said:

'What is it, then? What's wrong with her?'

'She needs hospital examination.'

'But what's wrong with her?'

'We'll find that out in hospital. I'll arrange for an ambulance.'

'When?' the Commander demanded.

'As soon as possible. Perhaps later today.'

'To hell with perhapses. We'll take her in in your car.'

'That's impossible.'

'Oh no, it's not. If I bloody well say we'll take her in, then we'll take her in.'

The truculence was undisguised. Bennett looked at him with equally plain loathing, but only said:

'Be reasonable, man. I have to fix things with the hospital first. There's no point in taking her in if we can't be sure of a bed.'

'There'll be a bed,' the Commander said. 'Go and fix it now, on the telephone. Then we'll take her in.'

'Look, there's no particular urgency about this. Any time in the next few days will do.'

'You've got it wrong, Doc,' the Commander said. 'It's urgent when I say it's urgent. Go and fix things.'

Rod sat in the back of the car with Hilda, while the Commander rode in front beside Bennett. The motor-cycle escort was doubled, two leading the way and two following behind. They proceeded at a moderate pace through the almost empty streets, and into the gates of the Pallister General Hospital.

Superficially, nothing had changed here. Rod remembered it from three years earlier, when Hilda's mother had been in for a gall-stone operation. There was the same impression of confusing but purposeful activity – the ambulances in the yard

– figures looking forlornly out from the top-floor windows – and the smell of sickness blanketed by antiseptic. He helped Hilda out, and took her arm to Reception. The Commander and Bennett went with them, and a crisply uniformed nurse said:

'We'll get Mrs Gawfrey up to the ward right away. If you wish to stay …'

'We'll stay,' the Commander said.

' … there is a waiting room just along the corridor. We'll let you know when you can see her.'

Bennett said:

'I presume it's all right for me to go now?'

He was looking at the Commander, who gave him a casual nod of dismissal. Rod went part of the way to the door with him. He said:

'Sorry about this.'

'Not your fault. They act as the humour takes them. You're lucky, finding that one in a protective mood. They can be just as nasty.'

'Yes,' Rod said, 'I realize that. Can you tell me anything – of how she is?'

'Not really.' He was not looking at him, Rod saw. 'We'll know more when we've got some X-ray pictures to study.'

Rod said: 'I see.' It was as though there were a hand inside his chest, squeezing. 'Well, thank you.'

The Commander tolerated the waiting room for a quarter of an hour, chain-smoking cigarettes. He did not speak to Rod, and did not offer him a cigarette, either. At the end of this period, he strode back to Reception, and started demanding action. The nurse tried to soothe him with politeness and offers of tea, but he would not have it. They were taken upstairs and handed over to the Ward Sister, who explained that Mrs Gawfrey was being given a bath, and could not see them.

'Right,' the Commander said, 'then we'll see the doctor bloke.'

There was another attempt at putting him off, but it was given shorter shrift than before. The doctor came within five minutes.

He was tall and lean, in his middle forties, with a cold thin face. The Commander said:

'We want to get things straight. What happens now?'

'My name's Miller.' He acknowledged the Commander with a brief look, and turned to Rod. 'You're Mr Gawfrey, I take it. I had a few words with Dr Bennett on the telephone. We'd like to have your wife in for general observation. For a few days, say.'

The Commander said:

'Look at me, mate.'

The tone was peremptory. Miller did as he was bid. He was a couple of inches taller, and stared down expressionlessly into the boy's eyes.

'That's better. Now – you can have a look at her as soon as she's had that bath, and you can tell us something. OK?'

'I can tell you nothing of value until she's been X-rayed.'

'So fix it. How long will that take?'

'We can have plates within an hour.'

'Right. Do that. I'm going out for a drink. I'll be back in an hour's time, and you'll be able to say something. OK?'

Miller drew in breath. 'I hope so.'

The Commander turned and headed for the lift. Rod and Miller watched him go. Rod said:

'I've already apologized to Dr Bennett …'

'He's not related to you, is he?'

'No.' He gave Miller a brief outline of the events leading up to this. Miller listened, and said:

'I tried categorizing them at one time into mother-seekers and father-seekers, but the types overlap. This one, for instance. On alcohol, I gather?'

'They get through a lot of whisky.'

'I had the liquor boys down as father-deprived, the acidheads as hunting for mother. And the queers, of course, as father-deprived, mother-dominated. It amused me for a time. All nonsense, really. Except insofar as they are products of bad environment, and Ma and Pa are still the biggest influencing factors.'

'How do you manage?' Rod asked.

'At the hospital? They leave us pretty much alone, as long as we don't put any obstacles in their way. They are quite good at realizing how far they can push us. I suppose we are at working out how far we can retain independent action. A symbiosis, you might say. In general, we're too busy to bother much. Understaffed and overworked.'

'I heard that a lot of doctors have left the country.'

'Not all that many. To start with, of course, it's illegal under present regulations. You'd have to smuggle yourself, and if you have a family it's that much the harder. There are also some – quite a lot probably – who feel a loyalty to their patients. The good old medical ethos. I doubt if that applies in my own case. The public connived at getting itself into this mess, and those of us who go on maintaining essential services are conniving at its continuance. A genuine breakdown would shake things up, and we might get somewhere.'

'You have children?' Rod asked.

'Boy and a girl. Boy's taking A-levels in summer. He's down for my old place – Thomas's – and I suppose he may go there, if he doesn't decide there's more prestige in becoming a Knight of the Road. Funny how standards change. I was one of those who took a strong line about the over-prescribing of drugs … would have had the chaps struck off, and perhaps prosecuted in the courts as well. We've got a gang round the corner that's on heroin. They come in here for their supplies. I have no option about complying, of course, but I suppose I need not enjoy handing it out as much as I do. Several of them are on more than twenty grains a day, and the dosage is increasing steadily. It's a joy to watch them going downhill. Ah well, I'd better alert the radiologist about your wife. You'll be staying for the time being?'

'Yes,' Rod said, 'I'll be staying.'

He had half an hour alone with Hilda before the Commander returned: she had been put in a private room on coming back from X-ray. They had talked a lot, about the children chiefly, so as not to have to face the intimations of silence. The Commander's arrival was a small relief and a monstrous intrusion. From somewhere he had got hold of a box of liqueur chocolates, hothouse roses, and a bottle of Cordon Bleu brandy. He spread these out on her locker, and stared at her. When she thanked him, he said:

'That's all right. Doctor been back yet?'

'Not yet.'

'It's an hour. I'm going to get him.' He nodded towards Rod. 'You might as well come, too.'

They found Miller in the ward. He said:

'Ah yes, I was coming to see you.'

'You've seen what it is, on the X-rays?' the Commander asked.

'The radiologist and I have looked at the plates, yes.'

'Well, then?'

'We agree there should be an exploratory operation.'

'What for? What's wrong with her?'

'We shan't know that until we make a physical examination.'

'Look, come off it!' The Commander lit up a cigarette directly opposite the sign saying NO SMOKING, and blew out smoke in nervous exasperation. 'You've got some idea what it is.'

Miller looked at Rod. 'There's a shadow in the region of the cervix. Quite a large one. It could be a malignancy. I'm sorry.'

Rod did not answer. The Commander said:

'Malignancy? You mean cancer?'

'It could be carcinoma. I gather there's been a weight loss.'

The Commander stared at the doctor. His long white face, at once stupid and alert, showed anger and suspicion. It had seen violence and death and taken them for granted, but this threat was different, more subtly and more fundamentally a challenge to the assurance of triumph and power. He said:

'When can you do it? The op?'

'We can fit it in tomorrow morning.'

'Not before then?'

Miller spoke with patient clarity. 'The patient has to be pre-pared. And there's a limit to the hours that the surgeon can work effectively. I take it you are anxious to have the job done properly. We'll put her in at the top of tomorrow morning's list.'

'Yes. Well.' He looked at Rod, including him voluntarily for the first time. 'We'll stay around. I'll get a suite at the Royal. I'll 'phone and tell them we're staying in Pallister.'

'We should know some more by mid-morning,' Miller said to Rod.

'Right,' the Commander said. 'We'll be here.'

IX

AFTER HILDA WAS TAKEN AWAY, Jane went around in a daze. Work occupied her physically but did not, this time, do much for her mental condition. She could not believe that there was anything seriously wrong, but had been shocked by Hilda's acquiescence in the Commander's plans – by her weakness generally. It was all unlike her. They were a healthy family, and she could not recall Hilda having anything worse than a headache. Her pregnancies and confinements she had taken unconcernedly and, as far as could be seen, easily. Jane thought of the Commander returning to the house, with an unfamiliar dread. She had come to accept the yobs through him, and him through Hilda. It was, she knew, silly to feel like this, but she could not shake it off.

The hours dragged by. In the end, she got to the telephone and rang the Hospital. They told her of the operation that was scheduled. She was frightened, and angry with Rod for not having let her know. A little reflection made her see the injustice of that. Even if he had telephoned, the yob who answered might not have bothered to pass on a message: they rarely did. That left only fear, and stronger than before. It tired her, so that she wanted to lie down. She put her hand down on the Pembroke table, steadying herself, and saw that one of the yobs was watching her from the other end of the hall – the one who had been there when she took the call from Walter.

He said:

'Boy friend again, then?'

She steadied herself. 'No.'

'I bet it was.' He came towards her, and she told herself

that nothing had changed. The Commander and Rod would be back soon, Hilda in a few days. This was just an oafish boy – a nuisance, no more. 'You look proper fed up,' he said. 'I reckon what you need is a bit of consoling. You want something better than five minutes' talk on the telephone, a big girl like you.'

He stood between her and the stairs. She said:

'Let me pass, please.'

'A little smoocheroo first. One for the road.'

Fear was controlled by contempt. She said:

'Get out of the way, or I'll complain to the Commander.'

'You'll have a job. He's staying the night in Pallister.'

'Then I'll see him in the morning, as soon as he gets back.'

He moved to one side, and she walked upstairs. He called after her:

'What I like about you is, you're classy. You've got a good back view, as well.'

It still worked. Much as she disliked the Commander, it was something that the rest of the yobs feared him, and that his writ continued to run in his absence. Things could have been a lot worse, without that.

She did not attempt to use the main kitchen, but prepared a meal for them all on the little cooker. The winter night had closed in, and it was dark outside the window. The kitchenette adjoined the room in which her parents were sitting. The wireless was on, playing the inevitable pop music, and her mother was knitting something with old wool, unravelled from an ancient jumper. Her father simply stared ahead of him.

Jane was engrossed in the cooking. It was an activity she quite enjoyed but could never do with Hilda's apparent casualness and ability to divide her attention. In her case it was necessary to watch everything – even, when there was nothing specific that needed seeing to, the pot simmering on the hot plate. It was not until everything was more or less ready that she went looking for the others.

Peter and Micky were in the second room, both reading. She asked them where Stephen and Linda were. Peter looked up absently. Micky said:

'Stephen's somewhere round the house. He said he was going downstairs.'

'And Linda?'

He gestured towards the door through which Jane had come. 'Isn't she in there?'

The remark exasperated her. 'Would I have asked you, if she were?'

'I'm sorry. I thought that was where she was. I'll go and hunt them up.'

'Never mind. I'll do it.'

He put down his book, though, and came with her. She resented that at first, but not when they reached the bottom of the stairs and heard the noise of festivity ahead. It had a distinctly drunken note. It was coming from the green sitting room, which was their preferred place for drinking sessions.

The room was full of yobs and their girls. She sought for Linda, and saw her being talked to by one of the younger ones, a fair-haired boy who looked more weak than vicious. She pushed her way through the mob, and said:

'Supper time, Linda.'

Linda glanced up from her drink which was, Jane was relieved to see, a Coke. It crossed her mind to wonder where the yobs got them from – the Americans weren't sending them as part of the bounty, surely? Probably old stocks. Not of great importance, anyway.

Linda said:

'We've been asked to supper down here.'

Jane glanced dismissively at the boy. 'Very kind, but supper's ready upstairs.'

'I'd rather stay, though.'

She was on the point of snapping something back when she was jostled from behind, and a voice said:

'It's Miss Classy. What are you drinking, honeybag?'

She recognized the voice and, without turning round, said: 'Nothing, thank you. I'm just collecting my niece.'

He took her arm, pulling her round so that she had to look at him.

'You can't do that. This is old Cha-Cha's birthday. Old Cha-Cha's nineteenth. She's accepted an invite. Turkey and stuff. Champagne. Old Cha-Cha's birthday. Everybody's invited. You, too. Have a drink, honeybag.'

'No.' She tried to free herself. 'I don't want one. Come on, Linda.'

He put his other arm, protectively, on Linda's shoulder.

'Don't bully the kid. It's a free country.'

Linda was staring at her mulishly and leaning against his arm. Jane looked for Micky, and was overwhelmingly glad to see him crossing the room towards them. The yob said:

'You want to relax. You're not too old to enjoy yourself a little. Stop crabbing, and have a drink.'

Micky reached them. He said:

'Sounds a good idea. I think we'd both benefit.'

The yob looked pleased. 'I'll get you some. Back in no time.'

Linda turned back to the boy she was with. Jane said to Micky, in a low intense voice:

'I thought you might help me. What a fool I was!'

'I'm doing my best.'

'Are you? I suppose it's possible.'

'Look,' he said, 'Linda would jump to it if Hilda told her, or Rod. You're only her aunt, and she's enjoying it all – the noise and excitement, and being flattered. She wouldn't go willingly, and if you tried to take her unwillingly there might well be trouble.'

'I'm prepared to risk that. It's not all that much of a risk, either. I've already smacked that little bastard down once today.

He's scared of the Commander. They all are.'

'The Commander isn't here.'

'He will be tomorrow.'

'He isn't here now. And they're on their way to being drunk. Have you seen Stephen?'

'No. Where is he?'

'Other side of the room, and pretty well drunk already.' She made the beginnings of a move, which he stopped with the tight pressure of a hand on her wrist. 'He's with Ape. There really could be trouble if you interfere there.'

'Are you telling me we're not to do anything at all about it? Just stand here and watch?'

'Better watching than not being able to. The least they're likely to do is throw us out and keep the kids here. If you stick close to Linda … there might be an opportunity of easing her out a little later.'

'And Steve?'

'I'll keep an eye on him.'

'But if they're making him drunk …'

'Not much making, as far as I can see. He's managing it on his own. Most young men do, sooner or later. It doesn't do a lot of harm.'

'Is that the best you can offer?' He shrugged. Dropping her voice lower still, she said: 'I can see why you needed the uniform. You're not much without it, are you?'

She turned away towards Linda, not waiting to see how her words affected him.

Although his refusal to help in getting the children away had angered and disgusted her, she realized that she had no alternative but to do as he had suggested. Linda was the one that mattered. She stayed with her, and accepted the drink which the other yob brought back. It was almost straight Scotch, but he fetched water for her when she asked him. He insisted on knowing her name, and he told her his own was Mouser. They all had nicknames – the one with Linda was Seedcake.

Cold roast turkey and pork were brought in by the girls, and put out on a table, along with a couple of big dishes of roast potatoes. There was a pile of plates, and they helped themselves. A certain amount of scrimmaging took place, but it was good-humoured. Soothed by the whisky, which she had sipped slowly, Jane felt that it was not too bad really. Some of the language was foul, but a fifteen-year-old girl these days was inured to that. Behaviour otherwise was reasonable. She had looked for Stephen, and seen him, as Micky had said, in the group surrounding Ape. He seemed glazed and withdrawn. Ape, she noticed, was drinking steadily, with little apparent effect. The only departure from his normal behaviour was that he was not, for the moment, picking his teeth.

They sat on the floor or on the arms of chairs to eat the fork supper. Several bottles of champagne were brought in, and Cha-Cha and another went around dispensing it, pouring it into the glasses they already had, in some cases on top of the previous drink. Jane finished her whisky, and accepted the champagne. It fizzed over the edge and soaked the sleeve of her frock, at which Cha-Cha laughed uproariously and Mouser went through an antic of licking it off her arm. She saw that Linda had been given some champagne, but not very much. She made a face, too, when she tasted it. She had never cared for wines, of course, which was a blessing. The champagne was terrible, anyway – almost warm.

The violence broke out without warning, and she did not at first realize what was happening. There had been exhortations to Cha-Cha to make a speech, and at last he was prevailed upon. He stood on the far side of the room, near Ape and Stephen, and took a swig from the bottle of champagne he had in his hand. It foamed out, running down the grey patches of his beard, and they all laughed. Cha-Cha laughed, too, swaying on his feet. He began to speak, incoherently, stopping now and again as laughter convulsed him. They cheered him on. Then Ape must have made a comment – or Cha-Cha thought he did – because he swung round and leaned down to where he was squatting on the floor.

'The old Ape,' he said incoherently. 'More like a bloody chimp … bloody ginger nutted monkey … cut off me legs and call me Short-Arse.'

Jane thought it was still good-humoured joshing. Ape smiled slightly, as he said:

'Sooner be a monkey with nuts than a billy goat without.'

It was a reference to something which the others understood. They howled with mirth. Cha-Cha's face flushed above the beard. He put his hand out and up-ended the champagne bottle, its contents streaming out over Ape's face and head. Then, as he started laughing in turn, Ape grabbed his ankle and twisted it, bringing him heavily to the ground.

He got to his feet more quickly than Jane would have thought, in view of the way he had crashed and his intoxication. He had clearly been hurt, but he tried to smile.

'Shouldn't have done that, Ape.'

His right foot lashed out and caught Ape's right arm and side, sending him spinning. Ape rolled over and came up, cat-like, on his feet. They faced each other, Cha-Cha so much the taller and bigger, Ape crouching slightly so that he looked even smaller than usual. Even if he were holding his liquor better, he was hopelessly inferior physically, Jane thought. All she wanted was to get Linda out of the way. There were people in her path, though, and the fight was on the other side of the room. They had grown quiet, and she heard a sigh, a general murmur whose meaning she could not read. She looked back at Ape, and saw the gleam of steel in his hand.

Cha-Cha pulled a knife out of the sheath at his own side. The crowd moved back. They circled each other with an almost ludicrous slowness, crab-fashion, foot after sidewise foot. Then Ape made a small move forward, Cha-Cha flung himself at him, and they closed. It lasted no longer than that. There was a single sickening grunt, and Cha-Cha's legs buckled. One of the girls screamed in the silence. Blood was gouting out, like champagne, from Cha-Cha's white silk shirt.

X

THERE WERE SO MANY NEW ONES. Some Martin knew, because he had brought them in himself, but most of them
were strangers. Strangers in the flesh, but brothers in the Holy
Spirit. They filed in to the dimly lit vastness of the Odeon Cinema. This was their latest meeting place, after outgrowing the
Scouts Hall and then the furniture depository. The Manager,
who had been converted, had closed the cinema to the public
for this evening. The Wurlitzer played the notes of the Kyrie,
its swelling strength underlining the massive rhythm of their
voices, the sound intoxicating the mind as it rose and echoed
back from the high gloom of the walls.

Meditation followed. It was not possible to kneel, because of
the closeness of the rows of seats, but they rested their heads on
the backs of the seats in front. So many, Martin thought. So
many souls united in the love of God, the service of God! He
prayed, and strength flowed into him, God's strength.

The organ began to play again, very quietly. He recognized
the tune. Handel: 'I Know that my Redeemer Liveth'. Very
quiet, and very slow. The auditorium lights glowed and winked
out. There was blackness, except for the single light on the organ. Minutes or ages of blackness, but followed by light. The
great beam struck from above and behind, dazzling, pouring a
pool of brilliance out on the stage; and on Brother James.

He was speaking even as the light came.

'Christ lives!'

They gave the response as he had taught them, a thousand
throats acclaiming:

'And brings, to all who will abide his Truth, Life Everlasting!'

He spoke, exhorting them. Great things had been done – were being done – but more remained. There could be no slackening, no resting, while the true word of God remained unknown to any man. Success, even in God's work, was a snare, a potential damnation, unless it spurred them on to greater effort still. For the world was vast, the heathen uncountable in their millions. Without the security of knowing that the truth must prevail, one must despair, seeing one's own puniness, and the enemy's might.

He paused, and the silence was like a sea, unbroken by the faintest stir.

'Listen,' he said, 'I will tell you a story.

'The Word of God was a garden, full of flowers. The flowers were sweet and simple, in white and red and blue and gold, balmy and fragrant; and people walked in the garden, in the beauty and perfume, and gardeners tended it, in diligence and holiness. So it was, by God's will. Until the day when the Devil moved like a wind, a foul miasma, an invisible mist that settled on the garden. The flowers were stricken by blight and disease, and grew in twisted, stunted, sickly forms. And the gardeners, infected themselves, no longer strove for simple beauties but grew monstrous exotic plants, which drooped and dazzled in dashing sensuous colours, and bore strange blossoms, some like the faces of evil women. And the people who walked in the garden were first entranced and then sickened, so that they turned away, abandoning what had betrayed them. After that, winter fell. The storms came, breaking down and crushing, and the rain beat the plants into the mud, and when the rain stopped there was frost, destroying them root and stem. Then men looked at the Garden of the Word of God, and saw a bare wilderness, and believed this was the end.'

His voice had grown softer, though every word was clear still in the hush that attended him. Now he paused, for long moments, and they waited, waited.

He said: 'But God is not mocked, and God's Word cannot be

destroyed. The frost killed the plants that grew from the days of sickness in the garden, but the true plants stayed rooted in the soil. They are there, waiting for God's spring, and for gardeners who will tend them. Brothers, that spring approaches! Winter is nearly over. It is time that the gardeners took up their tasks.'

As he spoke he held out his right hand. In it, there was a black clod of earth, and, growing from the earth, the fragile green spears and small white bell of a snowdrop.

He let the silence stretch longer; then said:

'Brothers, I am leaving Pallister.'

The protest drawn from them was inarticulate, a groan. Even in the ecstasy of his private knowledge, Martin was almost moved to join them. Brother James said:

'I go to carry God's word to other places. There are those who have been chosen to go with me, to travel the land and plant the seeds which will grow in the Garden that is to be made over and renewed. Those of you we leave behind have your own duties. Do God's work, spread His Truth, and wait for the time that will come. Our lives are worthless except insofar as they serve God. Let this be done in patience, bearing hardship and affliction, until the sunburst of action. And when that comes, let our lives be offered to God as a final sacrifice if He so wills, fearing no man, nor death neither.'

The organ began to play softly. Brother James said:

'While we are singing the hymn, those who are to go with me will come up to the stage. Give them your prayers.'

Martin arose from his seat and went into the aisle. He walked forward; in darkness, but towards light.

XI

THE ROYAL HAD BEEN PARTIALLY taken over by a gang with whose chief the Commander was on good terms: he was provided with a first-floor suite having balconies overlooking the park. Rod went with him as part of the entourage, and shared a room with two of the motor-cycle escort. They took the beds by the windows, and paid him little or no attention. He was even less concerned about this than usual. His mind was on Hilda, swinging dully between disbelief and sick despair. He slept in snatches, and had vivid unsettling dreams.

In the morning he went automatically with the others to the Commander's room for breakfast. He could not eat anything, but drank tea – even that was nauseating. The Commander ate greedily, and talked a lot while he wolfed the food down. The telephone rang, and one of the yobs brought the instrument to him.

Rod did not pay much attention until he realized that the call was from Bridge House, and that something unusual, perhaps shocking, had happened. After that, he listened, but could not make much sense of it. The Commander said:

'Why wasn't I told last night? Because you're scared of him, you mean. That little bastard! ... OK, OK. I'll see to it, when I get back ... Some time today ... All right, ring off ... I'll remember you called me.'

He put down the instrument and stared at his plate of sausages, fried eggs, kidneys and bacon. One of the yobs asked:

'Something up?'

'Ape.' He forked a kidney and chewed it, but with less enthusiasm. 'He put a shiv into Cha-Cha last night. That was

Spoonbill calling. Sneaked to the telephone to tell me.'

'Is he bad?'

The Commander sucked down tea. 'He's dead.'

They sat in silence for a moment. One said:

'Could have been an accident, I suppose.'

'Then why didn't Ape ring me himself?'

'Maybe he was scared, too.'

The Commander slammed his cup down into the saucer, so that tea splashed over the white cloth. His face was set and angry. He said:

'If he was, he had good reason to be! Sticking old Cha-Cha. On his birthday, as well. By God, when I get back there …'

'Are you going back right away, Commander?'

'No. We want to see how Mum's coming along. The bastard can stew for a few hours. Give him time to say his prayers. He'll need to. Old Cha-Cha was with me right from the beginning. By Christ, by the time I've finished with him …'

The Commander stared blindly across the room.

'Pour me some more tea out.'

Miller's eyes, as he entered the room, sought out Rod, and there was a moment of hope. The first syllables, spoken with a brisk clinical coldness, destroyed that. He was a man, Rod realized, who had come to terms with this part of his role by rejecting any suggestion of evasion.

'Mr Gawfrey.' He nodded to the Commander. 'I must tell you that it's bad news.'

Rod nodded himself. It was a ludicrous acknowledgement, but it made speech unnecessary. The Commander said:

'What sort of bad news? Let's have it.'

'I've had a word with the surgeon who operated. It's a carcinoma, and a big one. There was absolutely nothing he could do.'

'You're not telling me she's dead?'

'No.'

'But he didn't cut it out? Why didn't he?'

'Because Mrs Gawfrey would not have survived the operation.'

'He's just sewn her up again?'

His eyes, deliberately withholding compassion, were on Rod. He said:

'Believe me, there was no alternative.'

The Commander said abruptly: 'I want to see him. Your surgeon bloke. Get him along here.'

'I can't. He's in theatre …'

'I want him!'

' … Operating on someone from the Glendale Gang. He came off his bike this morning, and he's in poor shape.'

The Commander looked as though he were going to challenge the truth of this; then said:

'I'll see him when he's finished.'

'Just as you like.'

'What about …' He struggled for the word. '… the lady. She still under the anaesthetic?'

'Yes. She could be seen late this afternoon, probably. She will still be feeling drugged, of course.'

The Commander nodded, and turned away. At the door, he said:

'We could get another surgeon … one who might know more about this kind of stuff.' Miller looked at him, without replying. 'All right. Fix it that I see him.'

When he had gone, Miller said:

'It's bad enough for you, without having it soiled by things like that.'

Rod shook his head. 'It doesn't matter.' He hesitated. 'How long will it be?'

'Not long. A month or two, perhaps.'

'Can she come home?'

'I'd advise against it. She'll need care. The one good thing I have to say to you is that, with proper supervision, there's no need for pain in terminal carcinoma. She's had pain already – a great deal of pain – and put up with it. You won't want her to suffer any more. We've got the drugs to prevent that. I promise you she'll go easily.'

He was with her alone for a while before the Commander came up to the ward. She looked very tired, but her eyes were bright. They did not talk about her illness or the operation. Each behaved as though assuming that it had been put right, that there was nothing to worry about. Watching her eyes smiling at him, he knew that she did not believe this. She knew or guessed the truth. He wanted to lie to her, to bind up her hurt with deception, but could not. She was stronger than he, more truthful, more honest. If he spoke about it at all, she would see through what few threads of illusion might remain.

They talked about the children, and home. He had not meant to tell her of Cha-Cha's death, but it came out; under the pressure, perhaps, of the things he dared not say. She listened, and said:

'Poor Cha-Cha. He was silly, but one of the better ones.'

'What do you think will happen now?'

As he asked it, he had a glimpse of the time when she would not be there, to answer and reassure him, and was overwhelmed by it. He turned away a little, glad that at the moment she was not looking at him. She said:

'I don't know. But it will be all right. You just have to stick things out.'

There was no reassurance, because she was talking now of him having to stick it out on his own, without her, and they both knew this. He took her hand which lay on top of the bed, kissed it, held it between his own. The door opened, and the Commander came in.

He had more roses, more chocolate, a plastic bag filled with apples. Hilda said:

'I don't know where I shall put them all. Thank you.'

He stood awkwardly by the bed, staring down at her.

'How are you, Mum?'

'I'm fine. I'll be out in a few days.'

Nothing the doctor or surgeon had said had convinced him, Rod saw, until now, when her bright dismissal told him that it was true. There was another angry red spot forming under the Commander's chin, and he put his fingers over it, as though to rub it away. He was angry, and baffled, and even less articulate than usual. He said:

'I'll come in and see you.'

'That's kind of you. Will you bring Rod?'

He nodded. 'The kids, as well.'

'I'm not sure. I'd like to think about that. Reg, there is something I'd like you to do for me.'

Rod had not known what his first name was, or that Hilda knew it.

The Commander said: 'Whatever you say, Mum.'

'Look after them all for me, will you? Till I get back.'

'Yer.' He wiped the back of his hand across his mouth. 'Don't worry about anything.'

She shook her head, smiling. 'I won't.'

It was dusk as they headed up the Broadway out of Pallister. They drove without headlights. There was a couple of hundred yards' visibility, and the road was deserted.

Rod sat pillion behind the Commander, fingers tucked into the belt of his white leather jacket. The Commander had thought of taking a taxi out, but in the end had decided to commandeer a bike from one of the others, telling that yob to double up with his mate. He had ordered Rod to get up behind him, and Rod had obeyed. He felt indifferent to everything except that he was leaving Hilda behind in the hospital. It was necessary to go back – it was what she wanted – there were the children, and the old people. None of it meant anything.

They travelled at speed. He felt the reverberation of the big machine, the jolt as they hit uneven patches in the road. Not much was done nowadays by way of repair, and pot-holes were developing. He wondered how far the roads would be let run down before the gangs decided to do something about them. Presumably they would eventually, if they wanted to stay mobile.

The bikes crossed the top of Meredith Road, where the traffic lights still stood though no longer functioning, and blazed through Cowford on their way to Gostyn. They passed a bus, sweeping round it in noisy arcs. The day was darkening, and the Commander flicked his lights on, the other three following suit. The beams lit up the way ahead, but their illumination was blurred by the ebbing daylight, the sky still grey rather than black. Rod himself could see little but the white curve of the Commander's crouched back.

It was what she wanted, he told himself; and almost resented the children for needing to be looked after, she herself for having the strength still to want this more than the little aid he could give her.

They went through Gostyn, the village first and then the Estate. They were almost back. Then someone shouted something, and the bike reared and bucked under him, swung out with its back wheel, and started sliding. Automatically, he clung more tightly, twisting his fingers inside the belt. The bike broadsided, tyres screeching. There was a thin howl of metal as they hit something and were drawn along it, like a child's toy pulled by a string. The bike bucked again, and the belt gave. He felt himself spinning out and away, and was conscious of throwing an arm back to protect his head. He smacked into the ground with a force that almost blacked him out.

The darkness was chopped by segments of light from headlights tilted at unnatural angles. Rod watched, confused and trying to breathe. Other more purposeful lights snapped on from the road ahead. He could see the four bikes in the glare from them, and their riders. Two figures were lying still, two making feeble efforts to move, the fifth struggling to his feet. The front wheel of one of the crashed bikes was spinning quite fast. He looked for the Commander, and saw that he was one of those moving slightly. Someone was moaning – perhaps him. Rod himself could feel his arm now as numbness which was beginning to turn into pain.

He saw something else. A steel hawser lay across the road. The handlebars of one of the bikes seemed to be entangled with it.

Other figures came out of the light. There were half a dozen of them, led by Ape, his red hair gleaming unmistakably in the headlamp beams. He stood over the Commander, who made a jerking movement which could have been either an attempt at rising or one to pull the other yob down. His hand, anyway, fastened on Ape's wrist. Ape moved down towards him. Rod thought he was off balance, then saw that his free hand held a knife. The Commander screamed, and the scream turned into a grunt and was followed by silence. Blood spurted over the white leather jacket. Ape stood over him and lifted the knife. Rod had the lunatic thought that he might be intending to pick his twisted teeth with the point. Instead, he looked at it, took a rag from his pocket and ran it along the edge, and tossed the soiled rag on to the Commander's body.

Ape said: 'All right. Sort yourselves out.' His voice was unforced, casual. 'Shove him in the ditch for now. Get your bikes jacked up.'

Rod stood up along with the rest. Those who could: one of them lay there, moaning. Two of Ape's party picked him up, to the accompaniment of a howl of pain, and sat him on the pillion of one of their own bikes. They moved the Commander's body to the side of the road, and pushed one of the crashed bikes there. The other three appeared to be all right. The yobs mounted and stayed, waiting for a signal from Ape, who still stood watching operations. He looked round unhurriedly, as though checking that nothing had been overlooked. His gaze, traversing, came to Rod and paused for several seconds. The look was cold, not hostile except as part of a general hostility towards anything in the world which did not serve his purpose. In that moment, Rod realized what had taken place. The Commander was dead – long live the Commander. He realized something else: that his life hung on whatever whim prompted the mind behind the face of this young savage.

'All right,' Ape said. 'Let's go.'

He turned away, indifferently, from Rod, and walked to his own bike further on. Two of the yobs had rolled up the hawser. They mounted, and their engines kicked into life. They roared away up the road.

Rod's leg was hurting, and his left arm was on fire with pain. He risked flexing it, and found it was not broken. The last of the daylight had ebbed, and he walked towards a dark mound that was the Commander's body. Rod bent down, and confirmed that he was dead, eyes staring, shocked, up to heaven. One arm crossed his breast, reaching for the centre of the dark stain on the white.

Rod straightened up and began walking, painfully limping, along the road in the wake of the motor-bikes.

XII

IT WAS NOT EASY TO DEFINE the way in which the atmosphere had changed. The general routine went on much as before, the only obvious difference being that Ape had taken over Rod's old office. The yobs were subdued, of course, and so were the girls, but that could reasonably be attributed to the shock of the Commander's killing on the heels of Cha-Cha's death. By the end of the first day of the new regime, though, Jane felt there was more to it than that. There was an uneasiness abroad which was not part of the backwash of the knifings, but more fundamental. They had feared their old Commander and they feared his successor, but she thought they feared his incalculability more than his authority.

The Commander had had his lieutenants: Cha-Cha and Ape himself. There had been the illusion of a triumvirate, even though it was the Commander's word that was law. Ape did not choose any successors in this respect. He stayed for hours alone in his room. When he came out, he might completely disregard the people around him, or demand their company. In both cases they were at a loss. The attitude of the other yobs to him was one of ingratiating deference, which seemed to please him, twisting his small hard face into a smile. He accepted this equally from all of them, having no favourites.

Her first impulse was to wonder at their accepting his leadership so tamely; there was nothing to stop two or three getting together to overthrow him, if no single one felt capable of defiance. It was probably to do with the charisma of the assassin. They would see in him the authority that dared to destroy authority, and also, of course, his intimidating ruthlessness. Killing Cha-Cha had presumably been an accident, though one which demonstrated his ferocity. In browbeating half a dozen of them to join him in the ambush against the Commander, his determination and nerve had been of a different order. Once he had carried that through successfully, it was unlikely that anyone else would have the purposefulness and strength of character to raise a second revolt.

As for co-operation between them, there was the lesson offered by the country at large. The yobs ruled more by bluff and threat than by the exercise of real power. The weight of numbers was not always important.

Jane thought of this when she was bidden to the new Commander's side during the banquet which celebrated his accession. The Pembroke table had been brought in from the hall, and he sat there, near the others yet apart. She, with Rod, Micky and Linda, had come downstairs by royal command, conveyed by Stephen. There was an extra chair at the Pembroke table, and people were called there, then dismissed. Stephen had spent some time with him, and looked proud of the favour. She tried to tell herself that was not important; adolescent boys developed these infatuations, and grew out of them.

Ape said:

'Have some champagne. You ought to have brought your glass over.'

'I've had enough, thank you.'

He ignored that, and signalled to one of the waiting girls. She brought a glass, and Ape filled it with champagne from the bottle at his elbow. He had drunk a lot; his face was flushed but otherwise he did not show it. His plate was piled high with the white meat of chicken and chip potatoes. He said:

'Good health.'

She sipped from the glass, watching him.

'Good health.'

His next remark surprised her. He said: 'I like your voice.' She felt herself, idiotically, flushing, and at a loss for words. 'You sound like a woman I listened to on the telly once. She had your way of speaking – kind of clear and sharp, and as though she knew what she was talking about. Some cock about art or something, but I liked hearing her say it.'

There still did not seem anything she could usefully say. She felt flattered, despite herself. He was an unpleasant young hoodlum, physically repulsive. But he was also supreme in this small territory, the king who had killed the king.

'I thought at the time,' Ape said, 'that I'd like to hear her say things I wanted. You can do that for me.'

She was not alarmed. She asked:

'What do you want me to say?'

He leaned forward a little. The table was far enough from the others for their conversation to be private when spoken quietly. He did this now, his eyes intent on her face. The flush deepened, stinging her cheeks with blood. The sentence was grossly obscene, both in meaning and in the expressions used.

He watched her confusion. 'Go on, then,' he told her. 'Say it.'

She remembered how her open contempt had checked Mouser and wondered, for a moment, if it would work here, but a look into the raw bony face that stared at her, the jaws chewing on breast of chicken, made her realize that she lacked the courage to try. She said, awkwardly:

'I … I'd rather not.'

'But you will, though.' He picked up his glass, drained it, and poured more wine in. The small grey-green eyes came round to her again. 'You will.'

The words in themselves had not shocked her. They were not a part of her general vocabulary, but she had used some of them and heard the others from Walter's lips. What was horrifying was the form of the request, the circumstances, the eyes watching. She said:

'I'm sorry. I can't do that.'

He studied her, then shrugged. 'If you can't …' She felt a

relief that came close to being gratitude to him for not insisting. He returned to munching his food. He was a gross eater, as Walter had been, but in a mean and gobbling rather than a large way. He prodded half a dozen chips on to his fork, rubbed them in a pool of vinegar on his plate, and stuffed them into his mouth. He sucked and smacked as he ate, and broke off to say:

'You can go back, if you like.'

She started to get up. She was on the point of saying 'Thank you,' when he added:

'Send Linda over instead. She's got a voice a bit like yours. I'll get her to say it for me.'

'Please …' She struggled for words. 'Commander …'

'You choose,' he said. 'You say it, or she says it. I don't mind which.'

She sat down again. Looking away from him, she repeated the sentence in a low voice. He said:

'You remembered it very well. Now say it again, and just a bit louder.'

A Robey got on to the bus halfway to Pallister, and, seeing the white, she looked in case it might be Martin. But the man was much bigger, a burly black-bearded figure with a hearty North-Country voice. Above the noise of the bus he exhorted the passengers to forsake their old evils and weaknesses, and follow the truth. She presumed that Martin was doing the same sort of thing somewhere else; they had not heard from him since the yobs came.

The reception this one got was better than she would have expected. They listened to him, and a couple of women made assenting interjections. As they rocked through the outskirts of Pallister, he urged them to join him in singing a hymn. They nearly all did so. Herself apart, Jane saw only one other person who was looking blankly and uncooperatively away. The conductor did not ask him for a fare. When they reached the stop at the bottom of the Broadway, the Robey got off. On the step, he paused for a final homily:

'The day comes, friends,' he said, 'the day of deliverance, the day of judgement, the day when the Lord shall call men to Him. Be prepared for that hour – summon all your strength to meet it. For they that worked in the vineyard received every man a penny, whether he came late or had toiled through the heat of the day, but he that did not come received nothing. Bless you, friends, and hearken to the Lord!'

Jane got off two stops further on, and walked up the hill to the Hospital. By agreement, she and Rod did not both go at the same time; it was more important to look after things at home. The children did not come, either: Hilda still did not want to see them.

She was directed up to the private ward. The Commander might be dead, but this privilege remained. On her previous visit, Jane had asked Hilda if she would not prefer to be moved into a general ward; it must be lonely here on her own. She said no, and Jane had not pressed the matter. It was another sign of the psychological change which had come with her admission of the physical one. In the past she had been opposed to special medical privileges on principle. But this, like so much else, had become irrelevant to her. She accepted it as a means of helping her to withdraw from the world in which her time must now be so short.

She had been told of the Commander's death and Ape's take-over. She expressed some regret at the former; nothing over the latter. They had not, of course, told her of their growing fear of Ape, and what he might do, but Jane was surprised that she did not ask them about the situation. She asked after the health of the children and her parents; no more.

The contrast was chilling. The old Hilda had wanted to know things, and do things – had wanted to protect and guide. There had been a series of priorities – her children and Rod first, then the rest of the family, and so out to neighbours and friends, and the world in general. The one thing she had been bad at was letting others take responsibility for herself and hers. Jane had expected her to rage against this present separation, and its finality. Instead, she acquiesced.

In coming to the Hospital, Jane realized, her object had been only partly to offer comfort to Hilda. The other and larger part had been her own need for reassurance. She would not state her fears and misgivings, but Hilda would track them down and make them disappear. That was what always happened, and in the past Jane had even resented it, as an encroachment on her privacy. Looking at her sister's thin, serene, remote face, she desperately wanted it now.

Hilda asked her: 'How's Micky?'

It was a formal question as the others had been, put to make conversation rather than out of any desire for illumination. Jane said:

'Oh, he's all right.'

'Do you think you might marry him?'

There was more of curiosity in that, but the curiosity one might feel about the destiny of characters in a book that, on the whole, one was too tired to go on reading. Jane felt her irritation gather against this other, more legitimate target. She said harshly:

'I doubt it. He's less of a man than I thought he was.'

Hilda smiled. 'You won't know how much of a man he is until you take him on.'

'A man should be a man in his own right, without having to have a woman push and coax and organize him.'

'The ones that are, are generally inhuman.'

She thought more about it, and was frightened by what it seemed to involve. She said:

'You're asking a lot, aren't you? It should be the man who brings strength into a relationship.'

Hilda shook her head. She looked as though she were going to rebut the point; then said:

'Perhaps you're right.'

She closed her eyes: only for a moment, but it might as well have been forever.

The office was as chaotic as the flat had always been. The accumulation of untidiness and rubbish was only the result of weeks, but looked like that of years. She thought of setting to work to clear it, but realized she did not have the time: she had to catch the six o'clock bus back to Gostyn. She did clear the top of her own old desk, though. The debris included a number of American comic books, with a particular concentration on tortures and breasts, both graphically illustrated. She was glancing through one of these, when Walter came in. Holding it up, she said:

'Something of a new departure for you, isn't it?'

He looked harassed, she thought, and tired, a fat man who had grown used to thinner creatures snapping at his heels but had been made nervous by it all the same. He said:

'One of the boys must have left them. Where did you spring from? You didn't telephone.'

'There are difficulties. By boys, do you mean students?' He shook his head. 'The yobs, then?'

'I don't like that term,' he said irritably. 'I never did. Backward boy – a bit of cheap Music Hall wit.'

She ignored the remark, and said:

'So they come here, to the University? I thought you were concerned about keeping your official work and your – well, politics – apart?'

'Things have changed,' he said. 'You know that. They go wherever they like.'

'Yes, I know it. I didn't think it applied to you, though. Aren't you still the Chairman of the Committee?'

'There is no Committee.'

'But you're in touch with them – the leaders?' She put the

comic book down on the pile. 'They obviously bring their literature here.'

'I act as a sort of liaison officer – between them and the civil authorities.' He made an effort at looking happier. 'It's a developing situation. Each side has need of the other. This is an interregnum, but confusion can't last. There is a basic human drive towards stability. Things settle down.'

He was willingly deluding himself, she saw, as he had so often done in the past, propelling himself into a euphoria which discarded and disregarded everything that did not fit in with the immediate vision. She knew, at this stage, that her visit was pointless, but felt she must make the plea because she did not want to look at the alternative.

She said: 'We're in trouble at home.'

'Are you?' He looked at her quickly. 'In what way?'

'I told you about the Commander who had taken over.'

'Yes. The one with the grudge against Rod. There isn't much one can do about that sort of thing, as I said at the time. He probably won't do anything beyond humiliating him in small ways. And eventually he'll get tired of that, and move on.'

'It's different now.'

She told him what had happened. He listened, nodding at intervals in an abstracted fashion. At the end, he said:

'Well, you're better off then, aren't you? The matter of personal animus is out of the way. You have to put up with them in the house, but that has its advantages – decent food, and so on. Apart from that, all you have to do is not offend them. You can manage that, surely.'

'There is a difference. The Commander was nasty in a small way. This one is more evil and more ruthless.'

'You're exaggerating. He killed because he had to. A rat that's cornered is altogether different from one that has a free run.' She looked at him. 'As for asking you to whisper four-letter words … I shouldn't have thought you would have worried too much about that.'

'It was threatening to bring Linda in that bothered me.'

'He was bluffing. He's obviously not a rapist. If he gets his satisfaction out of listening to obscenities spoken by women, he can't be. It's an entirely different psychological type.'

Walter was busy convincing himself. Argument would have no effect, and the thought depressed her in any case. She said wearily: 'I'm asking you to help us. You must have some influence with the gangs.'

'Some.' He went to a box half lost in the clutter on his own desk, took out a cigar, and lit it. It was a solid, expensive-looking one. 'But not at the local level. They won't tolerate interference there.'

'You won't help, then?'

'I can't. Except …'

'Except what?'

'You could stay here. I don't suppose this one you call Ape would bother. It wouldn't matter if he did. I could protect you.'

'Never mind.'

'I don't see why not.' She could almost read his mind striking a balance between the minor risk of offending a leader of one of the smaller gangs and the advantages – sexual and otherwise – of her presence. 'It's the obviously sensible thing, as far as you're concerned. Just don't go back. I can pick up clothes for you.'

'I'm sure you could,' she said. ''Bye, Walter. I have a bus to catch.'

He blocked her way to the door, and then caught hold of her. His arms were round her, his hands pressing against back and buttocks. She did not try to escape, did not even avert her face from his kiss. He strained against her rigidity, trying to force response from himself if not from her. It lasted some minutes, uncomfortable but unimportant, before he let her go, accepting her contempt and his own impotence against it. She thought of Ape, and was not proud of her victory.

XIII

THERE WERE MORE THAN TWENTY of them travelling by train, but Martin was one of those who were with Brother James, in Brother James' compartment. They meditated or sang hymns while the fields of England, frozen in another frost, sped by; but the best times were when they simply talked together. He himself did not want to talk, only to listen to Brother James' words, but Brother James made him, drawing him out with power and gentleness.

They ate together on the way. It was only Frotein sandwiches, washed down with ordinary water from the flasks they carried, but they ate and drank in the joy of comradeship, of shared dedication to God's Word.

Brother James said:

'My flask is empty, Martin. Can I share yours?'

Too moved to speak, he passed over the old Army waterbottle, covered in khaki cloth, and watched as Brother James put it to his lips and drank. He was not thirsty, but when it was returned to him, he drank from it himself, pressing his mouth to the metal where Brother James' flesh had touched it.

'These are the crucial days ahead, Brothers,' Brother James said. 'We cannot be defeated, because God is with us, but the time and the road may be long if we fail in offering ourselves as sacrifices, or do not strike fiercely enough in the blows that will scatter His enemies. These are the days in which the battle can be won swiftly. They may not come again.'

Looking at him across the compartment, Martin wondered how he could ever have thought him physically insignificant. He was not a big man, but he shed the power that was in him

– almost visibly, as a radiance. Everything about him had glory and wonder, each feature, a distinctness and reality: not only the deep dark eyes, but the strong red mouth, bearded chin, the grooves in his cheeks that marked decision and will.

'Let us pray, Brothers,' Brother James said, 'silently, for God's might to reinforce our own weakness, so that His Will be done.'

They sat upright in the swaying train, and prayed. And when Martin opened his eyes, it was on him that Brother James' eyes were fixed.

They neared their destination. The train moved into the heart of the great city, which sprawled on either side of the line: a vista not of rabbit-hutch houses but of places where dwelt the souls who should be reclaimed. The immensity of it was a challenge that stimulated rather than alarmed. Its apparent emptiness was a promise. The train slowed, rattling over points, and a sign with an arrow said: EUSTON.

They came in under the shadow of the station's overarching roof. Martin's seat was by a window, and he could look out easily. The platforms seemed empty at first, and then there were people – two or three, larger groups, a crowd patiently waiting. Where their carriage stopped, the crowd was quite thick. Some wore the white robes of the Fellowship, others were in ordinary clothes. They moved, as though drawn by his presence, towards the compartment where Brother James was. They did not shout or cry out, but in their silence there was expectancy and joy.

'We are here, Brothers,' Brother James said, 'at the place and the time appointed. Are we ourselves prepared for what may come?'

They spoke their affirmation, and stood up.

'Yes,' Martin said. 'Yes, Master.'

XIV

ROD DID NOT KNOW ABOUT THE WHIPPING until Ape spoke of it. The family were having their mid-day meal together, when Ape came in with four of the yobs at his heels. There was no knock on the door. Stephen rose to his feet, and Rod did the same.

Ape said: 'Sit down.' He looked as amiable as he ever did. 'Just checking. You all right up here?'

Rod nodded. 'We're all right, thank you.'

He looked at Jane. 'How about it, Miss Classy? You get food from the kitchen? What you been cooking? A stew?' He picked up the spoon she had laid down and had a mouthful, smacking his lips. 'Not bad.' He grinned at her. 'You can cook, as well as talk pretty.'

She did not reply to that. Ape's gaze wandered from her along the table.

'Old folks OK, too? How about the kid?'

He was staring at Peter. To Rod's surprise, Peter stood up also, and said:

'Yes, sir. Thank you, sir.'

His voice was awkward and stilted. Ape's smile lingered, thinner, less pleasant. He said:

'Let's see how it looks.' Peter looked at him, silently. 'I thought you'd had your wits sharpened, kid. I said I want to see. Stand up, and take your shirt off.'

Peter rose from his chair, loosened his shirt, and pulled it over his head, along with the undervest. The action was painfully clumsy. Rod thought he seemed more upset than was necessary. It was just one of the small humiliations they were all exposed to all the time, which they had to learn to take. As long as the whims were no worse than this they could survive them.

Ape said:

'Turn round.'

Rod saw it, as they all did. The boy's white back streaked with angry red. He turned towards Ape, anger for an instant uncontrollable.

'You bastard! I'll …'

Ape's smile, surprisingly, broadened again. He said:

'So he didn't tell you about it? I like that.' He nodded at Peter. 'You did well, kid. But you tell it now, because I want to hear you tell it. You tell why you got a beating.'

Peter said woodenly: 'For being disobedient and … being rude to you, sir.'

Rod said:

'I've put up with a lot, but …'

'Shut up.' Ape's voice was sharp and cold. He was looking at Peter. 'Tell him who did the beating, kid.' Peter's eyes went from Ape to his father. 'Come on, then. This is an order.'

The boy's cheeks were flushed. He said:

'It was Steve.'

Ape walked to where the boy stood. He put his hand on his shoulder.

'Better not hit it where it hurts, eh? OK, kid. You can put your shirt on again.'

He stepped to one side to let him do this, and was standing behind Linda. He looked at Rod over her head.

'You want to watch it, Dad. You called me a rude name just now. You almost took a poke at me. I'll let you off this time because you was a bit ignorant. Don't trade on it, though. I might ask Steve to handle another beating. You get me?'

He was waiting for an answer. Feeling sick, Rod said:

'Yes. I get you.'

Ape put his hands to rest on Linda's shoulders. The nails were black at the ends. He said:

'How's it going, little Linda? You got any complaints?'

She was shaken, Rod saw, by what had just happened. She said in a small voice:

'I'm all right, thank you.'

'If you have, you come and tell me.' She was silent. His hands pressed slightly against her collarbone. 'Well, then, say you'll do that.'

'I'll come and tell you.'

'I like the way you talk. Like your aunt, only younger. Pretty. You know what I'd enjoy?'

She stared ahead of her. 'What?'

'Having you read to me. I like being read to. I'll tell you what – you come on down this evening, and I'll have a book for you to read. We'll sit and have a quiet read together.' He released her, and walked round the table towards the door. 'I'm going to like that.'

He stood in the doorway, flanked by the other yobs.

'Carry on with your dinner,' he said. 'You've all stopped eating. Six o'clock, Linda. Right? We'll have a read before supper. Don't forget, baby. I don't want to have to send and fetch you.'

As he turned away, Stephen said:

'Commander!'

'Yer?'

'Can I come with you?'

'What, now?' He grinned. 'You think it might be a bit cool up here, kid? Course you can come. It's a free country.'

Stephen got up quickly from the table. He did not look at the others as he followed Ape and the yobs through the door.

They did not discuss it until after the old people had retired next door, taking Peter and Linda with them. Then Jane said:

'We've got to decide what to do.'

The helplessness he felt focused on a single image: of Stephen walking away with his face averted. It was an acid burning him in so many different ways: horror for his son, misery over what

Hilda would have felt if she had known of it, bitterness and shame at his own inadequacy. He did not answer at once, and Jane went on:

'We've got to stop him getting Linda down there. I know what kind of book he will force her to read to him from – exactly what kind.'

Rod thought about that, and found his whole body squeezing in on itself with anger. He said:

'There is only one way.'

She asked: 'What's that?'

'I'm going to kill the rat.'

She said:

'Be sensible. He's more careful than the Commander was. He goes round with that bodyguard, and the guard outside his room have to stay on their toes. You wouldn't have a chance. He'd love you to try, probably.'

He looked at Micky. 'Two of us …'

'Would be no better than one. They've got guns. Jane's right. He's probably hoping that you will try something.'

Jane said:

'Whatever his motives, I'll concede that Micky's right, too. It would be quite hopeless.'

Her voice was cold. Three of us, Rod thought, despising our-selves and each other. No wonder the yobs had won so easily. We were rotten, and are rotten still. He said:

'As long as I can get my hands on his neck for half a minute, I don't give a damn what happens after.'

'But you wouldn't get that far,' Micky said. 'As for not caring what happens after, he's the kind who would make it last.' He paused. 'And use Stephen as part of the proceedings. Not to mention what might happen to the rest of the family.'

'It's not your family,' Jane said. He looked at her. 'So far it's been what we can't do. What about suggesting something that we can?'

Micky said:

'You could make a break for it.'

'You didn't get far last time.'

'They were tipped off, and after that they were watching. I don't think they're watching now.'

Jane said:

'If Ape caught you, he wouldn't be as lenient as the Commander was.'

Micky shrugged. 'If. I think it's the best chance.'

'No.' Jane shook her head. 'It isn't possible. The old people couldn't do it. Dad's sick. He wouldn't get a hundred yards without collapsing.'

'I didn't mean them.'

She said with contempt:

'You mean, leave them behind, on their own?'

Micky said evenly:

'I thought I might stay with them. You and Rod take the children. They're going out on a food sweep this afternoon – I heard some of them talking about it. I can manage some sort of diversion with those that are left, so you can slip away. Get the bus into Pallister, and a train from there. By the time they realize you're missing, you'll be too far away for them to have a hope of catching you.'

Jane said:

'It might work. But we can't leave you with Mum and Dad. They're …'

'Not my family? Does it matter all that much?'

Jane looked at him in a different way. 'No. But to us, I think. Rod can take the children. I'll stay here.'

Rod said:

'Why don't you take them, and I'll stay?'

'Because you're a man, and their father. Micky can go along as well. It's the best idea – he's right. But we don't need more than one to stay.'

'My idea,' Micky said, 'and I'm staying.'

Jane said:

'We mustn't bicker. Do you know what time they're going off on the sweep?'

'No. But we'll hear them.'

Jane stood up. She said to Rod:

'I'll go and get things packed up, for you and the children.'

XV

JANE WAS VERY CONSCIOUS of their being alone together. Her parents had retreated into the other room, and she could hear the distant sound of the radio through the wall. They were not fond of pop music, but her mother preferred it to the silence there would be otherwise, with her father staring in front of him. She would be knitting: the jumper which she said would do either for Hilda or Linda, and which it was unlikely that either would ever see, even if she finished it.

She looked across at Micky, as though seeing him after a long absence. Watching him diminished her anxiety. He was whittling a piece of wood, and she noticed how good his hands were – well formed, with tapering fingers, altogether his most handsome feature. The knife was a Swiss Army one. It suited him, she thought. Simple on the outside, but hiding complexities. And yet, at bottom, simplicity again.

The yobs were back. They had heard the motor-bikes roar in through the winter's dusk almost an hour ago. Since then she had been waiting for something to happen. It was not fear she felt so much as isolated moments of panic. Between them, she kept control by refusing to think about any of it – Rod and the children, Ape, what might happen ... She concentrated on the fact which strengthened: his presence here with her.

After Rod had gone, taking Peter and Linda, he had made another effort to persuade her to leave as well. She had said no, simply and finally, and he had not tried to press the matter. It was strange, she thought, that the long period of misunderstanding, of being estranged, should end so abruptly. A kind of *coup de foudre*, but at the end rather than the beginning. If they got through this ...

I'm going to marry him, she thought. Or do what passes for marrying in this chaotic world. Live with him, and love him. Bed, but a lot more than bed. She contemplated her past self, and was amazed by it, by her blindness chiefly. There had been so much she could have had, so much which he had offered her but which she had not noticed he was offering. She tried to tell herself that Walter had spoiled her for him then, but knew it was untrue. She was getting perilously close to persuading herself that Walter had seduced her, when she knew the truth to be almost exactly opposite.

She had chosen Walter not just for the surface qualities – the apparently powerful character and personality – but for what she sensed lay beneath: the weakness. It had been an intellectual and emotional exercise, something in which she could participate and yet still remain fundamentally free of, superior and observant. Not even involving her body, except in a superficial and unimportant way. Least of all her body.

With Micky, on the other hand, it was her body which had involved her. She had tried to write it off as sex; more pleasurable by far than anything else she had known, but of the same order. A sensual gratification, no more. But accident, the batterings of the world breaking down, had forced them more closely together, to a point where she had to regard him as a person rather than a sexual partner. And her mind had followed the same path as before, searching for weakness. She had even persuaded herself that she had found it, identifying it with the prudence and watchfulness which were at the core of the man.

There was an emptiness in him, she saw, though it was not the absence of strength but the absence of purpose. She remembered the barrack-like flat in which he had lived, and her speculation that his first marriage had failed because he had tried to make his wife conform to his own ideal of discipline and efficiency. That was wrong. Micky himself had been nearer the truth in saying that she wanted a man who would make something out of her. He could not have done that, because he was waiting to be made – to be given purpose – himself.

Her own strength, which she now admitted, would do this. They complemented each other. He had known this, sensed it perhaps, but she had not. They could give to each other, creating a unity that was more, and so much stronger, than the sum of their separate parts.

As the door opened, she said quickly: 'I love you.'

He did not have time to reply, but his eyes met hers briefly, in reassurance and response.

Ape said:

'All right, where is she?'

Jane said:

'Who?'

'You know who I mean. Linda. I said she was to come down to my office at six o'clock. It's after that.'

Micky whittled on the stick. Jane said:

'I don't know where she is. Somewhere in the house, I suppose.'

He had four yobs with him. Two of them at least carried guns. Ape's gaze ranged the room.

'Just the two of you. What about your brother? And the kid?'

She did not reply right away, and he began walking across the room towards the next door. She said quickly:

'There are only my parents in there.'

He pushed the door open, looked inside, and slammed it again. He turned to look at her. He was beginning to be angry, she thought, but also curious. Micky got up from his chair and moved, apparently casually, between her and Ape. The knife was concealed in his hand. She read his mind, and was horrified. Relieved, she saw Ape move back to the shelter of his men.

He said again:

'Just the two of you. And the rest somewhere in the house, you say. I reckon you'd better come on down and help find them.'

His tone was reasonable. She glanced at Micky, and caught a small nod of assent. Once more she felt a flurry of panic, but told herself it was silly. She said, indifferently:

'If you like.'

She stayed close to Micky as they went downstairs, wanting to touch him but not doing so because Ape was behind them. He directed them towards the green sitting room. She remembered going there for the trial of Rod and Micky which the Commander had put on. They had been afraid then, but things had worked out all right. And there was no explicit threat this time. She felt her legs trembling, moistness in the palms of her hands.

There were a lot more yobs, sitting about, smoking and listening to pop music on the radiogram, and a few of the girls. Ape said:

'Switch that bloody noise off.' He looked at Jane. 'Right now. You was going to tell us where your brother and the kids had got to.'

They were watching her with curiosity and expectancy. The silence pressed in. She said:

'I said that as far as I knew they were somewhere in the house. I haven't seen them for a while.'

'You're not worried, though?'

'Why should I be?'

Ape considered that for a moment. In his reedy voice, he asked her:

'How long's a while?'

'I don't know.'

'Half an hour? An hour? Two hours? You must have some idea.'

Endure the badgering, she thought. Keep calm. Be casual. She allowed herself a quick look towards Micky.

'It could be a couple of hours,' she said.

'You remember what you was doing a couple of hours ago?'

'Not exactly. Nothing much, I imagine.'

'Three hours, then?'

'The same.'

'Mouser's got a better memory,' Ape said, 'haven't you, Mouser? You was down here. Talking to the boys. Very friendly, Mouser says. He was struck by that. You played the piano for them, and got them all on a sing-song. I'm sorry I missed that. You're not like that usually, are you?'

She said nothing. She wondered how long the baiting would go on, and what would happen after. He had brought them down, she saw, as a show – less formal than the Commander's trial but no less threatening.

'You know what I think,' Ape said. 'I think that maybe while you was giving the boys this sing-song, your boy friend was helping your brother to get away, and the kids with him. I think you was leading them on.'

She kept her silence. It was easier than replying, easier to hide a tremor in the limbs than in the voice.

'They oughtn't to have let you do that,' Ape said. 'I was thinking at first I ought to take it out of them for not being bright enough to spot what you was up to. But you're the one that's really been naughty, ain't you? It's more fun thinking up something for you, too. I was going to have that niece of yours read a book to me, and now I can't. So you'll have to take the job on, won't you? You listening to me, Miss Classy? You'll have to do the reading.'

Relief was as weakening as fear had been. She strove to keep her voice level. If this were all ... one could tolerate this, treat it as unimportant.

'If you wish,' she said.

'I do,' Ape said, 'I do. I want to listen to you reading this book I've got, in that snotty voice of yours. But I've got other ideas as well. I'll tell you something else you're going to do, apart from just read. You're going to …'

He recited it calmly, his eyes watching her face. The thin voice spoke obscenities that this time were not a meaningless sentence but describing specific actions. There was a murmur from the yobs – part shock, part admiration, part amusement. Ape broke off, and said:

'You're blushing, Miss Classy. I like that. I never knew you sophisticated women could blush. Will you blush when you're doing it, too? Because you're going to. You're going to …'

He started the recital again. There was expression in his normally blank face, his lips twisting round the words. She was nauseated and wanted to look away, but dared not. Then Micky said:

'Just a minute.'

He spoke quietly. Ape stopped in mid-flow to say:

'Shut up, you, you stupid bastard. I'll come to you later on.'

'There's something I want to point out to you.'

He had started going forward as he spoke, both action and speech unhurried, giving no cause for alarm. He had his right hand in his jacket pocket. No-one moved while he got within a few feet of Ape. One of the yobs beside him began lifting the gun he was carrying. As he did, Micky flung himself forward the remaining distance, his hand coming out from his pocket with the open knife in it.

Automatically, Jane ran to help him. Two of the yobs had her before she had gone three steps. They dragged her down, and one of them gripped her breast cruelly. She was forced to the ground and could not see what was going on around Ape: there was shouting, confusion, a scream from one of the girls. All she could see was the yob pinioning her, the one who had dug his fingers into her breast. It was Mouser, and his face was full of idiot's laughter. She would have liked to spit in it, but her own face was held against the carpet. A voice cut through the uproar: Ape's voice.

'Have you got him? Hang on to him, then. And her. Let her up, but keep a hold on her.'

She was dragged to her feet. Half a dozen of them were on to Micky, who was still trying to struggle, but getting nowhere. Ape had the Swiss Army knife in his hand. He looked dishevelled, but was obviously unhurt. He said:

'You tried to kill me.' Unemotionally, he mouthed more obscenities, his eyes on Micky. 'If it had been something bigger than a pen-knife, you might have done it, too. Christ, you're going to know all about it, mate! You're going to regret it like you've never regretted anything in your bleeding life.'

His face, Jane saw, was white, either with anger or shock. He paused, and swallowed.

'Right,' he said. 'Put him across the foot-stool thing. No, face down. With his arm out to the side. Yer, right out.'

He walked over, and stood looking down on Micky, whose right arm was stretched out and partly turned, with one of them kneeling on the upturned hand. She could see his face, and see that it was hurting him.

Ape said:

'You sodding bastard, I'll show you.'

Because of Micky's shoulders being raised, the arm formed an angle with the floor. Ape put one foot, almost delicately, on the straightened elbow, poised there for an instant, and then savagely stamped down. She heard herself cry out as the bone cracked. Micky made no sound, but she saw his head jerk, his face distorted with pain.

She said:

'Stop! Please stop. I beg you.'

'Beg!' He laughed. 'Now get one of his legs across there. Yer, the left leg'll do.'

She did not see this because she was struggling once more to get free. They mastered her quite easily; a third, coming from behind, caught her kicking leg by the ankle and lifted and twisted it behind her. She tried to bite the hand of one of them, but he got it away and slapped her hard across the face. She saw Micky. They had dragged him round and he was lying with one leg over the foot-stool. Ape, cursing him, tried to break it as he had broken the arm. He was hurting Micky, but failed in this. After several attempts, he stood back. She saw that he was sweating.

'Too much like hard work, that,' he said. 'Someone else have a go. Take a run, if you want to.'

The leg went with the second one who tried. He was heavily built, and he landed with both feet, tripping forward afterwards to laughter from the rest. The crack of breaking bone was duller, heavier, than before, and a cry of pain was dragged from Micky. He lay with his eyes closed, his face screwed up.

Ape said:

'What do we have next? The other leg, or the other arm?'

She cried:

'I'll do it! But only if you stop. Only if you let him go.'

Ape turned to her. He was grimacing rather than smiling, and there were beads of sweat on his upper lip.

'Do what, Miss Classy?'

'What you said.'

'What was that?' She looked at him in silence. 'Come on, then. Say what it was. Say what you're going to do. So everybody can hear.'

She started to speak, but a wave of nausea stopped her. The sickness was not from what she had to say or do, but from looking at Micky's body, the unnatural angles of leg and arm, the agony masking his face – from remembering the sound of breaking bone.

Ape said:

'She's changed her mind. Stretch the other leg out.'

'No!'

She forced herself to speak. The words meant nothing, any more than the grinning watching faces did.

'You said that well,' Ape said. 'You wouldn't try to get out of it, though, would you?'

'No.'

'So if I want it to be in public, right now …'

She stared at him. 'Whatever you say.'

There were cries from the others: derision, excitement, encouragement. Ape shook his head, in a grotesque simulation of modesty. He said:

'No. I'm shy. Not in public. Except that I might have old Knifer here along. He won't do much harm now, and it'll be something to take his mind off things. Yer, I fancy having Knifer along. All right, you can let her go. She won't bother us, either.'

She went to where Micky lay, and knelt beside him, touching his face with her hand. They stood round her, grinning and laughing, and she could not sob because all that mattered was to help him.

XVI

EVERY DAY THE CROWDS were bigger, and more enthusiastic. They were starved and avid for the Bread of Life, God's Word, crying out for it in their eagerness. They listened to any of the Brothers – Martin himself addressed hundreds at a gathering and felt them sway to his every syllable – but when Brother James spoke they were in a delirium of joy, a delirium hushed, attentive, full of ecstasy and peace.

There were attacks from the yobs. They no longer disregarded the Brothers. The radio programmes, in between the interminable pop records, poured scorn on the Fellowship. Martin had heard something of it once, passing a house where there was a loud radio: a stream of mindless and obscene vituperation. The newspapers copied the radio. And the yobs, from time to time, broke up meetings, throwing stones, occasionally firing guns. A number of Brothers, as well as ordinary people, had been wounded, some killed; but they recruited far more than they lost. The people of the city protected them as well as they could, helping the Brothers to get away, putting themselves between them and their attackers. Not all helped, but enough; and every day, more.

They moved, according to plan, through the inner suburbs, splitting up and coming together again at Brother James' command. A week after they had arrived, they were south of the river, in Brixton. They congregated in a billiard hall, with spotlights bright over oblongs of green baize, crowding between the tables to listen to what Brother James had to say. He spoke briefly. His voice was harsh with exhaustion, but vibrant still in the power and love of God.

'The days go by,' he said, 'each one requiring duty, sacrifice, labour in God's service. Each must be a victory, if the end is to be accomplished. Tomorrow is a word for new labour, new sacrifice. But sometimes more than that. Sometimes it is a bell, summoning us to a battle that is more than the ordinary battles, a day on which many days, perhaps years, perhaps centuries, will turn.

'We have no newspapers, no radio. We have only our own mouths, and the mouths of those who hear us and hearken. Tomorrow we will gather in the heart of the city, in Trafalgar Square. We will gather there, and preach God's Holy Word, and if our courage and resolution do not fail us, we may win a victory which is more than just a victory. We may secure God's triumph.

'I have little to say to you now. You have been patient and steadfast in the hard times, and I know you will not falter. In a moment we will pray together. But before that, is there any Brother who wishes to speak?'

Silence brooded for moments, before a voice asked:

'Brother James?'

'Yes, Brother?'

'The yobs know of it, too. I was told today: there have been warnings on the radio. That people must stay away, or take the consequences. Warnings of bloodshed.'

'This is true, Brother.' The harshness thrilled like a trumpet. 'And true that we are in God's hands, as all men are. Now let us pray, Brothers.'

They walked through empty streets in the cold grey dawn, down the long road to Kennington, the still longer one to the river. Martin was at the front, near Brother James: there were perhaps two hundred of them, white-robed, silent. They had prayed through the night, and had not broken their fast. Tiredness, dullness came in waves; but so did exaltation. He felt light-headed, and the tramp of feet sounded like a dull surf breaking on a deserted beach. From a dark sea to an unknown land, whose present shadows might hide a rich and fruitful country, or a wasteland.

Fear brushed him as they came in sight of Lambeth Bridge. To the right of their path, on the road leading to Westminster Bridge, half a dozen yobs straddled their motor-bikes. They made no move as the Brothers went past them and up the slight rise of the bridge, and did not jeer as they usually did. They merely watched, in as close a silence as that of the Brothers. It was a watchfulness more ominous than noisy mocking would have been. He looked at Brother James, marching ahead of him, and took courage.

They passed between the sombre hulks of Westminster Abbey and the Houses of Parliament, and into the broad thoroughfare of Whitehall. Close by Downing Street, a cat crossed the road. A few pigeons pecked in the gutter. Apart from themselves, nothing else moved. Horseguards Parade ... Martin remembered being taken to see the Guards as a child, being awed and scared by their magnificence. He wondered what had become of them, and their horses. Now there was Trafalgar Square, and he saw, to his surprise, that the fountains were still playing. He had not expected that.

More yobs were stationed at the corner of the Strand and Northumberland Avenue. They could have been the same ones, except that the racket of their motor-bikes would have been audible if they had come round from the bridge, and the drab dawn was hushed and peaceful. The Brothers moved into the Square, towards Nelson's Column. Martin glanced up at the small high figure, white-smeared by the pigeons, and as he did so felt a feathery sifting of rain. Cloud stretched, unbroken, to the surrounding roofs.

They gathered round Brother James and, at his bidding, sang. Their voices sounded weaker in the vastness of the Square, and their numbers looked fewer. As the hymn ended there was a roar of engines, and he saw more motor-bikes coming down from Charing Cross Road. They stopped on the perimeter of the Square. Nothing else happened.

Brother James said: 'We will pray now, Brothers.'

The day advanced, but did not lighten. The rain came down, not heavily but as a fine chill mist that soaked through robes and the clothes underneath; to the bone, it seemed. The yobs arrived more frequently, and in greater numbers. They lined the sides of the Square, but still took no action, still remained silent. A few people, citizens, began coming in on foot, and they did not try to prevent them. Some, Martin saw, turned back when they were faced by the array of white leather jackets, but others pushed through to the Brothers, and joined in the hymns and prayers.

He thought he could guess the strategy of the yobs. They intended this as an example, a crushing demonstration of their own power. He saw that movie cameras had been set up in places, to record what was happening, or what might happen. They were waiting until the time was ripe, and meanwhile letting people through. The demonstration was intended for everyone, not just the Fellowship. You let the boil gather before you lanced it.

The dark sky wept and for a moment, feeling himself wet and cold, his belly empty, he doubted Brother James. A sacrifice, yes – but a useless sacrifice? Or was he expecting a miracle … God's thunderbolt hurled from the top of the Column? But there were no signs, no miracles, and could be none.

As though answering him, Brother James spoke to them.

'We are in God's hands, Brothers. We are nothing unless we accept His Will, His Judgement. The hour is here when we face God's enemies and our own. The moment approaches when only faith in God will serve – in this life and as a passport to the life which is to come. Now above all we must be steadfast in His service, joyful in offering our lives, our deaths, to Him.'

And Martin knew, dazed, that this was so. There would be no miracles because the miracle in each human heart was enough.

Death did not matter – defeat did not matter – compared with this.

Gradually the crowd thickened round them in the Square. The numbers coming in were not slackening, but increasing. They came in through all the entry roads, but particularly those to the south and east, and he had a vision of all the others following them, making their way towards this place. It was then that the attack began.

It started with cries and catcalls, the old familiar vituperation. The yobs had brought loud-hailers with them, and their shouts and insults blared and echoed like the cries of giants or demons. They joined together in a song: 'Robey, Robey'. Its obscenities were bellowed above the hymn which those in the Square were singing. Following that, they moved into a sequence of questions and antiphonal answers, one of them with a hailer asking and the rest responding. Obscene, absurd, mindless, but savage and full-throated.

A shouted command, followed by a pause in which only the hymn could be heard. Then the single voice, hideously amplified:

'This is it, Robeys. We're coming in for you. Anyone who wants to get out had better get out fast. Anyone except the Robeys. They stay. But the rest of you … if you don't want your guts torn out, this is your last chance. Move out, and we'll let you through. Don't move, and you get it along with your Robey pals.'

The hymn had not stopped. Out of the corner of his eye, Martin looked for movement in the throng surrounding the plinth. There was none. They stood and sang in the rain.

The first shot came from in front of the National Gallery, isolated and awful. It was followed by more, a ragged increasing fusillade. The hymn faltered, as someone screamed, picked up and then broke off. Martin saw a spreading star of red on the robe of a man near him, the man himself being held up by those who stood on either side. Nearby a woman dropped, showing a bloody hole in place of her left eye. There were screams and shouts all round, rising against gunfire and the more distant exulting shouting of the yobs. He felt bewildered and uncertain, but not afraid. Something was growing in him: an urge to action. He did not mind the crack of guns, the whistle of bullets through the air, the cries of the wounded, as long as there would be release from the tension of waiting.

Brother James climbed to a higher step, so that he stood above them all. He was a target, Martin realized, for those who were firing at them, but God's shield was in front of him and round him. A bullet chipped the stone a few feet from Brother James' head, but he paid no heed to it. He shouted, in a voice that for those near the foot of the Column rose above the row:

'Brothers, the moment is here! Go forward! Smite the heathen in God's name. God puts power into your bare hands to tame the animals with their guns. Fight not for yourselves, but for God. Fight, Brothers!'

Martin heard his own voice shouting: 'Glory, glory, glory!' Figures moved, swelling outwards from the plinth, the message going ahead of them as voice on voice took up the gladness of battle, the meaning plain even where the words were lost in the uproar. Progress was slow at first, for they were hemmed in by the others outside. The shooting continued, and a man in front of him doubled up, groaning. Martin said a quick prayer for his soul, and stepped over him. He reached one of the fountains. There was a body in it, head downwards, near the edge, and the water was dull red. The firing was less for a moment, and then heavier. There was a little clear space in front of him, and he broke into a run. He was shouting, but he did not know what he was shouting any more.

There was a hold-up again by the steps, with fighting going on at the top. People formed a pyramid to scale the wall nearby, and he climbed up over the backs of others. He stood on the balustrade at the top, and saw the seething mass fighting all round the top of the Square. Many of the yobs had retreated to other vantage points: one was firing from the top of the Washington statue. But more were enmeshed in hand-to-hand fighting, slashing with their knives. He saw one of them gripped from behind by a white-robed figure, while a man in a blue suit punched and kicked him from the front.

The yobs were fighting hard – fighting, in reality, for their lives – but the wave of God's followers was relentlessly spilling over them. Power into our bare hands, he thought. And people were still coming into the Square, turning the flank of those yobs who continued to maintain some kind of order. Even as he looked, the porch of the National Gallery was stormed, to a new roar of triumph. Someone had got hold of one of the loud-hailers, and was shrieking through it, over and over:

'God's victory! God's victory!'

He felt a blow in the arm, almost spinning him backwards off his perch. He looked down and saw a hole, with blood welling out. It roused him to joy and fury. Leaping down, he battled his way towards the nearest yobs.

'Glory!' he shouted. 'Glory to God!'

There was no pain in his arm, but a terrible strength.

XVII

His original idea had been to get the first possible train out of Pallister, to put as great a distance as he could between them and Ape. He stuck to this resolution during the nerve-racking journey by bus, expecting at any moment to hear the roar of motor-bikes coming up in pursuit. There was the noise of them once, near the bottom of the Broadway, and he cursed himself silently for not having got off the bus earlier and walked the rest of the way in. But they proved to be coming from the opposite direction – a different gang, on an ordinary sweep. He shepherded the children down for the next stop, all the same, and watched the bus lumber on towards Pallister Wall.

They would have needed to stay on for three more stages to get to the nearest point to the station. Here they were closer to the Hospital. He stood, swept by unsureness. He dared not go in to see her. It was an obvious place for Ape to check. For himself the risk was worth it, but there were the children to be looked after. He must not, dare not, take chances.

But at the same time the thought of catching a train, leaving Pallister, putting himself in a position where he could not visit her if he wanted to, was unbearable. As long as he stayed here, there was the possibility of finding some way – if not to see her, at least to learn how she was. If he were to leave, she could die and he not know. Thinking this, he put his hand in his pocket and felt the key which Micky had given him. In an emergency – if the trains were not running for some reason – he had suggested he could use his flat, providing nobody had taken it over.

Peter said:

'Hadn't we better get off the main road, Dad? We can cut through to the station.'

'I've been thinking,' he said, 'that we might stay here for the night.'

'Not go to Uncle Arthur's?' Linda asked.

That had been the project. He was not a real uncle, but an old Army friend with whom Rod had kept in touch. He was running a small hotel in a quiet West-country village, and the family had stayed there several times. He would take them in until things improved, or they thought of some better plan.

'Not tonight,' Rod said. 'Tomorrow, maybe.'

There was no-one in the flat, and no sign of anyone having been there. They had brought a little food with them, and Linda prepared it. He thought, watching her, that she had a lot of Hilda's ways, and was reminded of the cell-like room less than a mile away. He had let her down, he knew, by his weakness in staying here. She would have told him: the children – they are what matter, in the most important sense all that matters. He knew she was right, as she always was about fundamentals. They would leave Pallister tomorrow, in the morning. It made no sense to delay.

In the morning, though, Linda switched on the wireless in the flat, and they heard of the trouble in London. The news was confusing, and it was necessary to read between the lines of the official version. This started with a vilification of the Robeys that was even more trenchant than had been the case during the previous week, and had a specific point. The Robeys were gathering together, and it was time they were put down. These nauseating Creeping Jesuses had been tolerated long enough; it was time they were swept into discard. If they had their way, there would be no fun in the world, so they must be stopped now. The white robes, the speaker said, were the targets. Music swelled up – martial, with a beat. Over it, a voice shouted:

'The motto for today, folks! Go get a Robey!'

By the time they had finished breakfast, though, and were clearing, the tone had changed. On a new bulletin, the Robeys were still an object of scorn and hatred, but the light-heartedness had gone. The Robeys must be defied, because they were out to wreck everything that mattered. They were fascists, reactionaries, trying to drag the country back a century. The speaker appealed to everyone – to youth in particular – to come out and prevent them from getting a stranglehold on things. If they failed, the future was unthinkable. No liberty, no dancing, no pop music. Religion thrust down everybody's throat. Slave labour camps …

Rod said:

'Someone sounds worried.'

Linda asked:

'Have you finished with that cup, Daddy? Do you know what time train we're catching?'

The pop music came on again, a dirge somewhat appositely entitled: 'You just shattered everything to pieces'. He said absently:

'There's one at half past ten.'

'Then we'd better get a move on.'

The briskness, the very tone of voice, was Hilda for a moment, almost overwhelmingly so. He wondered how she was this morning – if he dared ring the Hospital to find out. Before they left, he could. But then there was the thought of putting the telephone down and going away to catch the train.

He said:

'There's another train just after two.'

His daughter looked at him with faint exasperation. He reminded himself of the difference between a child's affection and that of the grown and battered person.

'Ought we to wait till then?'

'Something's happening,' he said. 'Something very important, possibly. I think we ought to wait for another news bulletin.'

She sighed. 'If you think so.'

Peter said:

'Can I go out – to have a look round?'

'No,' Rod said. 'Stay here for the present.'

The pop music played on. Rod studied his watch as the next half-hour came round. But this time, there was no bulletin. The programme, he realized, was probably recorded and would continue unless faded out for the News Room. For some reason, that was not happening. The delay became five minutes, ten. Linda was doing something in the kitchen, but Peter was getting restless, picking up the few books Micky had, leafing quickly through them, and putting them down again. Then, in the middle of a number, the station went dead.

They had been tuned to National, the London transmitter. Rod searched for regional stations, and found them still broadcasting. He stuck on the one nearest to Pallister, and waited. On the next half-hour, the music faded out for news. The items were about a film star getting a divorce, civil disturbances in China, a palace revolution in West Africa. Nothing about London, nor about the Robeys. The music came back, and he swung the tuning dial round.

It was towards the end of the next half-hour that the pointer passed over the National frequency, and he realized the station was back on the air. Not with pop music, though, but a voice. A man's voice, earnest and exhorting, but without the mid-Atlantic buoyancy that had become standard for announcers. He was saying, as Rod tuned back in:

'. . . national regeneration and dedication. We have all sinned, all strayed from God's ways. By His mercy, and under the guidance of Brother James, we will have an opportunity to cleanse ourselves and our beloved country of the stains of past years. But first we have to rid ourselves, finally and without shrinking from the task, of the evil ones who, for more than six months, have dominated and degraded our national life. London already is ours. Brother James calls on all God-fearing men and women through the rest of the land to accomplish a similar victory. Brothers and sisters! Join together, sweep the monsters from your path, be ruthless with all things that come between your soul and the service of God, between our nation and its renewal. Do not shrink from bloodshed, for without bloodshed there is no victory, and God's own precious blood was shed for us. Rise! Strike! And rejoice in the strength of God's right hand!'

There was silence for a few seconds after the voice ceased, and then organ music. Something of Handel's, Rod thought. He was dazed and excited by what he had heard – excited not only by the news, but to some extent by the call. Someone had done something. Better the Robeys doing it, than nothing being done. He wondered who Brother James was: presumably some sort of leader. All this would sort itself out as things settled down. There was a real chance, at last, of getting the yobs off the country's back.

Linda had come in from the kitchen during the harangue.

She said:

'What's happening?'

'I'm not sure yet. It sounds like revolution.'

'Fighting?' Peter asked.

He spoke neither with excitement nor fear, but warily. How far they had come in the last year.

'There might be,' Rod said. 'I think as far as we are concerned, we'll stay here till it blows over.'

'We're not catching the two something train, then?' Linda asked. 'Not leaving Pallister?'

'We may not have to now.'

They did leave the flat, though, in the middle of the afternoon. The food they had brought, and what little they had found useable in the flat, had run out; and it was essential to replenish stocks if there was a prospect of more violence and unrest to come. Rod wanted to go himself, leaving the children here, but they protested: they had been cooped up since yesterday. He had to admit that there was no sound or sight of trouble – the windows of the flat looked out on to an ordinary quiet close leading to a peaceful street. The rain, which had come down steadily during the morning, had eased off, and there were prospects of the sky brightening. In the end, he agreed to take them with him. If anything did go wrong, they could dodge it. Things seemed to have settled down for the moment. The National station was continuing to broadcast homilies and exhortations, interspersed with properly solemn classical music and a leavening of hymns. The regional stations, on the other hand, maintained a bland indifference to it all, presumably having decided it was wiser to play it down than to rouse people any further.

As they left the flat, a woman came from the stairs and passed them in the corridor. She opened a door further down and Rod, pushing the corridor door to, saw her standing there, looking after them. Someone who had known Micky, perhaps, and was curious about their presence. She was in her fifties, a tall thin woman in black. He followed the children, who were racing down the stairs, eager to be out.

There were quite a lot of people about, and he found that others had been taking the precaution of laying in stocks. The local grocer's was out of everything except Frotein, and said that the nearest place where they would still be likely to get rations was nearly a mile away – in effect, in the main shopping area. They checked another shop nearby, and had this confirmed. There was an undercurrent of excitement, and they heard snatches of conversation from passers-by in which the words 'yob' and 'Robey' figured largely; but it seemed to be an entirely verbal excitement. Sunshine was breaking through the clouds, and the day was warmer than had lately been the case. Rod saw a chestnut, showing the first burgeoning of sticky brown against the darker bareness of the branch. It lifted his spirits, until he thought of Hilda.

While they were in the shop, buying food, there was the

sound of shooting not far away. People serving, and the other shoppers, came alert. Someone said, in a tone of satisfaction: 'It's started now.' Someone else, an elderly man, said: 'I'll bet the little bastards are shivering!' They completed their purchases, and Rod hurried the children out and in the direction of the flat. They had to cross a main road, and he saw that on the other side a crowd had collected, including a number of men in the white robes of the Fellowship. He turned the other way slightly, and then stopped at the sound, distant but approaching, of motor-bikes.

He had a ridiculous fear that it might be Ape and his gang, and pulled Linda and Peter back into the concealment of a shop entrance: the shop was closed, but behind the shattered window there were travel posters with scenes of Spain and the Greek Islands. He watched the bikes roar up – thirty or more of them. As they came near the place where the crowd was, figures sprang out – mostly Robeys, but a few who were dressed in ordinary clothes. They put themselves in the path of the yobs, who swerved and skidded helplessly in an effort to avoid them. Rod saw the first figure go down under the wheels of the leading bike, which somersaulted, spilling its driver head over heels into the road. After that, it turned into a mêlée. The bikes were dragged to a halt and disappeared under a wave of humanity that poured in as soon as they were immobile. The yobs – those who had not been knocked unconscious – tried to fight, but it was hopeless. A howl of savage fury went up, punctuated by screams. Resistance did not last more than a few minutes, but they did not stop when resistance ended. The victors, the women in particular, were like wild animals, tearing and rending. He saw one yob, the nearest to them of those that had fallen, pinioned while a woman, screeching, put her hands like claws to his face. He saw what she was doing, and that the children could see also. Peter was staring at the scene. Linda, sickened, had turned her head away. She was trembling violently.

Rod said:

'Come on, let's get back. Don't look at that.'

There was noise in the city now. On their way, they heard bursts of gunfire, the roar of engines, occasionally cut short. When they were nearly at the flat, they passed the scene of another skirmish. Motorbikes and white-jacketed bodies lay in the street, wrecked in different ways. The mutilations were sickening, and Rod saw, bile rising in his throat, that just inside a front garden there was one white-jacketed figure that ended at the neck in a bloody gaping hole. He hoped the children had not seen it. They turned back in their tracks, and found a way that did not lead them through the battlefield.

Linda said:

'What's happened? Have they gone mad?'

'A bit, I think.'

It had erupted with such suddenness, a boiling up of vengefulness and insanity. Presumably the yobs had stayed out of the city during the earlier part of the day, and then had come in, either as a demonstration of strength or because they had been lulled into thinking that it was safe now – that whatever had gone wrong was confined to London and did not affect them here. But the calm had been deceptive, and a few Robeys, sacrificing themselves, had whipped the rest of the populace to a fever of blood-lust. It could last for days, whether or not the yobs were able to put in a counter-attack. Rod was glad they had food to last forty-eight hours at least. The sensible thing, the only thing, to do was get into the flat and hole up there.

The peaceful street was peaceful no longer. A procession, led by three or four Robeys, was marching up the centre, singing a hymn. Others were standing, watching and cheering. At one point, a small group clustered round a man in a dark, typically Civil Service suit. He was holding up his long black rolled umbrella, and the staring head of a boy of about twenty surmounted it, blood dripping from the hacked-off neck on to the black oiled silk.

There was no hope that the children had failed to see that.

Peter put his head down and vomited in the gutter. Linda was saying, over and over: 'Oh, no ... oh, no ...'

At least, they were only fifty yards from the entrance to the flats. He wiped Peter's mouth, and they went on. The entrance was clear, and they headed for the stairs, since the lift was out of order. As they were passing the lift, though, Linda said:

'What was that?'

'What?'

This time Rod heard it: the groan of a man too stupefied to know what he was doing. It came from the lift, where the gate was half-open. Before he looked, he guessed what he would see – a white leather jacket, a huddled body.

Linda said:

'He's not dead.'

'No.'

What he most wanted, he admitted to himself, was to run for it. He thought of Hilda, and justified himself: it was the children who needed protection. While he was thinking this, Linda had darted forward and wrenched the gate fully open. She went in, and knelt beside the yob. After a brief moment, she looked back at him in just the way, peremptory and unhesitating, that Hilda would have done. She said:

'We've got to get him upstairs.'

He had various cuts and abrasions – a deep scratch down one cheek oozing blood – and was concussed. Colour came and went in his face, and his awareness of what was going on varied with it. In his more lucid moments, he complained of a pain in his chest. Rod felt for broken ribs but could find nothing, though there was an area, at the bottom right, which was extremely tender. Linda bathed his wounds, but there was not much else they could do. She had put the kettle on to make tea for him.

He muttered:

'Got away from them … you see what they did to Glenn? Bastards … Robey bastards … Commander said … make a bonfire and fry 'em … '

Cleaned up, his face was small and looked vicious, an inverted triangle leading down to a black Vandyke beard. His eyes were light brown, hard even when they were not focusing. He looked blearily at Linda.

'Could fancy you … need to get me strength back first … Robey bastards …'

Rod said:

'We can't keep him here.'

He took that in, and said strongly:

'Do as I bloody well say, or I'll knife you.'

Cries, and the ragged harmony of hymns, still came in from outside, though faintly. Linda said:

'We couldn't send him out there yet, even if he were all right.'

The yob bared his teeth in a grin. 'You fancy me, too, babe? You and me …' His face paled suddenly, and he blanked out for a moment. 'Fry the bastards … big white candles … set them alight …'

There was a confused noise outside in the corridor, and the doorbell rang. Peter, who was nearest, went to answer it. Rod said: 'Wait a minute …' but it was too late. As the door opened, a white-robed figure pushed his way into the room, followed by others. Among them, Rod saw the tall thin woman in black, who had watched them leave the flat earlier. She cried:

'I told you they'd brought him up here! I told you …'

They moved towards the yob, whose hand went to his belt but was gripped before it could get there. Rod said:

'He's sick.'

'He'll be sicker,' someone said. Several of them laughed. The yob started to scream, inarticulately but obviously in an appeal for mercy. Linda threw herself forward at those who had got hold of him.

'Stop it! Leave him alone …'

The Robey who had led the way in, a big red-faced man, looked at them, as though noticing them for the first time.

'Yob-lovers,' he said.

'We brought him up because he was ill,' Rod said. 'He should be in hospital.'

There was more laughter. A man casually punched the screaming boy in the face. The Robey said:

'Yob-lovers. Take them in. They will face God's justice.'

The court was held in the Council Chamber of the Civic Centre.

Three Robeys sat in judgement, while another Robey presented each case to them. The room was full of people. Some, standing, wore white brassards, signifying that they belonged to the Vigilantes, the new police force that was springing into being to enforce the Robeys' rule. Two of them stood behind Rod as the charge against him was read out. He had tried to help a yob to escape from the rightful justice of the people. There were witnesses who could be called, if necessary.

The Robey in the centre of the trio asked him:

'Do you deny the charge, Brother?'

He had spent the night, shivering and wakeful, on the floor of a locked basement room, unlighted and unheated. This morning he had been given tea, and a hunk of bread and cheese. He was tired, stiff, dazed. He had expected the atmosphere of the court-room to be one of feverish and rabid emotionalism, but so far it was not like that. The Robey who had asked him how he pleaded spoke in a calm, reasonable-seeming voice. He said:

'I wasn't helping anyone to escape from anything. He was ill and needed attention.'

'Are you a doctor, Brother?'

'No, but it was obvious that he was ill.'

'Why did you not seek proper care for him, in that case?'

'Because I thought the most important thing was to get him out of the way, before he was lynched.'

The Robey smiled down at him. 'Then you knew, Brother, that the people were seeking him?'

'Yes, but ...'

His voice trailed away, as he saw that he was being ignored. The Robeys conferred together in quiet voices. Then the spokesman said:

'You are found guilty. The sentence is one year in a work battalion, where you can make amends, by helping in the reconstruction of this great country, for your defiance of the people's will. Submit your body to the people, and your soul to God.'

Stunned, he said:

'I have a family to look after.'

'The Lord will provide.'

'But ... my son and daughter were with me when I was – arrested. Where are they?'

'They will be taken care of.'

'But I must see them!'

The voice was still calm, but took on a harder edge.

'You have been dealt with leniently. Opposition to the will of the people under God is a crime that can be punished by death. Your children will be taken under the people's care, and trained in the paths of godliness and duty. In the new society, the innocent need have no fears. God tempers the wind to the shorn lamb.'

He said:

'Please let me see them. And my wife. She's in hospital – dying.'

'That is a better attitude,' the Robey said approvingly. 'But your request is no concern of ours. You may put it, in due course, to the officer in charge of your work battalion. Constables, take the prisoner away.'

The Robey brought his hands together in front of him, his companions following suit.

'Justice is done,' he said. 'Praise be to God.'

XVIII

THEY WERE TAKEN to Pallister on the back of an open trailer, pulled by a farm tractor. Their hands had been tied together behind their backs, and their feet roped in pairs to discourage any thought of jumping off and trying to run for it. As an extra precaution, four Robeys on horseback rode on either side of the trailer and behind. It was a sunny morning but the wind was from the east, and, wearing only their ordinary indoor dresses, they were all blue with cold. One of the girls near Jane had been wanting to relieve herself almost from the time they set out. She had called to the Robeys, in appeal at first and then, when they took no notice, coarsely and insultingly. This phase had passed, too, and she merely sat and moaned.

Many of them had been defiant at the beginning, but the cold and discomfort had worn them down to silence. The one whose feet were tied to Jane's was a chunky blonde girl, broad-faced with somewhat slanting eyes. She had a bruise on her cheek which was the result of a blow sustained in an attempt to defend the yobs, and her favoured one in particular, during the assault on Bridge House. There were others who had managed to sneak out and join the attackers, but they were here, also. The Robeys made no distinction between any of the women they had found there. At the front of the trailer, two sticks, nailed on, supported a sheet painted with their description. The straggling scarlet letters simply read: THE WHORES.

As they moved into the city, clusters of people gathered to witness their progress. Some stared in silence; others jeered. A few, mostly children, threw things. A boy, aiming badly, hit the horse of one of the accompanying Robeys. The Robey turned silently, staring at the child, who scuttled away into the crowd. Men, for the most part, shouted insults at them, in lechery and anger. She tried to shut her mind to all that was going on around her, and to some extent succeeded. The physical torment helped.

From the Broadway, the procession went on to the ring road circling the Civic Centre. There were more people here, and the jeering was much louder. They were taken round to the other side, where the car-park had been. A dense crowd had gathered, and she could see, over their heads, what they were concerned with. The stocks, which the yobs had reintroduced, were there, and there were girls in them. But there were dozens of others, tethered in a makeshift way: their hands and legs tied, and the rope secured to metal stakes driven into the tarmac. The crowd was mocking them, and pelting them with rubbish. The girls had all had their heads shaved; their skulls gleamed like marble boulders in the sunlight.

She thought she had braced herself for anything, but this touch – the sight of that defenceless nakedness – brought her down. She felt her own tears on her cheeks, warm at first and then cold like everything else.

At night they were taken in, untied, allowed to wash in cold water and tidy themselves, and given a supper of bread and a thin Frotein stew. Robeys came and said prayers and sang hymns over them, and one preached a sermon, telling them that even they could pass from sinfulness to grace, but the way was long and must be arduous. Then they were left, with one blanket each and the floor to sleep on. The night passed slowly. There was some cursing but more crying. They had been locked in without sanitary facilities and the girl with the weak bladder, who had wet herself in the cart, moaned and wet herself again. Eventually, banging on the door aroused the guards. They listened to the complaint, and took four of the girls away. They returned, some time later, with a variety of containers – large tins, buckets, an old zinc bath – which were put in place near the door. They seemed to be in constant use after that.

In the morning there was more bread and stew, more prayers and hymns, and then they were taken out to be tethered as they had been the previous day. It was a little less cold, but the sun had gone; clouds rolled in from the west with a feel of rain in the air. Gradually the crowd collected, as before, and the jeering and throwing started. One could move a little, to dodge things, but often they came from behind. Someone had provided paper bags which, if they were filled carefully, would hold liquid for a time – long enough for them to be lobbed into the circle at a human target.

Jane did not break down again for several hours – not until she saw Micky, in fact. He pushed his way through to the front of the crowd, and she could see him looking for her. He had his broken leg in a plaster, one arm in a sling, and the crutch on which he supported himself under the other. She wept silently, but did not call to him. At one point she thought he was going to turn away without having seen her, but then his eyes fixed on her, and he began hobbling forward, picking his way between the tethered girls.

He managed, with great difficulty, to lower himself to sit beside her on the ground. Insults were called out to him, but no-one, not even the guards with the white arm-bands, tried to stop him. He put his free arm round her shoulder, squeezing her gently, and said:

'You're cold, love.'

His compassion made her sob helplessly. He slipped his overcoat off his shoulders, and awkwardly, with one hand, covered her with it. She said:

'Go away. Please, Micky. There's no need for you to be here – no point in it.'

He said:

'I heard it said they'd brought you here. I got out of hospital first thing, but I didn't come right away because I was trying to get hold of someone who could let you out. There wasn't anyone. I tried to explain, but it made no difference.'

She shook her head. 'It doesn't matter.'

'I found out it's only for three days. They're releasing you all tomorrow night. Can you stick it?'

'Yes, of course. But go now. Please go now.'

'I never knew I had so much hate in me.' He looked down at his leg. 'It's a bad time to be helpless.'

'I don't know.' She had just begun to appreciate that he was truly here beside her, that the coat on her shoulders was warm with his warmth. She tried to smile at him. 'You can't get into trouble so easily. And we're all helpless, really.'

He said: 'Stick it.'

'And you.'

The crowd had been watching them, and now began to take a more direct interest. They began throwing things at them, mostly the paper bags. One landed at the back of Jane's neck, spilling its contents all over her, and there was a roar of laughter. Micky got a handkerchief out and tried to dry her head. He said:

'Sorry I'm so clumsy. They broke the wrong arm.'

The touch of his hand made her aware again of her shaven head, and in her shame she averted her eyes.

'Don't …' she said. 'Please don't look at me.'

'Why not?'

'A naked skull …'

His hand caught her chin, forced her round until their eyes met and she could see that he was looking directly at her, and smiling.

'It's a good skull,' he said. 'The best I know.'

There was a burst of laughter and mockery from the crowd as he kissed her.

PART FOUR

A DAY OF REJOICING

Today, the birthday of our LEADER, Brother James, is rightly seen as a day of rejoicing for us all. It is also, by a directive of his senior associates which has the enthusiastic support of the entire nation, a public holiday. There will be thanksgiving services in churches throughout the land. In the afternoon there will be recreation in the form of healthy and constructive sports. There will be sober feasting. The meat ration has been increased by two ounces per person, one more sign of the way in which Brother James is leading us forward into strength and prosperity.

It is a day, also, during which we must take time for private meditation. We should remember the past, which we have put behind us, recognize the blessings of the present, dedicate ourselves to the building of the future.

We dwell, after long tribulation, in peace and order. We have police, who protect the citizen by enforcing the law with diligence and rigour. We have the beginnings of a new Army to defend our beloved land against any attack. Unemployment, with its soul-destroying curse of idleness, has been abolished: there is constructive work for every man. Above all, we have an awareness of our own value, under God, as the people of a Britain that is truly Great once more. Our factories are humming again, our fields bear the bloom of good husbandry. The land is in good heart.

Inevitably, there are the few who stand in the path of progress, who say nay to decency and good government. We should give thanks that they are few indeed, and powerless against the people's will. The so-called Revolt of the Liberals was quickly over. These 'Liberals', who did nothing while the yobs were terrorizing honest men and women, attempted to bring back anarchy, and failed miserably. They will have time enough to ponder their defeat, and their own wretched wickedness, in their new homes in the Scottish Islands. The Fellowship has named these places of corrective training the Isles of Hope, a signal mark of generosity and goodwill. For, as Brother James would remind us, there is hope for all sinners, however depraved, providing they bend their souls to God, and their bodies to cleansing discipline.

For the rest of us, the overwhelming majority of Britons, this is, we repeat, a time of rejoicing. We have turned our backs on vice and folly. Such measures as the closing of cinemas and public houses on the Sabbath are universally welcomed. So is the measure requiring youth to salute its elders – that salute which we already gladly give to the Brothers of the

Fellowship. We allowed an entire generation to go astray, and our licence resulted in terror and bloodshed. We shall not make the same mistake again.

Today also marks the opening of the second half of an eventful year. Under Brother James' guidance, we can look forward to the months and years ahead with confidence and joy.

I

DURING THE MID-MORNING BREAK, Rod sat, as usual, with Whitey. They were companions because they had opposite bed-spaces in the tented camp down in the valley. Apart from this accident of proximity, they had nothing in common. Whitey was fifteen years Rod's junior, an East End Cockney and a Jew. He had been a cab-driver, inheriting the taxi from his father, and grandfather before that. He was quick-witted and voluble, foul-mouthed, always – despite the guards' insistence on tidiness and hygiene – a bit on the scruffy side. Under normal conditions, Rod thought, they would have nothing to say to each other, no point of contact. Here they were friends, and the friendship was as real as any in his life had been: a great deal more important than most.

From somewhere, Whitey had got hold of a cigarette. They were completely forbidden in the camp, but there was some illicit traffic. Rod himself had made no attempt to smoke. There was a temptation, with the monotony and hardship of the life here, to do so, but he could not face the thought of scrounging and bargaining which it would involve. He humped his back, though, on the grass, so that Whitey could burrow down behind him, his face close to the ground, and take a few surreptitious drags, blowing the smoke into a rabbit-hole. The guards, with their dogs and guns, were thirty yards away, but watchful.

Above them, the Citadel rose against the blue sky. It was based, as were the Citadels being built all over the country, on a design which had come to Brother James in a vision. It was relatively simple, consisting of four battlemented walls enclosing a courtyard with a chapel at its centre. A tower rose at each corner. In the case of this Citadel, two of these had been completed, and a third was rising rapidly. The fourth was a source of hope and anxiety to Whitey. His aim, as a personal act of dedication, was to defecate in the foundations of each one of them. He had succeeded with the first three, though in the case of the third coming within a hair's breadth of being spotted by one of the guards. The fourth represented for him the final challenge, which he was determined to meet and overcome.

From behind Rod's back, he said:

'Hear about Maxie?'

'No. What?'

'Joe was telling me. They got him for the Islands.'

'For being late on parade?'

It was a shock, terrifying in its implications.

'Persistent late,' Whitey said. 'It wasn't just that, though. Silly bugger talked back when they had him up. You'd think the stupid bleedin' sod would know better.'

'How long did he have to go?'

'Three months. And now he's on the bleedin' never-never.'

Detention in the islands, unlike that in the camps, was for an indefinite period. UR was the term for it – Until Rehabilitated. The prospect of being transferred was dreaded not only for this reason but because of the rumours about conditions of life there. Scourging with the cat-o'-nine-tails was said to be common, according to some reports not only for actual offences but as a ritual process of purification. There was no way of testing the truth of the stories: traffic between the camps and the islands was one-way. Deportation, to make matters worse, was not based on any specific crime, but was ordered, at the recommendation of the Brother who was Camp Leader, on a general charge of uncooperativeness in the ideals and purposes of the training camp.

Rod said:

'I think he was a bit mad. A couple of days ago I saw him cut his bread into tiny squares, and then crumble them up. Yesterday he didn't go up for food at all.'

A lack of interest in food was as plain an indication of derangement as one could imagine here. Although the food was bad, there was never enough of it. The body craved for a crust of bread as any addict's might have done for dope.

'Who sodding isn't?' Whitey asked. 'Heigh-up. One of the bloody bastards on the prowl.'

The guard came up the slope towards them, and they scrambled to their feet and made the prescribed salute. He was one of the less unpleasant ones, a big fair-haired man.

He said:

'You're wanted down at Camp Office, Gawfrey.' He tapped his red transceiver, a single spot of colour against the grey of his uniform. 'Better get down there.'

Whitey said:

'Cor, you're for it, matey! Hope you're a good sailor.'

Behind the mockery, there was concern. The guard said:

'You've got a visitor.'

'Christ!' Whitey said. 'A bleedin' visitor …'

'Blasphemy's an offence, White,' the guard said. 'I'm not going to warn you again. Next time you're on charge.'

'Sorry, sir,' Whitey said. He shook his head. 'I don't believe it, though. A bleedin' visitor. You didn't tell me you had that sort of pull, Roddy boy.'

He went down to the camp without escort. If he had wanted to make a break, there was no cover and the guards had telescopic sights on their rifles. The dogs, anyway, would bring down a fugitive in a matter of minutes. He was let in through the gate and went to the Camp Office. He reported his arrival, and was taken down a corridor in the hut to a small room, with a barred window, a table, two chairs, and a number of moral and religious maxims framed on the walls. 'Temper the Soul to Win the Crown' – 'A Little More Effort is Possible: Make it Now' –

'Jesus Saves'. He was staring at them when the corridor door opened, and Martin came in.

It had never occurred to Rod that he would have advanced so far in the hierarchy. His white robe had the dark blue collar and cuffs of the highest order of Brothers, and on his breast there was a blue monogrammed J, which showed that he was a member of the Council. He stared at him without speaking. Martin advanced, and offered his hand.

'How are you, Rod?'

He took it automatically. 'I'm … all right, I suppose.'

Martin said:

'It's bad news, I'm afraid.'

'Hilda?' Martin nodded. 'When?'

'During the night. I came down right away, to be the one to break it to you.'

He stared at him dully. 'You would be able to do that, of course.'

'She's at peace, Rod. With God. And there was no pain at the end.'

'I didn't see her.' His brain seemed to be working terribly slowly and awkwardly. 'You could have fixed for me to see her.'

'There are no exceptions to the rules, Rod.'

'You're making an exception now, aren't you?'

'No. Deaths of near-relatives are notifiable. I have the authority to do the notifying.'

'But not to let me see my wife, your sister, on her death-bed.'

'Discipline and the acceptance of the rules provide the strength of our movement. Once you learn resignation, you will understand that. There can be no weaknesses.'

Anger burned, behind his shock and grief. He forced himself to reject it. Other things were more important.

'Linda,' he said. 'Do you know what's happened to her?'

'She is in the care of the Sisters. Safe and well.'

'And Pete?'

'You can be proud of him. He has been accepted as a Junior Brother.'

'Stephen?'

Martin hesitated. 'You were told, surely?'

'Told what?'

'He was killed in the uprising. He had joined the yobs. I'm sorry. I thought you had been notified. You should have been.'

He said stupidly: 'So there are weaknesses, even in the system of the glorious Fellowship.'

'Error and weakness are not the same. We are all liable to error.'

'Even Brother James?'

Martin said gently:

'You do yourself no good by this attitude, Rod. You must learn to accept things. The Lord's rod can heal as well as hurt. It hurts the proud and stiff-necked, but not those who have acquired humility. You should pray more.'

He wanted to leave this room before he lost control and hit him. Striking a Brother could only result in a deportation to the islands. For a Blue, a J Brother, it would be worse still. Death, probably.

He said:

'Look, when I get out of this place …'

'Yes?'

'I can have my children back? Linda and Pete?'

'As far as Linda is concerned, that will be considered by the Discharge Board. They will take everything into account: the extent of your rehabilitation, your prospects … above all, Linda's best interests. In the case of Peter – I told you, he has been accepted as a Junior Brother. He will go to a Citadel for training.'

'For how long?'

'The course lasts four years.'

Rod looked at him. The white robe, he saw now, was also of finer quality than that of lower-rank Brothers: it looked like silk. Above it, the pinched face was a matured version of the unlikeable schoolboy whom he had loved, twenty years ago, for Hilda's sake. Below the blue cuff of the sleeve was the travesty of a hand, at the sight of which he had always had to master his repulsion. This had life still while her hands – thin, deft, lovely – were dead and beginning to rot.

'Call on God,' Martin said, 'and you will find help, and the courage to accept His will.'

Instead he called, silently, in anger and despair, on Hilda. Not on the dead, but across time and space, on the living breathing person. And got his answer as though she were in front of him, her warm voice speaking to him. Endure. Survive, and you may do something for our children. And if not for ours, for others. It is not finished yet.

He said:

'Thank you for coming, Martin. I suppose I'd better get back to the working party.'

II

TRAFFIC WAS GETTING THICK AGAIN. Jane tried to cross the High Street opposite Marks & Spencers, where there was no pedestrian crossing, and got trapped halfway by a sudden surge coming up from Pallister Wall. There were a lot of official cars, with different blazons – white of the Fellowship, grey of the Police, red of the Army – but there were also quite a number of private ones. There were hints that petrol rationing was to be abolished quite soon.

The pavements were crowded also, with Saturday afternoon shoppers. The grey-uniformed police seemed to be everywhere, and she came on two of them dressing down a couple of scared teen-agers. The rule about saluting their elders was not enforced in crowd conditions, but apparently they had also failed to salute a Robey. Their names and addresses were entered in one of the policemen's notebooks.

The first thing she saw inside the store was a sign that said: BANANAS ARE BACK – THANKS TO OUR GLORIOUS LEADER! But they were well out of her price range, as were most other things. She made her careful purchases, and dodged the Dress Department, to save herself from needless frustration. She pondered a kipper for Micky, and decided that, though she couldn't really afford it, she was going to. It would be a surprise for him for Sunday breakfast.

Coming out, she found that people had moved towards the edge of the road to watch something passing. She joined them and saw, with a shiver of remembered horror, that it was the latest consignment for the stocks. They still kept to the tractor and the open trailer. There were three people on it, with halters round their necks. Two, a man and a woman in their thirties, were side by side, and the signs they were forced to carry said ADULTERER and ADULTRESS. The third was a priest, and his sign was larger and more elaborate:

HE CLAIMED HE WAS A MAN OF GOD
BUT SPOKE AGAINST OUR LEADER.

Whatever criticism he had offered must have been mild, she thought, or he would be on his way to the islands. Though it was always possible that the stocks were merely a transitional stage.

The trailer moved at its leisurely pace towards the Civic Centre, and the cars queued up patiently behind it. The people on the pavement watched with a mild interest that was in some ways more disquieting than the earlier mob enthusiasm had been. They took all this for granted now – a show that they were used to. She turned away from the scene, to finish her shopping. A policeman looked at her, but did not say anything. Lack of civic spirit was an offence, and one open to all sorts of interpretations.

She paused by a bookshop. It carried, inevitably, a copy of *The Sayings of Brother James* in the centre of the window, flanked, in lesser display, by other religious and semi-religious works. But she was surprised to find, in a side window, a selection of paperbacks of novels. The purge that followed the Robey revolution had swept away fiction lock, stock and barrel – it had been easier for them to do that than to try to winnow it for what small portion might be regarded as suitable. All these new copies carried the four small turrets, linked by a circle, which showed they had the imprimatur of the Fellowship. The jackets had the gaudy melodramatic naturalism which was officially approved, and women, where they appeared, were decorously clothed and wearing expressions of patent sanctity or unspeakable villainy. A lot of them seemed to be romantic works, presumably with a good moral basis and an appropriately uplifting ending. There were also Westerns, she saw, and detective stories. She noticed, in the case of the latter, that some had no indication as to author. She was puzzled until she saw a familiar title, and remembered that the writer of the book had been one of those publicly tried for taking part in the attempted counter-revolution. She could not recall whether he had been executed, or had got off with deportation to the Isles of Hope.

The butcher's was the only important place of call left; she went to one down a side-road who was generous with the bones she bought for soup and had a good supply of cheaper cuts on the ration. On the way there, though, she had a brief attack of dizziness, and was forced to rest against a doorway. It was an electrical and TV shop, with a TV set in operation on the single National channel. She glanced at the flickering picture, and saw Walter's face, in close up, animatedly talking.

The last she had heard of him was when his name had been included in a list of those scheduled for trial as enemies of the State. She had not seen anything in the newspapers after that, and had assumed that his trial had been one of the many that were not reported, and that he had been deported to the islands. (She would have known if he had been given a death sentence; executions were always reported, generally in detail.) She stared at his mouth, opening and closing behind the plate glass of the shop front. Only a faint buzz of speech came through, mixed with other sounds, but she recognized the tone of confidence and assurance. She pushed the door of the shop open, and went in.

There were quite a few people inside, and a transistor radio being demonstrated. It was tuned loudly to a home frequency, but she heard the salesman promising the potential customer that it could receive Continental stations. She moved closer to the TV set, and listened. Walter was saying:

'... the importance of self-examination. This is the key to the whole question of readjustment. As our dear Leader has said, no sinner is too far removed from the Divine Love to be able to turn back from his wickedness. Two things only are necessary: vision and will. Vision to see ourselves as we are, in our human squalor and degradation, and will, with God's help, to make the long leap towards redemption.

'In my case …'

She realized what programme it was: part of the series called 'Confessional' in which figures either prominent or interesting outlined their past wickedness and pledged their future adherence to the ideals of the Fellowship. She gathered it was quite popular because the confessions were sometimes lurid about weaknesses of the flesh. There had been one ex-Socialist Cabinet Minister who had confessed to seducing a Duchess in his ministerial office. She wondered wrily whether Walter would proceed on similar lines, but he did not. He talked of his part in helping the yobs, and of his earlier role as a corrupter of youth.

There was an interviewer, a discreet shadowy earnest young man. He said:

'Professor Staunton, now that you are being restored to academic life, what are your aims and hopes in moulding the young people who will be under your care?'

'Very humble ones,' Walter said. 'To guide them towards true knowledge rather than idle and dangerous speculation. To keep them secure in the moral atmosphere which the Brothers of the Fellowship have formed for them at school. Above all, to teach them that our Leader's example and wisdom …'

The assistant who had been trying to sell the transistor came up to her, and said:

'Were you thinking of buying a television set, madam?'

His tone was unpleasant. Sets were very dear at present, and he did not have to be particularly astute to read poverty in her appearance. Jane shook her head.

'No.'

'Then I would point out, madam, that our show-rooms are not intended for free entertainment.'

'No,' she said, 'nor for inciting citizens to listen to foreign radio stations.'

It was an offence to listen to anything but home radio, and sets were supposed to have governors preventing it. She saw the quick leap of fear in his face and, nasty as he was, was ashamed of herself for using such a weapon. He said:

'I'm sorry, madam. Please stay as long as you like.'

'Thank you,' she said, 'but I've seen enough.'

Walter was saying: ' … a new and glorious future, based on discipline, diligence, devotion – the three Ds.'

It was the kind of phrase, she thought as she left the shop, that might well be picked up and used by the propagandists of the Fellowship. Walter, at any rate, looked like having a new and glorious future.

The two rooms they had were in a tenement building, and on the fifth floor. It was a drag climbing up but nothing, she realized, to what it would be later. On the landing below, a group of West Indian children were playing some sort of game which involved a lot of shouting and laughing. Her mother, when she let herself in, was immediately querulous: there was so much noise all the time, and the smell of their cooking … It was funny, Jane thought, that she had always seemed ill at ease at Bridge House, but found the loss of comfort and spaciousness more trying than anyone else. She reminded herself that changes must come harder when you were over seventy, and heard her out patiently. She asked:

'Did Dad get up?'

'No.'

He had kept to his bed for three weeks now. There was nothing wrong with him except that he was tired of living. That was understandable, too.

Her mother asked:

'Did you remember to get toilet paper?'

'Yes.'

'Having to go down a flight of stairs to share a lavatory with twenty others, most of them blacks, and having to take your own toilet paper with you because they'll just use yours and never buy any … it's not what I'm used to.'

'I know.'

'It will be different when Rod gets back.'

'I hope so.'

She was picking about among the groceries. 'Is this the best meat you could get?'

'There wasn't much of a choice today.'

'It's a pity you can't shop in the morning.'

'Yes.'

She had a cleaning job in the mornings, six days a week. Even this extra only just enabled them to keep their heads above water; she dared not contemplate what would happen when she had to give it up. The rooms, poor as they were, were dear, and there had been no increase in old-age pensions to cover the sharp rise in general prices. The Fellowship's preferred aim was an institutional life for old people, where they could be more effectively prepared for the life to come.

'Or let me do it.'

Jane did not answer that. Whatever she had been in the past, her mother now was a hopeless shopper, squandering money on small pointless luxuries. She looked at the tin alarm clock on the shelf, and thought: only another hour till he's back. It lifted her heart.

Sometimes, of an evening, they went out together – for a walk, or to make two half-pints of beer last an hour in a pub. She did not suggest that tonight; he was all too plainly dead-beat at the end of the week's work. He was a labourer on the roads, the only kind of job open to a man with a yellow-edged Insurance card. This had been given him after he had been identified as an ex-policeman, had been offered a position in the State Police, and had refused. It covered the categories both of low mentality and political unreliability.

She had cleared away after supper. Her mother had gone through to sit with her father. The radio, which she had taken with her, boomed through the thin wall – some kind of a play. Micky sat in the armchair, one of whose arms leaned out sideways, perpetually on the point of collapse, and Jane rested against his legs. The sky was still bright outside, faintly gold with the last sunlight of a summer evening.

He said:

'Looks as though the weather might hold.' She nodded, her head pressing his knee. 'If it's fine, we might get out somewhere.'

'Be nice.'

'I thought we might take your mother.'

'But Dad …'

'Mrs Styles on the ground floor said she'd sit in if we wanted her. I spoke about it the other day.'

'Even so …'

She stopped, realizing the selfishness of her true objection: that if there were to be an outing she wanted him to herself, the two of them alone together, free for a few hours of her mother's moaning. Micky said:

'We could get a bus into the country somewhere. Take a few sandwiches, perhaps. Do you think she'd like that?'

She herself at least got out of the tenement a bit; for her cleaning, or shopping, or those precious walks of an evening. She said:

'I know she would. I wonder …'

'Yes, love?'

'She said something the other day about the flowers that would be out in the garden now. At Gostyn. It will be a bit of a wilderness, but she might be able to pick some.'

'She wouldn't find it depressing, seeing the place?'

Bridge House had been fired, either by the yobs or by the Robey mob, during the assault. Part of it was gutted, and the rest had been left to rot. Jane said:

'We could ask her. I think she'd rather see it again in ruins than not at all.'

'You put it to her, then. And we'll hope for fine weather.'

They sat in silence for a time. She thought of Walter, and of her earlier self. A drinks party somewhere, and Walter holding forth about the reactionary nature of the conventional virtues. Progress, evolution, had come about through the restless and dissatisfied, the not-good. 'That's viewing it objectively,' he had said, 'but there is also the personal view. Good people are invariably insipid.' She remembered laughing at that; it had been what she regarded as an excellent party.

His fingers moved in her hair, still short, but growing fast. She said:

'You know what, darling? You're a good man.'

'No, just a lucky one.'

She laughed. 'Lucky? My God!' She looked round the room – the antique gas cooker and cracked sink in view, the broken-down divan which they converted into a bed at night, the worn linoleum on the floor, its bigger holes covered by bits of threadbare carpet. 'All this?'

His hand moved from her hair, to her face, her breasts, and stopped on the curve of her stomach.

'All this.'

'We don't even know whose it is – whether it's a child of love or hate.'

His hand stayed on her body, strong and comforting.

'Of love,' he said. 'There's no doubt about that.'

ALSO PUBLISHED BY THE SYLE PRESS

by Sam Youd as John Christopher

with an Introduction by Robert Macfarlane

THE DEATH OF GRASS

The Chung-Li virus has devastated Asia, wiping out the rice crop and leaving riots and mass starvation in its wake. The rest of the world looks on with concern, though safe in the expectation that a counter-virus will be developed any day. Then Chung-Li mutates and spreads. Wheat, barley, oats, rye: no grass crop is safe, and global famine threatens.

In Britain, where green fields are fast turning brown, the Government lies to its citizens, devising secret plans to preserve the lives of a few at the expense of the many.

Getting wind of what's in store, John Custance and his family decide they must abandon their London home to head for the sanctuary of his brother's farm in a remote northern valley.

And so they begin the long trek across a country fast descending into barbarism, where the law of the gun prevails, and the civilized values they once took for granted become the price they must pay if they are to survive.

This edition available in the US only

ISBN: 978-1-911410-00-3

www.deathofgrass.com

by Sam Youd as John Christopher

THE CAVES OF NIGHT

Five people enter the Frohnberg caves, three men and two women. In the glare of the Austrian sunshine, the cool underground depths seem an attractive proposition – until the collapse of a cave wall blocks their return to the outside world. Faced with an unexplored warren of tunnels and caves, rivers and lakes, twisting and ramifying under the mountain range, they can only hope that there is an exit to be found on the other side.

For Cynthia, the journey through the dark labyrinths mirrors her own sense of guilt and confusion about the secret affair she has recently embarked upon. And whilst it is in some ways a comfort to share this possibly lethal ordeal with her lover Albrecht, only her husband Henry has the knowledge and experience that may lead them all back to safety.

But can even Henry's sang froid and expertise be enough, with the moment fast approaching when their food supplies will run out, and the batteries of their torches fail, leaving them to stumble blindly through the dark?

ISBN: 978-0-9927686-8-3

www.thesylepress.com/the-caves-of-night

by Sam Youd as John Christopher

THE WHITE VOYAGE

Dublin to Dieppe to Amsterdam. A routine trip for the cargo ship *Kreya*, her Danish crew and handful of passengers. Brief enough for undercurrents to remain below the surface and secrets to stay buried.

The portents, though, are ominous. 'There are three signs,' the spiritualist warned. 'The first is when the beast walks free. The second is when water breaks iron … The third is when horses swim like fishes.'

Captain Olsen, a self-confessed connoisseur of human stupidity, has no patience with the irrational, and little interest in the messiness of relationships.

'I condemn no man or woman,' he declares, 'however savage and enormous their sins, as long as they do not touch the *Kreya*. But anything that touches the ship is different. In this small world, I am God. I judge, I punish, and I need not give my reasons.'

Olsen's philosophy is challenged in the extreme when, in mountainous seas, disaster strikes: the rudder smashed beyond repair, a mutiny, and the battered vessel adrift in the vast ocean, driven irrevocably northwards by wind and tide – until she comes to rest, at last, lodged in the great Arctic ice-pack.

ISBN: 978-0-9927686-4-5

www.thesylepress.com/the-white-voyage

by Sam Youd as John Christopher

THE WORLD IN WINTER

The Fratellini Winter they had called it, after the Italian
scientist who had first detected the decline in solar radiation.

The seasons pass and the cold bites ever harder. The Thames
freezes over, stocks of food and fuel run low, and London falls
under martial law. That first arctic winter, it seems, was only
the beginning, the herald of the incoming Ice Age.

Andrew Leedon has problems of his own. Forced out of his
marriage, he joins the exodus of the privileged few with the
necessary influence to escape to the warmth of the African
sunshine.

But gone, he finds on arrival in Lagos, are the glory days of
Empire. The desperate influx of European refugees has
enabled the natives to turn the tables on their former colonial
masters: it is white men now who, from their shanty-town
hovels, serve at table and labour on construction sites, white
women who empty the bed-pans and sell their bodies.

Their Nigerian bosses, meanwhile, looking towards the
lawless, ice-bound north, have their own plans for expansion.

This edition available in the US only

ISBN: 978-1-911410-14-0

www.thesylepress.com/the-world-in-winter

by Sam Youd as John Christopher

CLOUD ON SILVER

A disparate group of Londoners are brought together by
Sweeney, a mysteriously charismatic man of wealth, for a
luxury cruise in the South Pacific – they know not why.
Sailing far from the normal shipping routes, the ship drops
anchor just off an uninhabited tropical island. Whilst its
passengers are ashore exploring, the ship catches fire and sinks
beneath the waves.

With no means of communication with the outside world
and no hope of rescue, passengers and crew must find a way
to survive. In the scramble for power that ensues, the
distinction between master and servant becomes meaningless
as the more ruthless among them clamber to the top.

The inscrutable Sweeney, meanwhile, sits alone on a hillside.
Coolly aloof, he watches the veneer of civilization disintegrate
as his fellows fall prey to fear, desperation, barbarity …

As for Silver Island itself, with its lush vegetation and exotic
fruits, it had seemed like paradise. But as the days pass, a
subtle sense of unease gains momentum, and the realisation
gradually dawns that all is far from well in this tropical Eden.

ISBN: 978-0-9927686-6-9

www.thesylepress.com/cloud-on-silver

by Sam Youd as John Christopher

The Possessors

When the storm rages and the avalanche cuts off power and phone lines, no one in the chalet is particularly bothered. There are kerosene lamps, a well-stocked bar and food supplies more than adequate to last them till the road to Nidenhaut can be opened up. They're on holiday after all, and once the weather clears they can carry on skiing.

They do not know, then, that deep within the Swiss Alps, something alien has stirred: an invasion so sly it can only be detected by principled reasoning.

The Possessors had a long memory … For aeons which were now uncountable their life had been bound up with the evanescent lives of the Possessed. Without them, they could not act or think, but through them they were the masters of this cold world.

ISBN: 978-1-911410-02-7

www.thesylepress.com/the-possessors

by Sam Youd as John Christopher

A WRINKLE IN THE SKIN

One night, the island of Guernsey convulsed. As shock followed shock, the landscape tilted violently in defiance of gravity. When dawn came and the quakes had stilled to tremblings, Matthew Cotter gazed out in disbelief at the pile of rubble that had been his home. The greenhouses which had provided his livelihood were a lake of shattered glass, the tomato plants a crush of drowned vegetation spotted and splodged with red.

Wandering in a daze of bewilderment through the devastation, he came to the coast, looked out towards the sea …

There was no sea: simply a sunken alien land, now drying in the early summer sun.

Gradually, a handful of isolated survivors drifted together. But where were the rescue missions from the mainland? How far did the destruction actually extend?

For Matthew, whose beloved daughter Jane had recently moved to England, finding the answer was all he had left to live for.

ISBN: 978-1-911410-10-2

www.thesylepress.com/a-wrinkle-in-the-skin

by Sam Youd

THE WINTER SWAN

In 1949, Sam Youd – who would later go on, as John Christopher, to write *The Death of Grass* and *The Tripods* – published his first novel. As he later said:

I knew first novels tended to be autobiographical and was determined to avoid that. So my main character was a woman, from a social milieu I only knew from books, and … [with] a story that progressed from grave to girlhood.

When Rosemary Hallam dies, what she longs for is the peace of non-existence. Instead, her disembodied spirit must travel back and back, through two world wars and the Depression to her Edwardian childhood, reliving her life through the eyes of her husbands, her sons and others less immune than she to the power of emotion. And the joys and the tragedies which had never quite touched her at the time now pose a real threat to the emotional aloofness she has always been strangely desperate to preserve.

'You remind me greatly of a swan, dear Mrs Hallam,' her elderly final suitor had declared, '… effortlessly graceful, and riding serenely over the troubling waves of the world as though they never existed.'

ISBN: 978-1-911410-06-5

www.thesylepress.com/the-winter-swan

by Sam Youd

BABEL ITSELF

London in the late forties: strange shifting times in the aftermath of the war. A motley sample of humanity has washed up on the shores of the down-at-heel boarding house that is 36 Regency Gardens, their mutual proximity enforced by shared impoverishment.

Gentleman publisher Tennyson Glebe, no longer young, watches with mild interest as fellow residents go through the motions of seeking redemption, through politics, through art, through religion; the inconsequentiality of his present existence throwing the past into vivid relief.

And whilst Helen, as landlady, presides over the breakfast table, it is the unnaturally large hands of the diminutive Piers Marchant, Tennyson comes to realise, that seek to control the marionettes' strings – his own included.

Who was it, after all, who had decided that a séance or two might assuage the evening boredom before the nightly trip to the pub?

ISBN: 978-1-911410-08-9

www.thesylepress.com/babel-itself

by Sam Youd

A PALACE OF STRANGERS

*'It is always nonsense for us that says some are chosen and others
left to die. If that should be, it is better not to be chosen.'*

'You mean, we're all chosen.'

'No,' Dadda said. 'I mean, we are all left to die.'

A Sunday evening in 1921: open house at the modest
Liverpool home of Benjamin and Mary Rosenbaum, where
Isaak Rosenbaum, visiting from Germany, has been shaken to
discover that his brother no longer attends synagogue.

Solly Gruenblum sits down at the piano, and six-year-old
David watches spellbound as Jinny O'Neill – 'glorious and
the breath of life itself' – bursts into song. The following
February Isaak and Jinny are married at St Jude's Catholic
Church.

'We have fought a war, your country and mine,' Isaak
declares before whisking his bride back to Germany. 'It must
not happen again that two such great countries should spill
each other's blood.'

But with the rise of Hitler, Isaak and his family are forced to
flee to London, and in 1945, David, now a British army
officer, comes face-to-face with the reality of the
concentration camps.

Even in a post-war world, though, for David and his German
cousins, can the traumas engendered by their mixed heritage
ever really be put to rest?

ISBN: 978-1-911410-12-6

www.thesylepress.com/a-palace-of-strangers

by Sam Youd

HOLLY ASH

Holly Ash – once a straggle of rural cottages a tram's ride from Liverpool – has been transformed, Frank Bates discovers when he returns years later as local boy made good. Now a director of Amalgamated Cables, and son-in-law of the chairman, he is shocked to see that in place of Ash Cottages, his boyhood home, rises the red and gold façade of Woolworth's, the pride of a suburban shopping arcade.

Frank's childhood had been a solitary one until, exploring one day the abandoned lake pavilion of the Manor House, he first encountered the children of the new local doctor. The natural assurance of the Manson siblings threw into sharp relief his own reserve, his consciousness of the working-class poverty of his upbringing.

John, Patrick, Patricia and Diana, however, accepted him into their tight-knit circle with open-handed generosity. Little did they suspect, as the years passed by, the resentment their quiet childhood companion secretly nursed against their effortless superiority, nor exactly how Frank's bitterness would play out in their adult lives.

ISBN: 978-1-911410-16-4

www.thesylepress.com/holly-ash

by Sam Youd as Hilary Ford

SARNIA

Life holds no prospect of luxury or excitement after Sarnia's beloved mother dies: potential suitors vanish once they realise that marriage to the orphan will never bring a dowry. Yet her post as a lady clerk in a London banking house keeps the wolf from the door, and the admiration of her colleague, the worthy Michael, assures her if not of passion, then at least of affection.

Then the Jelains erupt into her humdrum routine, relatives she did not know she had, and whisk her away to the isle of Guernsey. At first she is enchanted by the exotic beauty of the island, by a life of balls and lavish entertainments where the officers of visiting regiments vie for her attention.

But Sarnia cannot quite feel at ease within this moneyed social hierarchy – especially in the unsettling presence of her cousin Edmund. And before long it becomes apparent that, beneath the glittering surface, lurk dark and menacing forces …

Her mother had scorned those of her sex who tamely submitted to male domination but, as the mystery of her heritage unfolds, Sarnia becomes all too painfully aware that the freedom she took for granted is slipping from her grasp.

ISBN: 978-0-9927686-0-7

www.thesylepress.com/sarnia

by Sam Youd as Hilary Ford

A Bride for Bedivere

'I cried the day my father died; but from joy.'

Jane's father had been nothing but a bully. His accidental death at the dockyard where he worked might have left the family in penury but it had also freed them from his drunken rages. He was scarcely cold in his grave, though, when another tyrant entered Jane's life.

Sir Donald Bedivere's offer to ease her mother's financial burden had but one condition: that Jane should leave her beloved home in Portsmouth and move to Cornwall as his adopted daughter.

To Sir Donald, Cornwall was King Arthur's country, and his magnificent home, Carmaliot, the place where Camelot once had stood. To Jane, for all its luxury it was a purgatory where her only friend was the lumbering Beast, with whom she roamed the moors.

Sir Donald had three sons, and Jane was quick to sum them up: John was pleasant enough, but indifferent to her. The burly, grinning Edgar she found loathsome. And Michael, on whom Sir Donald had pinned all his hopes, she disdained.

Sir Donald had plans for the Bedivere line – Jane wanted no part in them.

ISBN: 978-0-9927686-2-1

www.thesylepress.com/a-bride-for-bedivere

Printed in Great Britain
by Amazon

14996267R00182